Domina

Patrick Khayler

2018, Amore Moon Publishing
www.amoremoonpublishing.com

Domina
Copyright © 2018 by Patrick Khayler

This is a work of fiction. Names, characters, places, and incidences are either a product of the author's imagination or are used fictitiously. Any resemblance to any actual person, living or dead, events, or locales is entirely coincidental.

Edited by Terry Wright

© Cover Art by Terry Wright

Cover image by sakkmesterke/shutterstock.com

Published by Amore Moon Publishing, an imprint of TWB Press

ISBN: 978-1-944045-46-3

Chapter One

Unmet Needs

Samantha Keating crossed her legs in the soft recliner. After three sessions with Dr. Phar, she'd started to loosen up a bit. His office invited comfort. Wood paneled walls met floor to ceiling glass. An eagle's view of Phoenix. Thirty floors above the busy streets which stretched beyond the horizon.

A few simple pictures and degrees from prestigious universities broke up the empty space between custom shelves. Each shelf cradled books on psychiatry, psychology, relationship building and the latest techniques in psychotherapy. Personal knick knacks declared the doctor's humanity, representations meant to instill confidence and hope in patients who no longer possessed those attributes or had forgotten them long ago.

Deep pile, white shag carpet covered the floor, softening the tense footsteps of patients when they entered. An invitation to relax and embrace the surroundings. A small couch and two recliners called to the ill who entered. Leather upholstery and cushions so comfortable the occupant could melt into them. Sitting was for the world "out there". In this room, an hour of sanctuary from the twisted demons of the mind could always be found. Comfort. Relaxation. Nothing less.

Sam clasped her hands around her tanned knee and twirled her ankle. She waited as Dr. Phar finished writing his notes. He wore a light blue long-sleeve button up and a patterned tie just a shade darker than his shirt. A splash of white and red made his ensemble appear both striking and professional at the same time. His close-cropped hair failed to make him appear stiff and uncaring. Matched with his perpetual five o'clock shadow, rugged seemed a more appropriate eponym than academic. Handsome without question. Gorgeous even.

Sam watched the doctor flip through the pages in front of him. Jotting something here. Writing something there. She couldn't help but fantasize: He perused an unimaginably long list of beautiful girlfriends, selecting the lucky woman who'd be allowed to pleasure him for the evening.

Dr. Phar set his pen down and gazed at Sam with

a disarming smile. He interlaced his fingers and placed his palms on the desk. "It's so good to see you again, Ms. Keating. I apologize for keeping you waiting. If I don't get my thoughts down immediately, I lose the gestalt of my patient's session."

"I completely understand." Sam unclasped her hands and let her black three inch heels come to rest on the soft carpet. Realizing her hands clenched and unclenched the hem of her knee length skirt, she made a conscious effort to stop. She leaned back in the soft chair and gripped the armrests, trying not to squeeze too hard. *You're supposed to be thinking about me, not your "other" patients.* She forced a smile. "Take your time, Dr. Phar."

"How've you been over the last week?" He opened the beige folder she recognized as hers and turned through the pages.

"Good." Sam did her best to convince herself. "I feel better. The relaxation techniques help. I'm working on my novel again. Sending out resumes and searching online for something more lucrative than writing."

The doctor flipped another page. "Your last job...Kelly was your boss as well as your...boyfriend."

The name of the man she'd been doing her best

to forget made her heart race. It always did. She looked away from Dr. Phar and stared at her uncovered knees. She tried not to tap her foot in nervous distraction. "That's why I quit. Well, I never went back. It amounts to the same thing."

"How long were you two together?"

"About two years." Her foot began to bounce. She twirled her dark brown hair between her fingers. Tighter. Tighter. *One year, eleven months, and two weeks.*

"That's a long time to be with someone." His voice suggested a question rather than a statement. "Is that the longest you've ever been intimate with the same person?"

Samantha pushed her fingers beneath her hair and rubbed her neck. "Yes." *By about one year, eleven months and a week.*

"You look nervous, Ms. Keating. Do you still feel anxious every time you think of him?"

Her neck veins began to throb. Her heart pounded harder. The air became thick, hard to breathe. Saliva disappeared, her mouth felt like worn leather baked in the sun. "No. I told you. I feel better."

Dr. Phar stared at her with his deep blue eyes for a long time, then: "So it won't bother you if we talk a little more about him?"

"Sure. Shoot." Her voice shook. *Short and to the point.* Sam looked at the ceiling. She counted her breaths in silence and tried to center herself. Hyperventilation threatened to reveal her unstable emotional status. The foundations of her mental stability began to slip away. "Doesn't bother me a bit."

The doctor jotted something on a legal pad before he asked his next question. "Why do you think Kelly ended your relationship, Ms. Keating?"

"Isn't that what you're supposed to help me figure out, Dr. Phar?" She tried not to spit the doctor's name, but he seemed determined to rob her self control.

Fuck you, Doc. I'm not supposed to be treating myself.

"That's what I'm trying to do, Ms. Keating."

"Sam." She ran her palms down her skirt. Smoothing non-existent wrinkles and trying to dry her nervous hands. "My mother was Ms. Keating."

Dr. Phar leaned back in his chair. He raised a knee and cupped his hands around it. "I apologize, Sam. Several visits ago you'd asked me to call you Ms. Keating. I believe you said 'Sam' felt to familiar." He starred at her for a moment before continuing, "Why do you think Kelly ended your relationship?"

Breathe. One. Breathe. Two. In and out. In and out.

"I don't know."

Dr. Phar leaned forward and paged through a few more sheets in the file. "You're a beautiful woman, Sam." His voice warmed. The cadence slowed." I can't imagine any man taking his eyes off you for very long. Do you think Kelly appreciated how attractive you are?"

Confused by the question, Sam looked at the doctor and cocked her head. *If you weren't my doctor, I'd swear you were hitting on me.* "I think so." *Careful what you ask for, doc. I'm very comfortable with this particular subject.* "I've been blessed with big tits and hips designed for holding. My body stays slim and hard for all the wrong reasons." She giggled at her own joke and tried to make light of her rising tension. "Continuous stress and intermittent depression means I never eat. I walk for hours perseverating on the past. Drowning in self destructive introspection."

Sam watched Dr. Phar's hand slip beneath the desk before he brought it up to join the other again. The image of his cock hardening when she hadn't even said anything of importance dialed her anxiety down to a tolerable level.

Really? You've got to be kidding me.

Dr. Phar put two fingers beneath his collar and pulled outward. "You do seem to have everything in the right place. There's no arguing that. Did he appreciate it enough? As any man should..."

You are hitting on me, you son of a bitch.

She took a deep breath to mask the spark of anger he'd ignited. *I will not be manipulated. I'm the one in control here.* She focused on the pathetic excuse for a human being before her eyes. *I came here for help and you want to play.* The kindling began to smolder. *Fine. Let's play, Doc.* "I think he appreciated me." She smiled and leaned forward so he would be forced to look down her blouse. "He would suck my nipples until every nerve in my body fired simultaneously." She closed her eyes and moaned. "When he knew I couldn't take any more he would...I shouldn't be telling you this." She lowered her voice to a whisper as if sharing a secret. "He would rub my chest in coconut oil and fuck my breasts as I pushed them together. Jesus. It was the best feeling in the world, especially when his hot cum splashed on my lips and slid down my neck. An incredible sensation. Every. Single. Time."

Dr. Phar fidgeted in his seat. A comfortable position seemed to elude him and his ever adjusting hand. It took all of Sam's concentration to keep a straight face as he squirmed.

Just the beginning, asshole.

The doctor cleared his throat. "I see. Your body obviously wasn't the problem..."

"I don't think so either." Sam flashed her best seductive smile. "I hope I'm not making you uncomfortable." She tugged at the hem of her skirt, inching it upward. "But, you're my doctor and I know you'll keep this between us." *Dickhead.* She covered her mouth with her hand and twittered again. "I feel so naughty."

Dr. Phar walked around his desk. His hard cock bulged in his pants. "Of course, Sam. The doctor client privilege is sacred. I took an oath."

Why do I love to tease?

"Kelly loved my hips so much." Sam pulled the skirt to mid thigh. Her anxiety had left. A distant memory blotted by her desire to make him suffer. *Why does manipulation make me so wet?* Her voice purred, thickened by the honey dampening her panties. "When he fucked me hard from behind, he would hold so tight I could barely breathe. On my back...oh god, the memories are so fresh. He would push my knees up so high and hold them there until my pussy was positioned exactly the way he wanted it. Tight. Wet. His."

The doctor's strong hands caressed her shoulders. Rubbing. Kneading. Asking for more. "Did you deny him the things he wanted? As a man?"

The statement seemed ridiculous at first. As Sam restrained outright laughter, a sickening idea pressed its monstrous tendrils into the most protected areas of her subconscious. *No!* She couldn't deny he'd unmasked the core issue no matter how much she didn't want to believe. His hands squeezed tighter, sliding farther forward on her chest with each caress. Tortured thoughts rolled through her mind as cold truths poured from her mouth. A painful catharsis she could no longer restrain. "I thought I was every man's fantasy. I fucked him whenever he wanted. In any position. Anywhere. Because I wanted it. I sucked his cock in the car, at parties, in elevators. I loved the taste of his cum and couldn't get enough of it. I never wore panties. I wanted him to be able to finger me whenever and where ever he wanted. At home. In movie theaters. The car. Restaurants. I gave him everything any man could ever dream of. All he had to do is ask."

The doctor's hot breath brushed her ear. Closer. A delicious hiss as he inhaled the scent of her neck. "But he had his limits, didn't he? Tell me about the threesome he denied you. That hurt you, didn't it?"

Fucking lecher! You didn't understand a thing I told you. No one can deny me anything.

She stood and sauntered toward the desk with her purse, glancing backward only long enough to see him adjust himself before he stepped behind the recliner. She placed her purse in the middle of the writing surface and rolled her skirt upward. White lace panties remained the only thing between him and her wet pussy. The hard edge of the desk dug into her ass as she leaned back against it. A dull knife. *Why is this making me hot?* She lowered her voice and pushed out her lower lip like an innocent young girl who'd just discovered how naughty she could be. "I caught him watching a porn video of two men fucking one woman."

Dr. Phar stepped from behind the recliner, staring at the wet fabric between her legs with awe as he approached. "And?"

And he broke my heart, you asshole.

She rubbed her clit through the soft cotton with one hand and lifted a heel onto the desk, opening herself to his gaze. *You aren't going to like how this party ends, doc.* "I asked him if he wanted to share me with another man. I was ecstatic. I'd finally uncovered one of his secret fantasies." She ran her tongue over her lips and tried to push the images of Kelly away. She didn't want the wound to open again.

Dr. Phar stepped in front of her and began to pet

her thigh with his fingertips. His eyes never wavered from the outline her outer lips made in the wet fabric. A cleft of promise, soaked in pleasure. His voice became little more than a hot whisper. "But he didn't want that, did he? He denied you."

Dealing with years of self-imposed mental agony, Sam had mastered only one coping mechanism. Transient but effective. The torment would always return but, for a few moments, she could extinguish unbearable aguish without fail. A brief interlude of bliss. An ephemeral puff of hope in an endless expanse of suffering.

She hooked her fingers under her panties and pushed deep into her vagina. Her voice warbled with sorrow, not lust. "He blew up at me. I remember the exact words. 'You would! Wouldn't you?' Then he stormed out of the apartment." She fingered herself harder. Trying to push the pain away. Sex always released her. Empowered her. "I cried but he'd already left. I should've asked if he wanted to share me with another woman. Maybe then... Maybe...but it was too late."

His fingers traced the outline of her labia and inner thigh. "But he didn't bring another man into your bed did he? Even knowing it was what you wanted?"

I didn't want it, you fuck! You couldn't understand me if you tried. But, I understand you. I understand your kind all too well.

"No. The next time I saw him was...was...that night."

He tried to hook a finger under her soaking panties but she stood before he'd found his mark. "Tell me what he did to you, Sam. I can make it all better."

She walked to the other side of the desk, making sure he watched as she wiggled her panties to the floor and left them behind. *You worthless piece of shit.* White hot anger boiled in her chest, pushing away the trauma he wanted her to relive. "He asked me to meet him at our favorite restaurant. Our special place. I knew he wanted to tell me he loved me. That he wanted to move in or maybe even...ask me to marry him."

Sam rolled her skirt above her hips before pushing the doctor's files from the desk with a swipe of her arm. Dr. Phar gasped in horror as the critical papers fluttered to the floor. She spread her legs before he could protest and propped her elbows on the spotless desktop. His eyes focused on her again. She wiggled her ass. *So easy.* He'd become hers. A toy for her amusement. *You're about to have a very bad day, doc.* "I waxed my pussy. I bought a new dress and even did my hair. I'd never been happier in my life. I'd found love at last. The love I'd needed for so long. He was going to tell me I was his. The only thing he'd ever wanted."

Dr. Phar moved behind her. She stared at the shelves across the room. Waiting.

Death is too good for you. I have something so much better.

The sound of Dr. Phar's belt being undone ricocheted off the paneling. His zipper resounded like thunder. "But that's not what Kelly wanted? He didn't want you at all. Not like I do."

His hands clutched her hips. An illusion of control she granted him for a few moments more. The tip of his cock pushed at the opening to her dripping pussy. *My life doesn't have happy endings, you useless fuck.* "No. He said, 'Sam. I don't want us to be together as a couple anymore."

The doctor's plump cock slid inside her. Stretching wide. Thrusting back and forth. *Breathe. One. Breathe. Two. Breathe. Damn that feels so good.* "It's not you. It's me, he said. You gave me everything I wanted and desired. You fulfilled all my fantasies and I could never give you anything you hadn't already considered or tasted long before I came into the picture. It's killing me and I'm sorry, baby, I can't do this anymore." Sam choked back her tears, reaching for her purse as the doctor's powerful thrusts drove the sharp edge of the desk against her naked thighs.

"You have me now, baby." Dr. Phar pounded harder. "I'll give you what you want."

Is that a fact?

Sam, looked over her shoulder as she told him what he wanted to hear. "Yes, baby. Oh yes. You're so big. Fuck me harder." When his eyes closed in pleasure, she unbuckled the side pouch of her purse and pulled her phone free. *Damn. I'm going to cum you bastard. Why did you have to be good at fucking?* She waited until his groans changed to breathy moans. An edge he couldn't come back from. She screamed at the top of her lungs. "Fuck yes, daddy! Fuck your little girl hard! Fuck her so hard! Yes, daddy! Yes, daddy!"

His violent penetrations slowed. His voice changed to a molten whisper. "Shhh! You have to be quiet, beautiful. People will hear."

His pace increased again. *You should have thought of that before you started fucking your patient, doc.* She worked her phone with one hand, faking pleasure to the best of her ability given the circumstances. *Only partially false.* She flipped the camera to selfie mode, centering the frame on her face and the man about to cum inside her. His eyes remained closed in ecstasy. "Smile, daddy."

She snapped the picture. A blinding flash.

He stopped his penetration as if struck by a baseball bat. Ripping his cock from her soaking pussy, he scrambled backward, trying to pull his wayward pants from his ankles.

Sam stood quicker. She snapped picture after picture as she scurried to the other side of the desk. "Smile, daddy! Smile for the camera!"

He swiped at her across the desk as the flash continued to fire. His face turned beet red, crimson and then purple as he held his pants up with one hand. Blinding fury erupted from his lips. "Give me the phone, you fucking cunt!"

"Cunt?" She laughed out loud. "I thought you loved me, baby. I thought you were going to make it all better."

He ran around the desk as she moved to stay directly across from him. He looked ridiculous and she loved every minute more than the last. "Stop!" She held the camera high in one hand. "Take one more fucking step and you go on Snapchat, you worthless piece of shit."

He froze. His face left no doubt he would kill her if given half the chance. "Give me the fucking camera." He seethed as he buckled his pants. "Please!"

Sam continued to hold the camera high. She picked up her wet panties and twirled them on her finger before tossing them to him. "Here, doc. I want you to remember the smell of my hot pussy forever."

His facial expression morphed into one of pure panic. "What do you want? I'll give you anything, just give me the phone." He continued to move around the desk in slow steps.

Sam reflected every step, remaining on the opposite side. Her hands shook with volcanic fury. "What do I want?" Tears began to fall in earnest as her voice rose in choked sputters of maniacal rage. "I want to be whole again, you asshole! That's what everyone wants, you worthless prick!"

With the office door behind her, she sprinted across the room and threw it open. Her finger paused on the phone's screen again as he raced after her. "Stop!"

He froze. The color drained from his face. A gaunt ghost wondering when life had slipped from his greedy hands.

The lobby behind her overflowed with horrified people. Everything right and proper in the world crumbled before their eyes. Undeniable proof of society's iniquitous decay.

"Don't bill me for this session or any others. I've already paid!" Degenerate satisfaction stoked her molten anger. She gazed across the faces. They seemed to loathe her impropriety as much or more than Dr. Phar's destruction of their trust. *He did this to himself. I'm the victim here, you motherfuckers.* "If you ever see another patient again, I swear to god you'll be the next star of the six o'clock news."

Sam slammed the door behind her with a resounding bang. "Fucking dickhead!" The lobby had become quiet as a tomb. Every eye focused on her. Sam smiled, unable to resist the coup d'état. "Well, I softened him up for you but...I bet he'll get hard again. You just have to take his cock deep in the back of your throat and pump that bitch until he comes. Worked for me."

Sam sashayed toward the elevator. Every eye followed her. The doors slid open. She stepped inside and pushed the button for the lobby. She perused the pictures she'd taken on her phone. *Fuck this. You don't get to torture anyone else.* "Smile, Dr. Phar." She pounded the phone with her finger as she typed, slid, copied, pasted and typed again."Snap chat! Instagram! Facebook! YouTube! Yay! You're fucking famous, you soulless—" She screamed at the top of her lungs and raised her hand, intent on smashing the phone against the wall.

The doors opened with a metallic hiss. People stared at the fuming mad woman about to kill someone. Sam raised her lip in annoyance and cocked her head, daring someone to call her crazy. After shoving the phone into her purse, she stomped from the elevator. She seethed, shouldering the masses out of her way as she thundered toward the bank of glass doors.

Sam walked out of the expensive office building and into the blazing Phoenix sun. She tried to be happy, but destroying someone else's life hadn't made her feel any better. A Punic victory. Nothing more. Kelly had left. Her life still sucked and no one gave a shit whether she lived or died.

***

The soft asphalt yielded to Sam's footsteps like a wet sponge. Shimmering waves of heat dissipated as she crossed the packed parking lot. Transient illusions reformed in her wake. A reflection of her own happiness. Close enough to touch but forever out of reach.

Sam used two fingers to open her car door, minimizing the amount of skin allowed to contact the searing metal heated by an Arizona sun. She flopped onto the car seat and turned on the engine. Sweat ran into her eyes as she waited for the air conditioner to chill her flesh and cool her temper. With a heavy sigh, she pulled the door closed and backed out of the parking space. She merged with the busy traffic flowing toward a life that never changed.

Congested traffic made her commute interminable, but gave her anger time to recede. Without direction, her thoughts drifted back to psychiatrist's office and the orgasm she'd missed. She hadn't had a stiff cock between her legs for weeks. *Phar may have been an asshole but damn, he could fuck.* Leaving her panties behind only reminded her of how close she'd been to release. Cum now trickled down her inner thighs unimpeded. *I should be angry not horny, damn it!* She opened her legs and let her hand drift beneath her dress. The minute circles across her swollen labia increased her need, but the heavy traffic prevented her from fingering herself properly. She focused on her clit instead of deeper penetration, working herself into a state of near frenzy before pulling into her apartment complex.

Sam ran to her apartment. Unlocking her door, she jogged down the short hallway to her bedroom, stripping her dress on the way. She bounced onto her tiny bed and tapped the keys of her computer with single minded intensity. A final mouse click opened an array of thumbnail images at her 'go to' porn hub. Curling on her side, she opened the newest video and lifted her knee. The video loaded with glacial speed as her glistening pink fingernails glided downward, tracing the sensitive skin between her outer labia and cum slicked thigh.

The video started. A young blond with big tits answered a knock on her door. Her tight half-shirt showed off hard nipples. Short blue jogging shorts let half her ass hang out. The woman looked through the door's peep hole and gasped. Searching from side to side as if she might be spotted at any moment, she unlocked the door and opened it before placing a hand to her mouth in surprise. "Oh, Jimmy! You can't be here. My parents are home. You have to go."

Sam dragged her fingernail in a circle around her cleft. She liked to graze the top of her short brown hairs, teasing herself with a tickle that made her pussy clench. She breathed harder, dropping her finger below her opening, brushing back and forth across the tiny stretch of skin just above her ass.

The camera shifted. Jimmy pushed through the door. Despite his dark brown hair and clean shaven face, he didn't look a day under thirty. His Led Zeppelin t-shirt showed off muscled arms but didn't seem to fit with the tight jeans and cowboy boots. His stage whisper would have been heard outside a rock concert. "I couldn't stay away, Trish. I love you so much. I had to see you."

Despite the crappy dialogue, Sam could see Jimmy's massive dick straining against the faded denim. It became the camera's main focus. Sam pulled her finger across the flood between her outer lips, using her own juices to caress her hard clit. The sudden electric sensation made her ass pucker. It always did.

"Oh, Jimmy." Trisha fell into his arms and kissed him hard. The door slammed behind them. Their hands groped each other with fervor before Jimmy slid his hands into Trisha's pants. She moaned once and stepped back, looking down the hall to her left before turning toward him again. Her belly button ring caught the light. Her hand grazed his chest. "No, Jimmy. We said we would wait until we graduated high school. Our first time has to be special. I want to be a virgin on our wedding night."

Sam raised her eyebrow in disbelief. *You gotta be kidding me.* She let her finger slide downward, opening herself to the first knuckle of her finger before pulling back up and circling her clit again. *Start fucking already!*

"I know, baby." Jimmy hooked his fingers over the elastic in Trisha's shorts and pushed them downward. "But our love can't be constrained by our parents' rules."

As Trisha swooned and began unbuckling Jimmy's belt, Sam lifted her wet fingers and grabbed the mouse. With disgust, she clicked through the menu until she found the gang bang link. She opened the first video and fast forwarded until she could see something she recognized as penetration before hitting PLAY again.

Another big busted blonde gripped a worn couch as a thirty-something man covered in tattoos drove his cock into her pussy again and again. Sam released the mouse and began fingering herself with alacrity, timing her strokes with the man on screen. When he drew back to show his beast slipping from the woman's wide open vagina, Sam rubbed her clit. When he started thrusting again, Sam worked two fingers into herself, mimicking the cadence of his hips.

By the time the woman's pathetic screams of pleasure began grating on Sam's nerves, her own orgasm approached. She moved her fingers faster. Harder. Calling her release to the surface with practiced hands.

Sam bit her lip as the tattooed man pulled out of the blonde's dripping pussy and pumped his cock until thick cum spurted across her back. Without pause another man took over and began fucking the moaning woman again. Even harder than the first. Sam closed her eyes as the walls of her own pussy began to contract around her fingers. She pictured herself being taken by the men on screen and squealed as release washed over her body with violent contractions. She moaned in ecstasy as wave after wave took her mind to another place. A brief moment of bliss.

Sam's breathing slowed as the throbbing between her legs began to subside. The real world returned with the sounds of the woman on the video screaming, "Stop! No more!" before the moans of factitious pleasure began again.

Sam rolled over and slammed the laptop closed. A flash of sudden loathing. Self hate. She let her head crash back on her pillow and draped her arm across her forehead. Unbidden, thoughts of Kelly crept into her head and tried to erase the memory of the orgasm she'd just enjoyed. *Why would two men ever want me? I couldn't even keep one.* She tried to concentrate on her breathing but Dr. Phar's teachings repulsed her more than her current misery. Unable to drive the rising depression, hot tears began dripping down her cheeks. A herald of soft sobs always followed in their wake.

No!

Sam opened her eyes and sniffed her running nose clear. Sitting up, she slid to the end of the worn twin mattress, which had somehow managed to squeeze itself into the tiny apartment bedroom. The single bulb lamp on her bedside darkened her mood with its dull glow. Wiping her tears, she stared at the closet door and tried to decide how to change her life.

Sam stood on long, shaky legs. The cushion beneath the faded green carpet had collapsed to nothing long before she moved in. A mat of worn knots beneath her feet no longer resembling what they used to be.

With a sigh of resignation, Sam traversed the short hallway to her bathroom. She flipped the bathroom light switch. A sink, toilet, and shower shared the space with three steps of cracked tile.

She turned on the shower and pulled the vinyl curtain closed so the water could warm. Staring into the mirror, she hooked her long black hair behind her ears then wiped the remaining streaks of mascara from her cheek. The clear square of glass where Kelly's picture had stayed too long beckoned for her attention. She braced her hands on the sink and pressed her forehead against the cold glass until brown eyes and the dark circles beneath them became her entire world.

For the millionth time she berated herself for possessing the singular gift of driving every man she'd ever known away. She stepped into the shower and let the hot water beat down on her head. *Did I kill the excitement by granting every fantasy you ever had? Did I steal the mystery? The excitement? Should I have made you beg for every orgasm I ever granted?*

Sam rubbed shampoo into her hair and lathered her body with soap. Hot water massaged her back and shoulders. She found her mind sauntering back to Dr. Phar's office again and again. *Get out of my head!* She'd teased him mercilessly, without planning or anxiety, and he'd followed her like a puppy in heat. It'd been so easy to rivet his attention on every movement she made. Making him hard enough to drop his pants in his own office had been simplicity itself.

Sam moved her hand between her legs and rubbed her clit with a gentle touch. Her fingers slipped deep and returned to her clit again, pressing harder as the epiphany arrived.

His cock slid into my wet pussy because I demanded

it. My movement, words, voice, and body controlled everything he did. I wanted to be fucked and he had no choice except to obey.

She fingered herself harder. Reaching deep.

Maybe you saved me after all, Doc.

Chapter Two
Bargain

Samantha turned the radio down and stared out the windshield. A huge number of cars filled the dark parking lot. The nondescript building revealed nothing of its purpose or the secrets hidden within. The only indication of an active business hung above an unmarked set of double doors: a small circular sign with the initials P.C. lit by a flickering yellow fluorescent light.

Is this it?

She hunched down in her seat and watched a few couples walk to the club. With a smile, a middle-aged man in a worn brown suit opened the door for the patrons. He waved them inside before returning to a barstool set before a small podium. His phone came to life in his hand and lit his face with a warm glow.

Sam exhaled through pursed lips. She gripped

the steering wheel with both hands. Her heart pounded like a sledgehammer crushing her chest from the inside out. She closed her eyes and covered her face with sweaty palms.

I drove all this way. I'll just go inside and see.

The car door swung open with a noisy creak that grated her bones. Deafening. With furtive glances, Sam searched left and right hoping she wouldn't run into someone she knew. *Guilty of a crime I haven't even committed yet.* She gritted her teeth with resolve and stepped clear of the vehicle's protective metal shell. She plucked at her tight pink blouse with nervous energy and smoothed the knee-length white skirt for the hundredth time. *Turn back before you do something stupid, Sam.* She lifted a foot and checked the buckle on her six inch *fuck me* heels even though they weren't loose or uncomfortable. They meshed well with her outfit, but walking on them would be another matter entirely.

I look ridiculous.

The car door slammed with a resounding bang. She cringed. The man at the podium didn't even look up from his phone. Her anonymity had been preserved for a few seconds more. She stood up straight and pulled her shoulders back before wobbling toward the double doors on unsteady legs.

Behind her, a quick beep from her car declared its locks secure and cut off her retreat.

Forward. Always forward.

She counted her breaths with every step, trying to pretend she belonged.

Casual sex. It's just casual sex. I don't even need to know your name. You just have to do as I say.

As her heels clacked on the blacktop, the man at the podium looked up. He jumped toward the doors two steps away. With a flourish, he motioned her inside. "Welcome to Players."

Her stomach knotted. "Thanks."

The doors closed behind her with a gentle whoosh. She stood in a small room. A dim alcove to her right overflowed with skimpy lingerie and innumerable sex toys in shiny plastic packages. A short counter blocked the way forward. Her last chance to turn around and relinquish her dubious fantasy.

"New member?" The voice came from a young woman behind the counter. Tribal tattoos covered her arms, climbing upward to disappear beneath a tight blue tank top. Numerous earrings flashed in the low light.

Sam ran her hands down her skirt again, blotting away sweat she wanted to hide. She looked down with embarrassment. "Sorry. Yes. I mean...is it that obvious?"

The woman laughed. A disarming chuckle Sam needed to hear. "No, sweetie. You have to pay an admission fee if you're not a member."

"Oh." Sam ran her fingers over her neck. "I thought it was the way I dressed."

"Not at all, baby. You look fine." The woman looked at the closed door behind Sam. "Are you here by yourself?"

"Yes." Sam looked over her shoulder with a nervous glance. "Is that okay?"

"Okay?" The woman chuckled again. "Unicorns are always okay. You just don't see them very often." She held out a hand. "Can I get your driver's license?"

Sam opened her small clutch and pulled out her license. "A unicorn?"

The woman took the card and copied the number on a piece of paper attached to a clipboard. "You really are new. Most of our members are couples. A unicorn is a single woman who wants to get laid. You're more precious than gold, baby." She turned the clipboard around and handed it to Sam with a pen. "Uhm... You do know what kind of club this is, right?"

Sam took the clipboard and looked at the legal

disclaimer. It went on for three pages with multiple blank spots for signatures. Sam was too nervous to actually read it. She couldn't think of anything to say that wouldn't sound stupid. "Yeah. Of course. It's a...a sex club."

"Just initial the first two pages and sign the last one." The woman stepped to the cash register at the end. "Yes and no on the sex club. Sure, people have sex here and you're going to see a lot of shit that may shock you, but we're really all just here to have a good time. No one will make you do something you don't want to do. No means no. Period. Got it?"

Sam initialed and signed before handing back the paperwork. Her nervousness began to recede a little. "Yeah. I think so."

"Okay. Single females are always free but you have to pay a fifty dollar member fee for one month or a hundred dollars for the year."

Sam dug in her purse again. *Hope springs eternal.* "I'll pay for the year."

The woman took her cash and opened the register. "Do you want a receipt?"

"No, thanks." Sam couldn't figure out why she would need a receipt for a sex club...or whatever they wanted to call it.

The woman handed her license back. She pushed

a few buttons on another machine and handed over a warm laminated card with Sam's name and signature. "Welcome to Player's, baby. This is your membership card. Just bring it in with you next time and you'll get in free. I'll have Eddy find you inside and show you around. Have fun."

Before Sam could ask more questions, another chuckling couple banged through the door behind her. After a brief glance in their direction, Sam stepped out of the way and pushed through the swinging door at the end of the counter.

***

Sam's eyes adjusted to the dark. Music thundered in her head. Couples ground their hips in wicked appetence on the dance floor. Promises made by subtle movements in place of words. A sea of tables surrounds the rhythmic press of bodies. Every fashion imaginable from suits to jeans, pants to dresses, leather, lace, and nothing at all.

A gorgeous brunette, naked as the day she was born, smiled at Sam on the way to the bar. The shining belly button ring caught Sam's attention. Full shaved pussy lips and the tiny barbell piercing her clitoral hood held her pinned in awed fascination.

Did she just wiggle her ass at me?

"You must be Samantha."

The deep voice startled her. A short man in a white collared shirt, brown suit coat and red tie held out his hand in greeting. The brown derby hat pulled low on his close cropped hair made him seem both unthreatening and warm.

Sam hoped the low light concealed the crimson heat spreading across her cheeks. She offered her fingertips with trepidation. "How did you know?"

His laugh reminded her of Santa Claus. His long brown mustache twitched as he smiled. "I'm Eddy. I'm giving tours to the new members tonight. If that's okay with you."

With rising discomfort, Sam looked around. She wondered if people would gawk at the 'new meat' getting a tour, but conversations continued around her unabated. No one stared. No one pointed. Their discussion hadn't generated an iota of interest in anyone. "Okay. I guess."

"Don't look so enthusiastic." He laughed again, infecting her with his jocularity. "Let's start at the beginning." He gestured to the long bar on her immediate left.

A long counter stretched off ahead of her. People sat on the tall stools or leaned against the padded edge, watching the dance floor. More than one couple communed in deep, passionate kisses. A dark-suited man supported a luscious blonde between his open knees. Her back pressed against his chest, fingers behind his neck. She moaned out loud as he kissed her neck and worked his hand beneath her short skirt, oblivious to the crowd around them. Sam wondered if she'd allow a man to finger her as other people watched, but the wet heat rising between her legs told her the night hadn't even begun.

"Looks like they're starting early."

Eddy's voice pulled Sam back to reality. Her face turned hot. She looked away, as if he could read her thoughts.

Her tour guide stepped up to the counter and gestured to the deli cooler filled with soft drinks and bottled water behind the bar. A neon sign announced 'now serving' with the number 69 perpetually lit below it. Trailing off to the left and right, shelves of mugs and wine glasses filled the wall. "Mixers are free. Margaritas, Bloody Marys. You name it. Ice buckets and setups are yours for the asking. Tap water is free. Bottled water and soda are two bucks each. Margie."

An older woman with graying hair and a loose white blouse broke off her conversation with another customer. She stepped into the space across the bar from them. Her striking green eyes lit on Sam as she spoke. "What can I get ya, sweetie?"

Eddy leaned across the bar and kissed the woman on the lips. "Margie. This is Sam. Sam, Margie. She owns the joint. You'll see her here most nights."

The plain appearance of the woman surprised Sam. No tattoos or piercings. No revealing clothes. A twinge of guilt swept over her as she wondered how many men this unassuming woman had slept with over the years.

Worried her eyes revealed inappropriate thoughts, Sam looked down. She drew her finger on the wooden counter scratched by a thousand glasses and burned by a million cigarettes. "Can I just have a beer?"

Margie squinted. She looked at Eddy sideways before turning her attention back to Sam. "We don't serve alcohol here, baby." She spoke in an apologetic tone. "It's bring your own. Didn't anyone tell you?"

Way to fit in Sam.

"No. That's okay. I'll just have a bottled water." She lifted her clutch, digging for two dollars before they could see her embarrassment.

Eddy touched her shoulder. "What kind of beer do you like?"

Samantha pulled out two dollars and closed her clutch. "Any really. I'll remember to bring a six pack next time."

"Don't sweat it." Eddy called across the room to a table swarming with people. "Dave. Can you hook my friend up with a beer?"

Sam wanted to crawl into a hole and die. She grabbed Eddy's arm and dug her fingers into it. "No. It's okay. Really."

A giant six-five-if-an-inch man looked up in question before digging around in a huge cooler and pulling out a bottle of Sam Adams. He opened the bottle and strode through the crowd with an enormous grin. His long blond hair had been pulled into a ponytail. His beard and mustache were more platinum than gray. Bulging biceps ringed by tattoos rippled as he held out the cold beer. A white muscle shirt pulled tight across his chest declaring 'The only thing in here bigger than me is my cock'. "Here you are, beautiful." His voice didn't match his countenance. The refreshment of soft rain on a lonely afternoon. "I'm Dave." He motioned over his shoulder. "The hot brunette with big tits and pink panties is my wife. Melissa."

Sam took the beer and drank deep, trying to slow her pulse as a five-foot-zero woman wearing nothing but a half shirt, see-through French cut panties, and six-inch heels sauntered toward them.

Melissa hugged Eddy and kissed him on the lips. He grabbed her ass in one hand and squeezed tight. She held out her hand. "I'm Melissa. Are you new?"

Sam shook her hand, hoping her palms weren't sweaty anymore. "Sam. Yes. I didn't know it was BYOB. Can I pay you for this?"

"Don't be silly. We have two coolers and a fifth of vodka. Help yourself. What's mine is yours." She stood on her tiptoes and kissed Dave on the cheek. "I'm gonna dance with Tracey, babe. See you in a bit."

Dave smacked his wife's ass with a ringing crack as she walked away. She jumped with a playful squeak. Sam watched Melissa fall into the arms of a half naked woman on the dance floor. They swayed to the music and sucked each other's tongues.

The huge man turned his attention back to Sam. "Pleasure meeting you, Sam. Come over to our table when you finish the tour. We'll make you feel at home. I guarantee it."

"Thanks, Dave. I'll take you up on that." Sam watched the huge man move away and wondered if the adage "big hands big feet..." held any veracity at all. If so, he'd have to be hung like a horse. She tried to picture the giant driving his massive cock into the tiny brunette or better yet, into her. She licked her lips and sipped from her bottle. "Everyone seems so friendly."

Eddy gestured ahead, walking as he answered. "You seem surprised."

Sam tried to choose her words with care but wasn't sure what she wanted to say. "Well... I am. A little. I guess."

"How come?" His eyebrow rose with sardonic gleam. As if he'd asked the same question a million times and never gotten a different answer.

"Well, because this place is a...you know."

"What kind of place is it, Sam?"

She gazed around her at the half naked people again, not wanting to sound rude. "A club for...sex and stuff."

He laughed. "Think of it more as a do whatever the fuck you want and no one is going to judge you for it club. If sex is what you want, it's a sex club. If you just want to hang out with nice people who aren't hung up on the way they look or who they sleep with, it's a club for that too. You get out of the club whatever you put into it." He stopped in front of two pool tables. "Pool tables. There's free coffee over there. Always a pot on."

Sam tried to keep her focus on the pool tables but

a woman with a blouse and no skirt walked by and kissed Eddy on the lips. Sam sighed as the woman walked away. "I don't think I would ever feel comfortable dressing like that."

"Why not?" Eddy admired the retreating bottom as he answered. "No one is going to touch you without your permission. The women control the show here. There are less clothes here than any vanilla club you would ever go to but drunk guys won't be hanging all over you. I love it."

"Really?" With the truth all around her, Sam still couldn't believe.

"Really. No means no here. There are fifty guys who'll come to your rescue if you so much as raise a hand. Dave is fucking DEA with twenty-five years on the job. Doctors. Lawyers. Construction workers. Everyone is here to have fun. If the women aren't comfortable, we don't have a club."

"Well the women sure look...comfortable." She watched another woman walk by in nothing but high heels and panties.

"You have no idea. Wait until about eleven. That's when it starts hoppin'. When everyone starts to unwind, then you'll see *comfortable.*"

Sam followed Eddy through throngs of people. He introduced her to a variety of folks from all walks of life. The women greeted him with a hug or a kiss, the men with a firm handshake and a happy exchange of words. Without exception, every person smiled at her and offered a place at their table. Her unease continued to fall away with every step.

They passed the dance floor and moved to the far side of the club. Ascending a short set of stairs, they stood in a separate area five feet above the main floor. The space stretched right and left for the width of the building and extended another ten feet in front of them. Eddy passed through a curtain on the left to reveal a king size bed, a table and a few chairs. "This is the private area." Eddy pulled back sheer curtains blocking their view of the club so they could peer across the crowd of people below. "It costs a little more, but some people want to have their own space and still feel part of the group."

Sam cleared her throat as she looked at the bed again. She tried to appear only moderately interested. Her panties had become saturated, but Eddy didn't need to know that. She pictured herself leaning over the balcony as a man she'd just met fucked her slowly from behind. At her pace. The way she wanted. Eddy closed the curtains and showed her a few more rooms before leading her back down the stairs. He turned left again.

The wall before them hid a small alcove that turned into hall going left. A sign above the entrance stated: *'Couples Only*. Another sign announced: *'If You Enter Together, You Leave Together.*

Eddy stopped and turned to Sam. "This is the playroom. Anything goes but you can only enter with another person or a group. No solo forays. No still means no."

Her excitement rose as she followed him into the darkening hall. The walls muffled the music from the dance floor, turning it down to a slow pulse rather than a booming roar. A woman in a half shirt sat in a chair before another long hall in front of them. On the right, another room opened up just past a small bank of lockers. She could see indistinct silhouettes moving, but her eyes hadn't adjusted to the lower light levels.

Eddy pulled her attention from the towels she'd just folded and placed a hand on the woman's shoulder. "Hey, Chrissy. This is Sam. She's a new member."

Chrissy set the towels on a table next to a bowl filled with unopened condoms. She offered a hand. "Pleased to meet you, Sam. Welcome to the playroom."

Sam shook the woman's hand. A rising moan on

her right made her turn her head. She squinted, peering into the darkness with interest, knowing the sound but not believing. She could discern movement now, two or more figures with indistinct outlines.

"We have individual rooms down here."

Chrissy's words ripped Sam's attention back to the short blond woman. A new flush of embarrassment filled her cheeks. The woman pointed down the hall over her shoulder and had already risen from her chair. Sam tried to focus but the rising moans to Sam's right had become muffled grunts of "Uh! Uh! Uh!"

The blonde walked through a set of curtains with Sam in tow. Twin beds filled small curtained niches on both sides of the hall, one after another, each separated by another curtain but nearly touching. "You can get undressed and wrap yourself in a towel before you come in. You keep your stuff in a locker. Alternatively, you can get undressed on the bed and put your things on the floor. In either case, bring a towel to put underneath yourself, especially if you're a squirter."

Sam stopped trying to strain her hearing for sounds from the next room. "A squirter?"

"Oh yeah." Eddy raised his eyebrows in something akin to awe. "You would be surprised how many women have squirting orgasms. Like a fountain sometimes. I love it."

Sam tried to picture a fountain of liquid shooting from anyone's vagina let alone her own. The temperature between her legs rose to sweltering levels. She would scan her porn hub for squirting when she got home. *Can anyone squirt or just some women?* Not wanting to sound naive, she nodded to Eddy in false collusion.

Chrissy moved back toward the entrance. "Oh. By the way. Don't make us pick up your condoms. Police your own. That's just out of control and pure disrespect. If you wouldn't do it in your own house, don't do it here."

As they passed through the curtains again, profligate voices flew from the darkness again, calling to her in perfect clarity. "Yes! Yes! Yes!" Sam began to decipher guttural grunts from a deeper voice bouncing in synchrony with the reverberating passion pounding in her ears. She wanted to see the coupling with her own eyes. Ever since she started masturbating to bad porn, she'd dreamed of being asked to watch another couple fuck. Her fantasy was in full swing only a few feet away and she couldn't bring herself to tell her host. She could only listen and dream of sweet release.

Eddy moved toward the darkness and the scene Sam craved. "This is our voyeur room."

Finally.

Sam followed on rapid steps. She peered into the darkness with mounting excitement, willing him to walk faster. A small bench on the left had been positioned beneath a huge glass window. An audience could peer through the glass into a room with dim overhead lighting and filled with wall to wall mattresses, but Sam wasn't interested in the empty room. In front of her, a dark haired woman bent at the waist over a short leather bench. She screamed in pleasure as a tall man gripped her hips from behind and drove his dick into her with brutal force. Sam's mouth dropped open as she watched the man bare his teeth and grunt with every thrust. Sweat dripped down his powerful chest.

The woman screamed as her body shook. "I'm cumming! I'm cumming! Don't stop!"

With something just short of a growl, the man pushed in deep and exhaled as he pumped his cum into her. The release left him panting and nearly prostrate across her back. He kissed her skin, fighting for air before he laid his cheek on her back. The woman smiled in post-coital bliss. Her chest heaved. She turned her head, meeting Sam's gaze for the briefest moment before she received the man's lips on her own. "Thank you, daddy."

Sam couldn't tear her eyes off the couple even as Eddy's voice came to her ears. "By midnight it's wall to wall people in here. If you like to watch, there'll be plenty of people who want you to see. If you've always fantasized about being fucked in front of a crowd of onlookers, this is the place. Stay out here or go inside the orgy room. Whatever flips your switch."

Sam wanted to rub her own pussy. She wanted to be fucked and, for the moment, didn't think she'd care who watched. As the man pulled his hard cock from the woman and helped her stand, Sam could already picture herself draped across the bench. The couple embraced with another deep kiss before he wrapped her body in a towel and pulled another around his own waist. The woman winked at Sam with a knowing smile as they walked past.

Maybe this is my kind of place after all.

Eddy watched the couple open their locker before addressing Sam again. "Well that's about it. Do you have any questions for me?"

Sam watched the couple drop their towels and pull their clothes on, as if getting dressed in front of people after they watched you fuck couldn't be more normal. *How about getting someone to bend me over that bench?* "No. Thanks, Eddy. Not right now."

Sam followed Eddy into the main part of the club again, waving to Chrissy on the way out. The music and the crowd of people she'd totally forgotten enveloped her the moment they turned the corner. Melissa waved to her from the dance floor and flashed an inviting smile. Her bouncing tits had become uncovered since they'd left. Sam managed a shy wave in return. The sea of people swirling around her no longer appeared threatening in any way.

It's a do whatever the fuck you want and no one judges you for it club.

"Looks like you've got people to see, Sam. Let me know if you need anything. I have another tour."

As Eddy walked away, Sam merged with the flow of people. She walked toward David and Melissa's table, wondering what the night might bring.

***

Sam hadn't laughed so hard in months. She'd forgotten how to have fun. The club's atmosphere and the people she met pulled her into conversations with ease. Taboo had become fantasy. Men and women hugged, kissed, and fondled each other as they danced, drank or pulled each other toward the playroom. Sexual energy permeated the air and flowed without interruption.

Sam stopped drinking when a warm buzz muffled her thoughts. She didn't want alcohol to soften her inhibitions in an unfamiliar place. It's not like she didn't want to get laid. Her nipples had become solid points of steel pressing against the softness of her blouse. Her panties had become so wet, cum ran in rivulets down her thighs. Tired of adjusting the uncomfortable fabric, she'd finally tossed them in the trash so her pussy could throb without restriction.

She'd had more than her fair share of offers to 'go play' with other couples. Offers so hot she had to grit her teeth just to find the strength to say no. She wanted it to be her choice. She wanted the man or woman she chose to follow her to the back because they had no choice, not because an available bed waited for them in a club filled with lust.

Sam let her gaze trail over the bodies around her. Clothes had been shed or replaced with enticing outfits. Couples pressed and tasted each other's flesh in every direction she looked. *Why would a man crawl on his knees to devour me when there are so many delicacies to choose from?* She looked at David's imposing figure again as he cupped a young redhead's ass in his hand.

How could I ever control someone like that?

Anxiety began to tighten in Sam's chest. Before the tsunami could wash over her as it had so many times in the past, she walked away from the table and tried to gather herself again. *Maybe being a fuck toy is the best I can hope for.* Her eyes began to water. She looked for the exit across the crowd closing in around her. She had to escape the club's claustrophobic ambiance before the unwanted tears came again.

As she pushed through the naked bodies, the air became more breathable. Her skin tingled as if her clothes had been stripped away. Light fingertips bounced across the hairs on her arms until her whole body seemed to awaken for the first time in her life. A hot breath caressed her neck with electric pleasure. She pushed her hand beneath her hair and turned with lascivious expectation but no one was there. As she searched the crowd without understanding, the aroma of smoke, sweat, lust and alcohol faded away with a jolt. Rose petals floated in a vanilla sea. Comfort. Warmth. A lover's embrace. She exhaled and searched around her frantically.

Am I losing my mind?

"It's funny isn't it?"

Domina

The soft voice forced Sam to turn as if bitten. A petite woman stood by her side, but Sam had no idea where she'd come from. A stunning spectacle of beauty dropped from the sky. Impossible to look away from. The figure's long blond hair held a hint of curl, a soft wave that seemed to flow and move as if pushed by a gentle breeze. Intense hazel eyes flickered with tiny fires as they burned into Sam's gaze from another place and time. They drew her in as if taunting, daring Sam to decide their true color. Blue. Green. Blue. Green. The visitor's cheeks had a tinge of pink accentuating her Mona Lisa smile. Her full red lips looked damp, painted in juice squeezed from pomegranates touched by a perfect sun. A simple red dress flowed across her naked flesh. Hardened nipples on full breasts begged Sam to release them from the thin fabric's grasp. No less intoxicating, smooth hips flowed from her tiny waistline, aching to be held. To be touched. Tasted. The soft hem barely dropped across her mons. Alabaster legs of sculpted perfection poured into ruby red high heels.

The woman's beauty seemed palpable. Impossible. Desire itself wrapped in unfathomable seduction. Sam wanted to touch her. She needed to kiss her and feel her flesh press against her own. A simple taste would never be enough. The siren already possessed Sam in entirety, body and mind. Her consciousness wavered. Words wouldn't come. "What?" Sam looked around and wondered how many others stared. "Where did you...?"

The woman stepped closer. "I said, it's funny isn't it?"

Sam's mouth became a desert devoid of water. She'd never been attracted to women before and now, she couldn't think about anything else. Sam did her best to form an answer, but she still didn't understand the question. "What's funny?"

"All these people and not one of them knows what you really want, Samantha. I find that funny."

The woman pushed the hair back from Sam's face before gliding a fingertip across her neck and down between her breasts. Their bodies almost touched. Sam could no longer breathe. "Have we...have we met?" Sam gulped as the woman's soft hands came to rest on her hips. "How did you know my name?"

The woman leaned forward and inhaled the skin of Sam's neck. She touched her lips to Sam's ear and whispered. "I know everything about you, Samantha." She kissed her earlobe. "All your desires. All your needs."

Sam's legs threatened to collapse beneath her as the hot breath rushed against her skin. The woman's soft lips pressed against her neck. Sam's hands rose to the woman's hips. She closed her eyes and accepted. "Who are you? How do you...?" She couldn't speak. As the woman's lips trailed lower, Sam could feel the walls of her pussy throb. An orgasm sped toward her like a bullet.

The woman stepped back, sliding her finger across Sam's stomach. "I'm Nova. And you...you are breathtakingly gorgeous, Samantha. Just his type. I think you're going to work perfectly."

The small amount of distance opening between them allowed Sam to breathe. She'd never had anyone compliment her looks or suggest she'd be perfect for anything. "Thank you."

"For what?" Nova canted her head in question.

Sam couldn't hold her gaze. She stared down at the floor. "I just don't...I just don't get compliments unless someone wants something from me."

Nova's deceptive smile crawled across her luscious lips. "Who says I don't want anything from you?"

Sam jerked her head up in surprise. People around them began to halt in place, staring at Nova as if a new star had burst into life while they watched.

Mouths fell open and voices ceased. Sam tried to ignore the growing attention, but as more people turned toward Nova, Sam's anxiety made her heart skip beat after beat. The air became too thin to breathe. The familiar pain Kelly caused washed over her like a tidal wave. *What's wrong with me? What was I thinking?* The woman would be swept away by another and nothing Sam did would prevent it. Someone more attractive, more experienced, and more desirable than she could ever be.

How could I have thought someone like her would want someone like me?

Voices began to rise. The masses filled the space between them. Sam choked back her tears. She pushed through the bodies toward the exit. She kept her eyes on the floor as she shuffled away. *This was a mistake. I shouldn't have come.*

The music stopped as if cotton had been thrust into Sam's ears. Voices disappeared and the bodies around her froze in position. Nothing moved except the air. A cooling breeze wafted the air around her, filling her nostrils with lavender and spice.

The jingling of Nova's voice found her again. "Leaving so soon, Samantha? I thought I'd made an impression."

Samantha turned with fear-tinged hope. Nothing

moved. Smiles and grins were fixed on a hundred faces. Glasses and bottles touched lips but nothing spilled. A splice in time. A hiccup in reality.

Nova weaved between the human statues with a sway in her hips. Her lower lip pooched out in disappointment. "We just meet and you head for the door. How are you going to get me in bed if you run away without asking me to join you?"

I must be losing my mind. As far as Sam could tell, she and Nova remained the only beings with a pulse. *A dream. It's a dream. A dream I don't want to wake from.* "You see...you see this?"

Nova laughed and stepped to Sam's side. "Of course. I knew this was a bad place to approach you, but I couldn't wait another moment. When I came near you, the scent of the cum between your legs drove me wild. I couldn't control the fog anymore and the people around us began to crave my...company. I thought a little time to ourselves was necessary."

Nova had grabbed her heart and stolen the key. The statues around them no longer mattered. Only her. "A dream."

"I hope not." Nova sidled up behind Sam and placed her chin on Sam's shoulder. She pressed her pelvis against Sam's ass and slid her hands down her thighs. Her tiny fingers hooked beneath the hem of Sam's dress and began to move upward toward the uncovered wetness now dripping in earnest. "I haven't told you what I need."

"You did this?" The disbelief slipped away as Nova's finger touched her inner thighs. Her clit. "It's not... It's not..."

"It's not what, my love?"

Nova's voice melted Sam. She opened her legs and let the woman's finger slip inside her. It dove deep and slid back to her sensitive nub to circle again. "It's not..." Words had become useless.

"It's not what you want? This succulent little treat between your legs makes me doubt that. She seems to want my attention."

In and out. Rubbing. Sliding. Sam pulled her dress higher to give Nova better access. The frozen multitudes around them had been forgotten. Her entire body vibrated. Her pussy clenched around Nova's finger and released in spasmodic waves. Sam groaned as an orgasm broke over her. Her body trembled. Pulses of lust radiated throughout her body and threatened to sweep her sanity away. "Oh! My! God!"

Nova removed her fingers and stepped back. She smiled wickedly as Sam continued to gasp and sputter in pleasure. She sucked her glistening fingers. "I'm sorry, beautiful. You weren't ready for that yet. I couldn't resist. You're just too perfect for words. I couldn't have found someone better if I'd looked for years. The fact that you're so alluring when you come is just a bonus."

Sam gasped for breath. Her pussy still contracted in a steady quiver, pumping hot cum down her legs like a waterfall. "What did you do to me? I can't stop! Oh my god! I'm coming again!"

"Shhh, baby." Nova touched her wet finger to Sam's lips. "Breathe. Breathe, baby girl. I didn't realize you'd be so precious."

Nova's touch slowed the pulsations between Sam's legs to a dull roar. A warm rush made her legs falter. She sucked Nova's fingers as if commanded. A cum coated pacifier filled with strength.

"That's a good girl. Just breathe, beautiful. Just breathe."

When the world around her came back into focus, Sam realized she'd just had the most earth shattering orgasm of her life. Even the aftershocks exceeded anything she'd ever experienced. She sucked the woman's fingers with gusto and pulled herself closer. Touching her. Wanting more.

"Relax, beautiful. We'll have our time soon."

Sam gasped. She remembered they stood in a room of people frozen in space. Her cheeks warmed as she let the fingers slip from her mouth with profound regret. "What did you do? I've never felt anything like that." She looked at the immobile bodies surrounding her. "I can't believe any of this. It can't be real."

"I assure you it's real." Nova snapped her fingers and the room came to life again. The club returned to normal as if it had never stopped. Laughing. Drinking. Pressing. The area Nova vacated when the room had swirled to a stop became a confused mass of people. They looked perplexed by her absence for less than a heartbeat and then resumed what they'd been doing before she arrived. As if she'd never existed. "What's happening to me? What's going on?"

People near them began to notice Nova again. Conversations stopped. Men and women stared. Nova took Sam's hand in her own tugged her toward the entrance. "We have to go, Samantha. That last pause weakened me. Using my powers here is too draining."

"Your powers?" Sam stumbled behind Nova as the crowd closed in behind them. "I don't understand any of this."

"You will, my sweet. You will."

***

Nova climbed into the car. Sam ran to the driver's side to join her. Jumping in, she slammed the door and started the engine. The scent of the woman beside her blended equal measures of heaven and earth. Nectar of the gods. "Where too?"

"Your house." Nova let her hand move to Sam's knee. "Where else?"

The touch of Nova's soft skin against her own radiated upward. Sam's eyes began to close with acceptance. The blare of a horn pulled her back to reality. Blinding headlights flashed in the windshield. Sam yanked the steering wheel at the last second, missing the car by inches.

"Samantha. You must concentrate or we'll never arrive at your house alive. Our night will be over before it begins."

Sam inhaled through her nose and blew out through pursed lips. She nodded with vigor.

"That's my girl. Just breathe."

The pain in Sam's lip told her she'd clamped her teeth too tight. She relaxed her jaw before blood could pool. With concentration, she let the excitement of having Nova near her be enough. Her heart slowed and she could think again. "How did you do that?

Freeze all those people. Stop everything. That's not possible."

"You saw with your own eyes. Let's say, it's not common."

Nova's voice had a musical quality that made Sam want to listen. To believe. "Are you a witch or...something?"

Nova laughed. "Or something. A fairy perhaps. A sprite. Something else. Our names have changed over the millennia but our cravings remain the same. We have always been and will always be."

Nova's hand roved across Sam's leg. Her fingernails dragged upward and reversed directions before settling on the place Sam needed them to stay. Sam concentrated on the black road and the flash of passing cars. She pushed her hips forward. "And those cravings are?"

"The same as yours. Lust. Happiness. Fulfillment of desire. Love."

"Love?" Sam's voice cracked when the fingertip brushed her clit and slid downward.

"Of course. Physical desires are separable from emotion to a point but, in love, release can become infinite. In fact, that's exactly why I came to you. I need your help with a...problem."

Sam lifted her knee against the door to open

herself farther. Nova's finger entered her pussy, withdrew and found her clit again. Sam's breath quickened. "What problem could I possibly help you with? With your power?" Her juices flowed faster with each caress.

"What do you want most, Samantha?"

Sam began to pant. Her mind raced. "You. I want you."

Nova giggled and pulled her finger free. She licked it with the tip of her tongue, savoring every drop. "You'll have me. I'm what you want most at this instant. I want to know what you want most in this world, or the next."

Sam almost came as the fairy's finger left her soaking cleft. As the contractions eased off a bit, an answer came to her. "I want what you have."

"And what would that be, precious girl?"

She worried Nova would find her dreams childish but truth poured from her lips despite her hesitancy. "I want to have men..." She turned to Nova, licking her lips before letting her eyes drift back to the road. "And women desire me."

"You're a beautiful woman, Samantha. You already have that. You simply refuse to see."

Sam didn't want Nova to know about Kelly. She would never tell her about Dr. Phar. "You don't understand. I want them to need me. I want it to be impossible for them to think about anything except what I can give them. I want them to crave me the way they crave you."

"You want them to love you."

Sam remembered Kelly. He'd loved her once, but he walked away without a second glance. "No." Her arousal slipped away. She lowered her leg. "I'm done with love."

Nova's laugh echoed through the car's interior. Her mirth rolled on until Sam giggled with her even though she didn't understand why. "What are we laughing about?"

Nova caught her breath after another bout of hysterical laughter. "Oh my poor Samantha. If only it were that simple. Love drives everything we do. We may spurn it, hate it or even turn our backs on it but it always returns. Pain and pleasure. Inseparable. Lust and desire. Indivisible." She giggled again. "I'll make you a deal, Samantha. If I could give you seduction... If I taught you control... What will you give me in return?"

Sam's mouth watered. Her voice dropped to a whisper. "Anything."

"Ooooh. I believe we have an accord then."

Samantha pulled into her apartment complex as

Nova finished her strange statement. She parked and turned off the car. "What do I have to do?"

"Simply take what you want. Become what you need to be." Nova opened the car door, stepped out and closed it behind her.

As the interior light shut off, Sam exhaled in the dark. *Somehow I don't think it'll be that simple.* Outside her windshield, Nova crooked her finger and motioned for Sam to come to her. The embodiment of desire.

But I'm sure as hell going to find out.

***

The porch light didn't work anymore. Its absence only heightened Sam's nervousness. She fumbled with her keys, searching for the correct one in the darkness.

I'm actually going to sleep with another woman.

She jiggled the doorknob more than a few times and finally bounced her shoulder against the tired wooden frame before it opened.

If my hovel doesn't scare her away.

She tried not to draw attention to the dingy carpet and tattered furniture rational people would be afraid to sit in.

How will I get her to my bedroom after she sees this

place?

Sam shrugged off her apprehension. She slunk toward the diminutive nook she'd dubbed her kitchen and hoped the refrigerator wasn't on the fritz again. "Would you like something to drink?"

Nova's oppressive silence became unbearable. Sam turned with chagrin rising in her cheeks. Her mouth fell open. Nova stood in the hallway. Without so much as a hint of clothes, the buxom woman leaned with one hand on the wall and the other on her hip. Hard pink nipples lifted atop swollen breasts. The tight muscles of Nova's stomach drew Sam's gaze downward. A forbidden path leading to the swollen lips between her legs. Nova's tense clit, pink and succulent, peaked innocently from its sweetened cover, poised for display and already wet with cum.

Sam gasped. "You don't waste any time, do you?"

Nova touched her own nipple with a bright red fingernail, circled and slid south, opening her labia with a long stroke of a single finger. "Your first lesson comes without obligation, Samantha. Never waste time taking what you want. I want you. You want me. What's there to talk about?" She put the wet finger in her mouth, sucked deep and pulled it out with a soft pop. "Besides. Fucking is much more sensual without clothes." Nova held out her hand. "Come."

Domina

Never wanting anything more in her entire life, Sam moved in slow motion. She touched the woman's hand and let the beautiful stranger lead her down the hall. They stopped beside Sam's miniature bed. Nova released her hand and shifted closer. A ballerina's poise. She gripped the hem of Sam's dress and pulled upward. Sam lifted her arms in urgent hunger. Their skin brushed against each other as the material slipped clear. The heat of a thousand suns. More delicate than silk.

Without breaking eye contact, Nova held the dress in two fingers and let it fall to the floor. She bent at the waist and patted the bed. "Sit, baby girl."

Unable to resist the goddess's pull, Sam lowered herself onto the bed and its pained creak of ancient springs. Sam looked down in sudden distress. "I'm sorry the apartment isn't more—"

Nova touched Sam's chin with a single finger, lifting until their eyes locked in shared empathy. She lifted her leg and straddled Sam's lap, kneeling on the lumpy mattress. The naughty goddess wrapped her arms around Sam's neck and leaned in until their breasts nuzzled in a soft kiss, their lips a breath apart. "It's not the place. It's the lover you share it with."

The soft hair between Nova's legs tickled. Excited. The wetness of her pussy against the top of

Sam's legs mingled with the gentle rock of the woman's hips. Liquid warmth spread through her body. Her entire being. Sam's heart pounded in excitement. She looked upward with hope, searching for Nova's lips. Her own hands snaked around the nymph's back, driven by their own volition.

"Slowly, beautiful." Nova's voice had become a song. "You're first time with a woman has to be special. It has to be perfect."

"I can't stop." Sam pulled Nova closer, tight. "You've bewitched me."

Nova giggled, a simple chime blown by a hint of air. "No, precious. I prefer to begin the old fashioned way. Arousal by flesh. Touch. Words."

Sam pressed her mouth to Nova's as the woman's arms brushed behind her neck. Finding their pace. Their union. One body. One mind.

Sam leaned back on the bed as Nova devoured her. The wet lips between Nova's legs rocked across her abdomen. Hips thrusting forward and sliding back. Sam released Nova's ass with anguish, pushing against the mattress to slide them both higher on the bed.

Nova kissed her neck. Her chest. Lingered on her nipples. Sucking. Licking. "Listen with your body, Samantha. I'll teach you what it means to be a woman. To have a woman's touch."

Nova coaxed Sam's legs open and glided between her thighs. She traced the skin of Sam's swollen labia with a single finger. "Open, baby girl. Only a woman can understand another woman's needs."

Sam couldn't breathe. Nova bent forward and kissed her inner thigh. Somewhere between a tickle and a touch, Nova's hot tongue circled and then climbed upward, an Angel dragging Sam toward heaven. The trace across Sam's clit invoked an instantaneous moan. A mounting explosion before Nova's mouth descended the smooth skin between her outer labia and thigh. Nova didn't relent; she lapped at the flesh between Sam's ass and soaking entrance. Awareness. Every point between her legs became alive. She could feel the shape of her vulva as if staring at it in a mirror. Every fold. Every pore. Millimeters of sensation distinct but without separation. Sam's hips moved in rhythm with Nova's head. Her body's response to its own dreams and desires.

Nova mouthed her wet entrance, kissing a lover who'd been gone for decades and finally returned. A reunion between those never meant to be apart. Sam let her hands find the soft blond hair of Nova's head.

Pulling as the beauty pushed her tongue deep, rose upward and found her clit again. Each flick of the practiced tongue fired a jolt of energy into her pussy, radiating outward before starting again. Sam lifted her legs, rested her heels on Nova's shoulders, and pulled Nova's head toward her vagina. Wanting more. Needing more.

Sam's breath came in staccato shots as Nova's fingers slipped inside and found her G-spot. Stroke after stroke matched with deep suction on her clit and a vibrating tongue. Impossible pleasure.

Sam nearly broke when the first orgasm took her. Her eyes slammed shut. Her back lifted from the sheets. Every nerve firing in simultaneity. The muscles in her abdomen clenched and released. Contraction after contraction beneath her womb.

With a long, mewling cry, Sam's lungs filled and emptied with rapid, inadequate breaths. She whimpered as more fingers filled her. Thrusting in and out against the sweet spot at the top of her contracting pink walls. The spot Nova now owned with purpose. Sam's whole body vibrated with the incessant thrashing of Nova's tongue. Pulling her lust to the surface. Dragging another orgasm upward.

Sam screamed. Her knees slammed shut. Her body quaked. An arching back on the verge of breaking. Her fingers dug into the back of Nova's head, pulling her tight as wave after wave of uncapped fantasy crashed against Sam's body and tore her apart.

Sam's chest heaved. She forced her eyes open as Nova lifted her head and licked her cum soaked lips. The residua of Sam's climax still glistened on the gorgeous woman's cheeks. Nova moved upward like a predatory cat. She laid herself on top of Sam's body and kissed her mouth. Flavors recognized as her own filled Sam's mouth as Nova's tongue twisted with hers.

More. Give me more.

"Do you see?" Nova kissed her cheeks with whispered promises. "Do you understand?"

Unsure of what she'd agreed to, Sam could barely nod. She didn't care anymore as long as Nova stayed with her. Her breathing slowed. "I've never met anyone like you."

Nova giggled like distant bells from a forgotten church. She rose on her knees, shuffling forward to straddle Sam's face and braced herself against the wall. "Because there is no one else like me."

Sam inhaled the woman's scent. Strawberry promise on vanilla dreams. Rose washed memories. Calling her. A hint of pink inner lips called between alabaster labia. Drops of crystal dew on unfurled petals. Hiding. Asking.

Sam kissed Nova's clit with a light touch. Nothing could be that soft. Nothing could be so beautiful. She mouthed her sex, working her jaw to push her tongue into the wetness and pull upward. She clutched Nova's firm ass. Pulling her closer. Her thirst burned. The fount concealing her relief hovered above her tongue. All Sam had to do was swallow.

Nova moved her hips forward and back with Sam's attentions. "Drink, baby girl. Slake your thirst and crave me for eternity."

Sam didn't know what Nova meant. She didn't care. Sam took in her clit. Experimented. Hard. Soft. Slow. Fast. The sounds of Nova's moans guided her. The dripping cum demanded she continue.

More.

Nova's breaths came faster. "The pupil stood at the master's door, asking for instruction."

Sam explored with her fingers. Pushing inside. Circling Nova's ass. Her wetness. Sam's craving rose. A never ending trek across a barren desert without water. Oasis and satiety running drop by drop down her parched throat.

Nova moaned. "The master handed her a broom and closed his door."

Sam had no idea what Nova was talking about. She didn't care.

Nova's hips stuttered like an earthquake's after shock. She mewled in a feral squeak before oscillating the sweet tang over Sam's mouth again. The wetness came faster. Changing flavors. Thicker. Sweeter. A million candied dreams.

Another moan from Nova's lips. "The pupil swept the spotless porch every day. Rain or shine. Never asking why. She knew the things she desired would be revealed once she'd proved her worth."

Sam pulled the hard clit between her lips. Flicked. Released. Sucked.

It would never be enough.

With a gasp on warbling notes of rising pleasure, Nova's entire body trembled. She moved her knees backward and let her wetness rest on Sam's stomach. She smiled, staring into Sam's eyes. "One day, the gates opened."

Sam wanted to roll Nova onto her back, pin her against the sheets and drink forever. She didn't understand the woman's words but the lust they shared was real. Corporeal realization of uncountable fantasies.

Unseen hands gripped Sam's wrists and pulled them to the side, pinning them against the bed. As fear replaced her desire, ethereal bonds wrapped her ankles and pulled her legs open. She couldn't move. Her horror filled expression found Nova smiling with lascivious need above her.

Nova licked her lips and worked her hips against Sam's flesh again. "Search for me. Show me your desires are real and not a mortal's silly whim."

"What..." Words evaporated. A massive orgasm raked across her body. Sam bucked. Clenching her teeth. Straining against the bonds she couldn't see. A rush between her legs. Penetrated. Stretched. Continuous pleasure. She screamed. Every muscle in her body knotted with godlike contractions, released and contracted again. Orgasm after orgasm, the intensity of each continued to climb unimpeded. She couldn't see. Her own screams echoed in her ears. Her heart threatened to explode as each climax abutted the next. Unstoppable.

Stars raced across the skies.

Colors gyrated and scrawled themselves across her conscious mind.

Pulsing lights of incredible intensity.

Another world. Another place.

She left her body and floated in liquid pleasure. Undulating passion beyond experience. Beyond existence.

The universe began to flicker. Ripples tore the fabric of time, fading in and out across infinity.

Sam's consciousness broke. Everything she'd ever known or understood slipped away. Her entire world evaporated in a blinding flash of beauty without end.

***

Sam's eyes fluttered open.

My bed.

My room.

My house.

With aching muscles, she groaned and rolled to the side of the bed. The scent of Nova had left the air but her memory still burned fresh. Sam stood with slow pain. Everything hurt, from her chest to her toes.

It was real. Wasn't it?

She walked down the hallway, still hoping Nova would appear but knowing she'd already gone. Not even a hint of her presence remained. Before sadness could rinse away the pleasures she still couldn't comprehend, a splash of white on the kitchen table caught her attention.

Sam rushed forward and lifted the tiny business card with awe. The last remnant of a perfect night.

Complete pleasure faded into longing.

Stark white. On one side of the card, a simple line drawing of a flower decorated the thick paper. On the other, a string of numbers, black as pitch, seemed to lift themselves from the page and float in a hazy mist: 0112358132134. Sam blinked. She shook her head. An attempt to clear a sleep filled delusion. As her vision cleared, the numbers became solid again. A simple business card. Nothing more.

Chapter Three

A Beginning

*F*or the millionth time, Sam stared at the dog-eared card in her hand. A compact piece of stark white thrown into contrast by the bronzed skin of her hands and the blood-red polish glistening on long fingernails.

It'd been months since Nova shattered her world and left her hungry. *What did you want me to do with this?* The card had become an obsession, replacing recurrent thoughts of Kelly and the anxiety that accompanied them. She'd wasted too much emotional capital on a man who'd never hold a candle to the things Nova could grant her.

A sunflower.

0112358132134.

She could draw the picture in her sleep and recite the number in her dreams. *Why didn't you tell me what to do?* Forcing a breath through pursed lips, she beat back her own frustration and recited Nova's last words: "And then, one day, the gates opened."

Nova wouldn't have left her the card for nothing. Her cryptic words had to mean something. *"Search for me. Show me your desires are real and not a mortal's silly whim."*

The number didn't represent a phone number. Not only did it start with a zero, it had too many digits. *Too many combinations.* She had dialed variations until her fingers ached and stared at the card until the numbers seemed to pulse and spin.

What am I supposed to do?

Her eyes burned in frustration.

"Earth to Sam."

The gruff, impatient voice pulled Sam back to the planet she'd been born on. She looked up with a start. Trisha Summers, her only friend, sat across from her with open-mouthed incredulity. In truth, they weren't close, but they got together for lunch on occasion. Trisha provided her with human companionship but failed to relate to her on any subject with so much as a modicum of substance.

Trisha had picked the posh cafe. It was way too expensive for Sam's dwindling bank account. The eatery sat high above the Phoenix streets surrounded by glass windows on three sides. Cute wire-topped tables and comfortable chairs offered the illusion of a Paris street corner, if one chose to believe. The waiters wore black slacks, pressed white shirts, and bowties, a perfect match for the waitress's black skirts, pristine white blouses, and coifed hair. The food always reminded Sam of spring. Fresh baked bread imbued with a thousand scents. The wine flowed freely.

Trisha continued in an exasperated tone. "I swear to god, Sam, every time you take out that damn card you disappear. Did you hear anything I said?"

At the mention of the card, Sam opened her purse and tried to put it away. "I'm sorry, Trisha. It's just...well, you know. If I could just figure out what she wanted me to do with it."

"Give it to me." Trisha held out a manicured hand. Her wrist glistened with golden bracelets.

Sam hesitated. The precious card meant more to her than she wanted to reveal. She'd hinted to Trisha about her night with Nova without providing details. Especially with regard to her recent craving for women. *One woman at least.* If she spooked Trisha, she wouldn't have anyone to talk to anymore. Even if Sam decided to tell her everything, Trisha would never believe the details. She'd think Sam had gone around the bend at last. *I'm not sure myself anymore.* Sam caressed the card lovingly as she searched Trisha's eyes for intention. Benign. With a shaking hand, she passed the precious paper to her friend.

Trisha's fingers closed on the card and tugged hard before Sam relinquished it. Trisha harrumphed. "I just want to look. Jesus. I won't hurt it."

Trisha dressed in sexy clothes and flirted with every man they passed. Since her boob job, her blouses had cut deeper into her blooming cleavage and her skirts had risen higher. More than once, Sam considered taking their relationship further but her friend had never expressed any interest in women. A failed pass would ruin their friendship.

"We know it's not a phone number. You've told me that more times than I can count." Trisha set the card down in front of her and edged it back toward Sam with contempt. "Hell, it's not even very professional but what the hell do I know."

"What's that supposed to mean?" Sam growled before snatching the card back with lightning speed. She pressed it lovingly into her purse before speaking again. "Professional? It's a frigging number and a flower on a white card. What the hell do you want?"

"Wow." Trisha offered a smug expression before sipping her wine. "A little defensive aren't we?"

Sam pressed out her lower lip without thinking. Fighting back tears, she realized how stupid her reaction had been. "I'm sorry, Trisha. It's just... It's just... What does it mean? What did she want me to do with it?"

"Damn, girl. You've got to get your mind right. Men drool when you pass. You could have anyone you want and all you ever think about is the one that got away. What the fuck? Maybe the card doesn't mean anything at all."

"It means something. I know it does. I just have to figure it out." Sam wanted to change the subject, but couldn't bring herself to talk about anything else. "What did you mean about it not being professional?"

Trisha shrugged. "The number isn't even centered. It's like it was cut wrong or something."

Sam pulled out the card again, running her finger over the numbers with love. The off-center writing had never bothered her before but now she couldn't think about anything else. The digits started about two-thirds of the way across the card from left to right and had been displaced about two thirds of the way from the top of card to the bottom. The asymmetry became more obvious the more Sam thought about it. "It can't be cut wrong." Nova had been perfect. Powerful.

She wouldn't have made a mistake. It must mean something. Something I missed.

"I don't know what to tell you, girlfriend. It's a card. No doubt about it."

"Thanks for nothing."

"Did you try Google?"

"About a million times. At first I thought I was on to something. The numbers came up as the Fibonacci sequence."

"Fibo what?" Trisha almost choked on her wine.

Sam giggled. "The Fibonacci sequence. It's a series of numbers. The next number in the series is always the sum of the previous two. In this case you would have to add spacing to the numbers."

"I have no idea what you are talking about. Math is not what I excel at." Trisha watched a waiter with a cute ass go from one side of the room to the other. She turned back to Sam and smiled lasciviously. "I work the best on my back."

Sam rolled her eyes, no longer in the mood for wayward glances or small talk. "You're incorrigible."

"Come on, Sam," Trisha pleaded. "I'm sorry. This is obviously important to you. Tell me about the knocker sequence."

Sam laughed out loud. "Fibonacci sequence. Here. I'll show you." Sam pulled a pencil from her purse and unrolled a napkin. She wrote the number down from memory and added hyphens. "0-1-1-2-3-5-

8-13-21-34. 0 + 1 is 1. 1 + 1 is 2. 2 + 1 is 3. You see? It goes on forever."

"Okaaaaay." Trisha drew out the word before drinking the rest of her wine then looked around for the cute waiter again. "So. What's it supposed to mean?"

"I don't know."

"Wow, that's great. Good stuff. What about the flower?"

Sam flipped over the card and traced the flower with her fingertip. "It's a sunflower."

Trisha leaned forward as wine threatened to spout from her nose. "You know what kind of flower it is?"

"Of course. It's a sunflower. The seeds always form the same pattern."

"A sunflower, huh?" She guffawed. "Did you go back to school over the last couple of months or did I just get dumber?"

Do you really want me to answer that?

"Well, in this case, I think the flower type is important. The seed's pattern more than anything else." Sam saw the disgusted look on Trisha's face as she continued to explain. Her cheeks started to flush the way they always did when she was embarrassed. She shrugged and started to put the card away again.

I'll figure it out myself. "You can learn anything on the web. Look. Just forget about it. I'm not really hungry anymore. I'm going to head out."

Trisha reached across the table and put her hand on Sam's. Holding her. "Sam, I'm sorry. I knew you'd been thinking about the card a lot, I just didn't realize you'd become an expert in mathematics and botany. I slept with my professors. I didn't listen to the things they said. An A is an A right?" She laughed. "Go ahead. Wow me with your flowers, Teach."

Sam groaned. "Sunflowers. I think they're important because of the way the seeds develop."

"The seeds? Of course! Why didn't I think of that?" Trisha finished her glass of wine and filled it again.

"Just listen. Give me one minute without laughing. Just one."

Trisha waved her hands. "Go ahead, professor."

"Okay. Sunflower seeds always grow in the same way." Sam showed her friend the picture of the sunflower on the card and traced the spiral with her finger as she spoke. "The tiny ones in the very center are first ones formed. As the flower grows, each new seed formed is bigger than the one before it. With the changing size they can only fit together one way. The bigger the sunflower gets, the more seeds it forms and the bigger the spiral becomes. You see? The seeds spiral outward like the spinning arms of a galaxy."

"Great. A sunflower and Funacelli's number. So what?"

"Fibonacci. This is where it gets weird. To me at least. It turns out that the size of each new seed when compared to the size of the last seed formed is always the same. Dividing the size of the larger by the size of the smaller one gives you a ratio of 1.618. This is called the Golden Ratio. Since the ratio is always the same, the spiral the seeds form will always have the same shape. A Golden Spiral." She smiled, almost laughing at how easily she could explain it now. "You see it in nature all the time. In flowers and shells. People have used it throughout history in art and architecture because of its perfection. Cool, right?"

Trisha turned the bottle of wine upside down over her glass. When the last drop fell she groaned. "You and I have very different ideas of what's interesting, Sam. The only thing less interesting than a Golden Spiral or Golden Ratio would be a Golden Shower." When Sam glared at her, she held up her hands in self defense and set the wine bottle down. "I know, I know. Go on. I'm listening but only until this glass is empty. You have that long to convince me I care. What does this Golden stuff have to do with

Fabio's numbers?"

Sam didn't correct her this time. "It turns out that the Fibonacci numbers can be used to create, if you didn't guess, a series of Golden Rectangles."

Trish raised her lip in disdain. "Yeah...that's what I was thinking. Of course."

Sam flipped over the napkin and began drawing again. "It starts with a square and the first number in the sequence, one by one. You extend it to the first golden rectangle, which is the next number in the sequence and the one you just used, two by one. Go to the next number and you get new rectangle, three by two. Do it again and you get five by three. On and on and on. Each of the Fibonacci numbers one after the other. They fit perfectly on top of each other because they approximate the golden ratio, just like the sunflower seeds. The rectangles form a rough spiral with corners. If you draw an angle through the boxes from corner to corner like this..." She sketched a rough spiral. "A perfect golden spiral. So, sunflower seeds form a golden spiral because each seed is bigger than the last by the golden ratio. The Fibonacci numbers can be used to draw an interlocking series of golden rectangles. When you draw an arc through the corners of the rectangles you get a golden spiral. They're all connected." She pointed to the card."The sunflower." She flipped it over and pointed again. "The Fibonacci numbers." She placed the napkins next to each other. "The golden rectangles and finally another golden spiral. You get it?"

"Sure." Trisha drained the last of her glass and signed the check her cute waiter had brought over. "So how does that help us understand the card?"

Sam's lip quivered. "I don't know."

"Great. Fascinating presentation, professor." Trisha put her credit card away.

Something about the asymmetry of the number tugged at Sam's brain but she couldn't bring it forward. Sam blurted out before she thought about what she would sound like. "She said to search for her."

"Search for who? The mysterious woman you keep talking about?" Trisha chuckled. "She wanted you to search for her? What the hell does that mean? Sounds like a nut-ball to me."

Sam realized she'd said too much and couldn't take it back. She couldn't explain the details. Trisha wouldn't understand. "I don't know."

"Wow. I've never seen you so flustered. Is there something you didn't tell me?" Trisha smiled mischievously. "Did you sleep with her? You little tart."

Sam tried to smile back but her expression looked more ill than happy. *Yes I did and I'll never stop trying to find her.* "Stop. Of course not. You're making me blush."

"I know what you need. A sleepover will make you forget all about your...girlfriend." The corners of Trisha's mouth turned up in an expression that could only be described as pure lechery.

Trisha loved 'just girl's nights'. For Trisha, Sam's house provided both an excuse and location for her extra marital affairs. Over the last few years, Sam hadn't been home when she'd loaned the place to Trisha. She'd always been with Kelly. Now *human* lust no longer excited her. Nova had ruined her forever. Mortal men may still be able to push her to the brink, but her newly discovered needs far exceeded any past desires.

"Maybe." Sam attempted another facetious smile. "Not tonight though. I think I'm going to turn in early." She counted out the cash for her share of the check and pushed it across the table while Trisha flirted with another young waiter.

Trisha gathered up the cash and her things with a sigh. "Well, I have to be getting back anyway. The husband expects me to cook for him and the kids every now and then. One must keep up appearances.

Are you sure you don't want to go out tonight? A proper fucking would do you more good than an early bedtime. My two cents."

"I'm sure." Sam couldn't stop thinking about the Golden Spiral and the off-center numbers. "This weekend, I promise. Okay?" Sam stood and pushed her chair in.

"Okay. But we have to come back here. I want to ride that waiter to the ground."

Sam laughed. "Which one? You've probably slept with most of them already. Just saying."

"Are you calling me a slut?" Trisha gave Sam a hug and kissed her cheek. "The tall guy with close cropped blond hair over there. With the tattoo on his neck."

Sam searched across the tables until she spotted the waiter Trisha lusted after. "I think he's wearing a wedding ring."

"I'll make him forget about his wife."

"You're unbelievable."

They walked through the doors together.

"Are you saying you want a shot at him?"

"No! That's not what I'm saying at all."

"Then what are you complaining about? If you aren't going to sleep with him, I will."

Sam kissed her cheek and looked across the

parking lot for her car. "I have no doubt, Trisha. I promise I won't get in the way. He's all yours."

"You're too choosy, Sam. You need to get laid a little more often. It'll make you forget about Kelly and this new...girl."

Sam waved as she headed across the black top. "Call me, Trisha! This weekend. I promise."

"Count on it, girlfriend. Love ya."

Her friend's voice faded as Sam pulled the car door shut and turned on the ignition. The air conditioner started with a roar but the temperature hadn't started to drop yet.

Sam couldn't stop herself. She pulled the business card from her purse again. *I know the answer is here.* With longing, she pulled her fingers downward across the middle of the card. *Somewhere.* She drew her finger sideways, feeling the raised letters from left to right. *Somehow.* As the blare of a car horn jolted her back to reality, she looked up and waved to Trisha pulling out of the lot. A flicker of light caught her eye. She looked down with a start. A simple white glared back at her.

Great. Now I'm fucking hallucinating on top of everything else.

***

Golden Spirals.

Fibonacci Sequence.

Asymmetric placement.

Golden rectangles.

That's it!

With a pounding heart, Sam drove to her house. By the time she turned the key in the door and pushed it open, her hands shook. She kicked off her shoes and closed the door with her foot. She pulled the card from her purse and tossed the bag onto the ground before jogging to her bedroom.

Progressing through every cuss word she knew, she banged her drawers open one by one, rifling the contents and throwing them on the floor. On the edge of a nervous breakdown, she finally found an old ruler and dived onto her bed.

She stabbed her finger at the power button on her open computer repeatedly. "Come on. Come on."

The computer flickered to life with interminable slowness. She traced the card again, refusing to take her eyes off of it this time. *I'm not crazy. Draw a line from top to bottom touching the numbers on their left side. Bisect again from left to right across the numbers.* The numbers flickered and lasted long enough for her to trust her sanity. *Yes!* A ghostly twinkle of ethereal green radiance pulsed before it faded against brilliant white again. Her breathing quickened. She repeated the action of her hands again. Another flicker. Weaker. Fading faster than the first time.

"No. No." She pleaded for the card's light to strengthen. She traced again. Added another line but nothing could make the flash stay longer. Exasperated, she went back to her computer, clicked again and launched the browser.

She searched Golden Rectangle and Fibonacci Sequence and scrolled through the same files she'd seen so many times before. Changing her attention from the screen to the card and back again, she searched frantically, trying to find the page that would trigger the part of her brain screaming at her. The solution to the puzzle just out of reach.

There.

She opened a page showing how to construct a golden spiral from golden rectangles derived from the Fibonacci sequence. She laid the ruler on the card and drew a line from top to bottom just touching the left side of the numbers. The line created a large box on the left and a slightly smaller box on the right. She tried to slow her own pulse as she measured the width of the card and the width of the smaller box. She pulled up a calculator and divided the larger number by the smaller number and then shrieked in glee. *1.618. The golden ratio.* The line abutting the number had divided the card into a golden rectangle.

Her hands shook as she laid the straight edge of the ruler on the card again across the middle of the number. She drew a line from left to right, perpendicular to the line she had just draw from the top of the card to the bottom. The card now had three rectangles. A large one to the left of the numbers. A smaller one in the top right quadrant above the numbers and an even smaller one on the right below the numbers. She measured the two rectangles on the right and divided their lengths. Another golden ratio, another golden rectangle.

The number divides the card into golden rectangles! I knew it wasn't a mistake.

After bouncing on the bed with joy, Sam looked at her computer again. Using the Fibonacci numbers, she began drawing a series of golden rectangles on the card with her ruler starting from the center. One by One. One by two. Three by two. Five by three. Eight by five. The rectangles spiraled outward from the center and meshed with the original two she'd drawn to perfection.

She glanced at her screen one more time. Starting at the center again, she began to draw one continuous arc connecting corner after corner of each rectangle. A perfect golden spiral.

Now what?

She touched the center of the card and followed the spiral outward with her fingertip. She stopped breathing as the numbers pulsed. Iridescent green alternating with blue. She moved to the center of the card and traced the spiral again. The numbers began to spin. She gasped. Blood red. Emerald green. Blue. Spiral upon hypnotic spiral.

Yes! Yes!

Not wanting to stop, she traced again. Faster.

The card began to hum at a frequency she felt in the pit of her stomach.

She traced again.

The room vibrated.

The air in her lungs disappeared. Sucked clear with burning fire. Unable to breathe, terror replaced excitement. She clawed at the bed and prayed for life. On the edge of madness, the room faded away with a grinding rush that pounded at her ears with bone shattering decibels. Unbounded pain.

Her stomach lurched. Darkness wrapped its cloak around her with silent finality. The world faded away.

Chapter Four
A Task

Sam floated in another place. Enveloped in never-ending spring, birds chirped a twittering song meant for her ears alone. Bubbling water of perfect clarity cascaded across rocky streambeds. Vanilla, lilacs... Aromas from a million dreams teased her brain, pulling her back with forgotten memories.

She moaned. Her long black eyelashes fluttered as she tried to open them. Soft hands stroked her forehead. Impossibly smooth. Beyond warm. Light stabbed her brain. She blinked, trying to rise on her arms.

"Shhh, Samantha." A familiar voice. A melody constructed from a thousand exquisite tones. Resonance of comfort.

The woman above her came into focus. Long blond hair fell about her shoulders. Alabaster skin carved from unblemished stone barely a breath away.

Hazel eyes possessed of depth so vast, a mere glance would never unveil their secrets. Full crimson lips begged for a kiss anyone would sell their soul to taste. The scent of roses. "Nova?"

"Of course, Samantha?" The woman smiled. "You were expecting someone else?"

Sam found her voice as the cosmos continued to steady around her. "I didn't know what to expect. I thought I'd never figure out what to do with the card. I didn't know what it meant. I almost gave up."

"Posh." Nova leaned forward and kissed her lips softly. "I knew you would understand. I'm very patient."

"Where are we?"

Nova's long fingers circled Sam's hardening nipples through the soft fabric pulling against them.

The pink silk of Nova's thin negligee pulled tight against her ass as she sat up and motioned in the air with an open hand. "*That* is a difficult question. We're in neither your world or ours. The In-Between, if you will."

Stone walls surrounded Sam on all sides. Each was broken by a single hallway leading off in another direction. Multicolored frescoes of men and women engaged in various forms of intimate congress decorated the walls. Marble columns stretched into the darkness far above her, support for a ceiling she couldn't see. Light flashed from sconces set in every wall. Without smoke or oil, their light flickered and danced, neither too light or too dark. Mood itself had been cast across the surrounding stone.

Sam sat up on an enormous bed. The mattress molded to her form with its feather-soft embrace. Unmarred by flaw or wrinkle, silk sheets flowed beneath her. Sam looked at her clothes as she slid off the bed. She'd been adorned in a light white shift. Almost transparent, it revealed every curve she possessed.

"I loved the way it fit you the moment I saw it." Nova stepped forward and rested her light hands on Sam's hips. "The feel of it against your skin. I loved removing your clothes and dressing you while you slept. It took everything I had to keep my tongue and fingers focused."

Sam closed her eyes. She gasped as Nova's hot mouth bathed her neck in tender kisses. Her own hands found the toned flesh of Nova's ass beneath the pink silk. She squeezed, pulling her closer until their breasts pressed against each other, separated only by cruel fabric. Wet heat dampened her pussy. Blood rushed into her clit. Nova nibbled lightly, dragged her tongue across her throat, between her breasts and headed lower. Sam entwined her fingers in the blond hair with a moan. "Yes."

Nova raised her head and kissed Sam's lips. Their tongues probed softly and then deeper. Sam's heart began to race. She pulled harder.

Nova stepped back and moved away. "Our time will come soon, Samantha. It's time to meet your charge."

Sam wanted Nova to take her to bed. "My charge?"

Smiling sweetly, Nova held out her hand. Her perky nipples tented the silk of her pink negligee. Sam had never wanted to kiss anything more.

"Your charge, Samantha. You can't learn to be a dominatrix without a charge. This one is...how should I say this...particularly surly. He'll make you work for your mark, but the rewards are beyond measure."

Sam took the tiny hand in her own. So warm. So perfect. Her head spun with questions as the nymph pulled her down bright hallways intermittently lit by lamps or sunlight pouring down from open-air sections. "What is it I'm supposed to do?"

"You asked if I would give you seduction. If I would teach you to control. Do you remember?" Nova's voice remained soft, almost inaudible.

Sam stared at the floor as they walked. "Yes."

"Do you remember what you promised in return?"

The words came back in a rush. Sam's voice dropped lower. "Anything."

"Good girl. You're going to fix my...situation." Nova giggled. She placed her hand on Sam's lower back. "Try not to look so upset. He'll be the perfect man for you to hone your skills. If you can tame him, you can own any man."

With confusion splashed on unanswered questions, Sam let herself be pulled between ornate columns and towering walls of dressed stone. They passed several men and women as they walked. Each more delicious than the last.

The women seemed hewn from dreams. Breasts both large and small. Hips wide and narrow. Blondes. Brunettes. Redheads. Each stepped to the side as Nova and Sam passed. Their faces filled with smiles and giggles. Sam's cheeks pinked with embarrassment as the succulent women followed them with interest.

The men were just as magnificent. Tall or short, their arms bulged with sculpted muscles. Never too much. Never too little. Their chests and abdominal muscles would be described as lickable, nothing less would do them justice. With few exceptions, they each wore a simple wrap around their waist, dropping to mid thigh. The loin covers seemed designed to outline and display the swollen members they failed to hide. More than once the hard bulges beneath so many wicked cloths seemed impossible. Sizes that brought her to open-mouthed standstills time after time until Nova tugged her into motion again.

"You can sample the fruit whenever and as many times as you want later, Samantha. After you meet your charge."

"Sample?" The pounding in Sam's chest became more intense.

Nova turned and walked backwards, puckering her lips with exasperation. "Of course. Each of them is here of their own accord. Desiring only pleasure. Simply ask and they are yours for as long as you need them. They will fulfill each of your fantasies, and by doing so, you will fulfill theirs."

Daydreams of enjoying her choice of multiple men and women left Sam speechless. Any ménage of her choice. Hundreds of beings surrounded her, every one willing to grant her any desire. She didn't want to squander a single minute.

They turned into a courtyard surrounded on all sides by other buildings. A pool of topaz blue filled a marble basin. At its center, the serene mirrored surface was broken by two naked women locked in a loving embrace. Sunlight accented their shining bodies, dark skin against light, their lips pressed together with longing. Overhead, the sun warmed the space to perfection, providing life to the small trees reaching upward to accept it.

A man squatted at the edge of the pool. He waded in as she watched. His arms appeared cut from rare mahogany, hard, massive and meant for control. The tattoos encircling his upper arms seemed to writhe and move the longer she stared. Outlined by tanned skin, every muscle in his back bulged as if cut from stone. His ass, unclothed and defined, simply delicious. A veritable anatomical sculpture of man. Gods would hide in shame at his appearance. Sam had never seen anything so beautiful. Long platinum hair flowed over his powerful shoulders inked with an X-shaped picture too far away for her to see in detail.

"He's heavenly, isn't he?"

The sound of Nova's voice forced a blush across Sam's cheeks. "He is. Do you know him?"

Nova kissed her cheek. Her voice dropped to a breathy whisper. "He's my husband."

"Your husband?" Sam looked at the ground and

turned away from the pond, glad Nova couldn't see her thoughts. "I'm sorry. I didn't mean—"

"Didn't mean to want him?" Nova interrupted her. "To taste his flesh with your eyes? Don't apologize. The perfection of his form has driven my lust for centuries."

Sam turned to stare again. The man shifted his attention between the women in the pool with him. Grabbing their asses. Kissing their lips and chests. Running his fingers between their thighs. Forgotten fervor began to rise between Sam's legs as she longed to be in their place. She twirled her hair as her mind wandered. "Doesn't it bother you he's with other women?"

Nova tilted her head as if Sam had asked the strangest question she'd ever heard. "Of course not. We love each other. Always. He has his needs and I have my own." She motioned with her hand. "Love has nothing to do with...this."

Sam didn't understand but, then again, the idea of him taking whomever he wanted excited her. The warmth beneath her shift changed to damp necessity.

Out of my league.

"So you accept?"

"Accept what?" Sam stared at the beauty beside her.

"Your charge."

Sam closed her eyes and shook her head before letting them open again. "I have no idea what you're talking about."

"I will teach you control and you will make him submit. To you."

Sam's mouth fell open in shock. "Your husband? What... Why would..."

"Stop being difficult. We are creatures of pleasure. Why should we deny ourselves? Why should we deny others? He's lost his way and you will help him find it again. He has used his powers to manipulate mortal women for the last time. It will no longer be tolerated by the council."

"The council?"

Nova raised a hand and waved the question away with exasperation. "The details of our world and its politics are unimportant. He's been given his final ultimatum."

Sam couldn't believe Nova's words. Nothing made sense any more. "Why me?"

Nova touched Sam's hips and pulled her closer. She starred into her eyes before kissing her lips. "Because you're perfect and, I have no more time." She turned her head and raised her voice. "Gage. Your mistress has arrived."

Sam's face sweltered like the surface of a star. "No. Oh my god." She tugged her hair and stared at the ground, wishing she could crawl under the tree's sheltering shade and die.

As Nova spoke his name, the man turned his chiseled face toward her. With a stern glare, his black eyes became coals burning across eternity. He growled with deep-seated vitriol. Boiling spit. "So. She has come."

How did I invoke such hatred in a person I've never even met?

Gage stood slowly. His massive cock hung to mid thigh. Huge even before erect. The pain his tool could inflict had her pussy flowing with a Pavlovian response she hadn't expected. His luscious abs glistened with sweat and pulled her toward his unmatched masculinity.

Gage gripped himself hard. He stroked his beast to life as he approached with purpose. "Am I to submit to this tiny slip of a girl? A woman I could fuck into oblivion without thought?"

Excuse me?

He laughed with something on the wrong side of hatred. "I will turn her on her knees and fuck her ass until she knows who the master is. When she pleads for mercy, I'll wrap my fingers in her hair and fill her with my cum." His voice rose with bitter hate as he closed the distance. "Kneel, little girl. I need a new fuck toy anyway. I suppose you'll have to do."

"Enough," Nova screamed in fury. She lifted her open hand in the air. "Your insolence bores me." She closed her fist and Gage crumpled as if made of paper. He screamed in immortal pain, writhing on the ground like a gutted fish.

Nova's fist tightened until her knuckles turned white. "You will obey the council's wishes or I will expel you myself."

A primal screech poured from Gage's lungs as if his soul had been severed from his mortal shell. Pain beyond measure.

The naked women in the pool screamed in terror. They fled into a distant building as the sound of Gage's horror tore through Sam's skin and pounded her bones. She grew lightheaded as he contorted on the ground. He shriveled into a fetal ball and shrieked without cessation. Torture spewed from his lips. Perpetuity passing in slow motion.

As tears rolled down Gage's cheeks and pooled on the ground, Sam couldn't take any more. "Nova, stop. You're killing him."

Nova turned to Sam. She scrunched her eyes in question and tilted her head to the side. "Interesting."

She opened her hand without taking her gaze from Sam. Gage's screams transformed into raking sobs that continued to claw the air around them.

Sam stared at the wounded animal who'd been Gage only a moment before. "Why did he say those things to me? Why did he want to hurt me?"

Nova stepped forward and placed her hand in the small of Sam's back. "Set him on the correct path again."

"What?" Sam turned on Nova with a start. "He hates me already."

Nova's warm finger traced circles through Sam's shift. An attempt at comfort now lost in confusion.

"What path? Why is he being punished for using his power to seduce? Is that wrong? Isn't it what you did to me?"

Nova let out a peal of laughter. An amazing sound of music, played by a thousand angels.

Sam hadn't meant to be funny. "Why are you laughing?"

"Because you're cute." Nova lifted Sam's chin and kissed her on the lips. "He used his powers inappropriately for lust and conquest. Seduction is fine. Compulsion is not. The council frowns on magical beings who abuse their privileges. Especially if they weren't born with those powers."

"He wasn't born magical?"

"Of course not." Nova laughed again. "Does he look like one of the fair folk?"

He looks like a god to me.

"I guess. I don't know."

"The answer is no. He was human, just like you. I became infatuated with him hundreds of years ago. His looks. His purity. I seduced him and made him mine. After that, I couldn't give him up. I traded many...favors to get the council to allow him to age with me. They relented and he has been my lover ever since."

"And now you want me to save him? How am I supposed to do that? He's your husband, for god's sake."

Nova grabbed Sam's ass and pulled her in tightly. Pressing their chests together. "You're so precious, Samantha. I could just eat you up."

Sam's lips found Nova's again. She wanted to be eaten.

Nova stepped back. She ran her finger across Samantha's chest as if absorbed in her own thoughts. "Gage used his powers to compel. He forced women to give him anything he wanted. He hadn't earned their lust with seduction. He took it by force. Manipulation of another's mind is forbidden. The council warned him repeatedly and he refused to obey our laws. His punishment has been decreed. It's non-negotiable. I cannot save him this time. He will be an example. Submit or be broken. The choice is his."

"And I am his...punishment? That doesn't sound very flattering." Sam already regretted their agreement. She closed the distance between them, caressing the blonde's back as their lips touched again. Barely a breath between them. The scent of promise on her tongue.

Nova's voice dropped to a whisper. "He must submit. He must bend to his Mistress willingly. Gratefully." A wicked look lifted the corner of Nova's mouth. "You, Samantha, will bend him to your will."

The implication of Nova's words struck Sam hard. She forgot how wet her pussy had become. She pulled back, terrified by the impossible request. "Me? That's ridiculous. I've never seduced anyone in my life let alone someone like...like him." Her gaze flashed backed to Gage struggling to find his knees.

"On the contrary. You seduced Kelly. Many others. Should I go on?"

Sam's head spun. *How could she know?* "No." The pain of Kelly's loss crept into Sam's head. "They seduced me. I chose to participate."

"I see." Nova chuckled. "You didn't try to entice them?"

"Of course, but..."

Nova reached for the shoulder strap of Sam's shift and pulled it low, exposing her breast. "Is that what you're doing now?"

Sam's mouth went dry. "You've been watching me? How else would you know?"

Nova tightened her lips, choking back a grin. "Perhaps you only wish to submit? Is that what you want? To give your lovers what they need without ever addressing your own desires?"

Nova's words confused Sam. She'd turned everything around, backwards and inside out. "No." Blood rushed between her ears with an audible thrum. A dizzying swirl. "I was the submissive. I did whatever he asked."

"The submissive is always in control, Samantha. You either failed to understand that simple concept or chose not to believe."

Shaking her head, Sam pulled her shoulder strap back into place and stepped away. "No. That's not true." She couldn't face the possibility of being the source of her own misery.

Did I drive them all away?

Nova raised an eyebrow in disbelief and

sauntered closer as Sam continued to back-peddle. "Am I in error? Is there something about the statement that isn't correct? Is it flawed in some way? I'm always eager to learn something new. What about the good Dr. Phar? Did you simply choose to participate? A wanted tryst between consenting lovers? How fascinating." She clapped her hands in a parody of excitement, bouncing on her toes with factitious glee. "Do tell. I want to know more."

Gage moaned, drawing the attention of both women. Sam began to hyperventilate. "I-I can't."

"You can." Nova let her face soften with understanding. Pleading. "I'll teach you and you will return my lover to me again."

"But—"

"Stop, Samantha." Nova clutched both of Sam's hands in her own and stared into her eyes, drawing her gaze away from Gage. "Listen to me. I've chosen you. You have to."

"Have to?" Sam tried to sound indignant but her heart wasn't in it. "I thought this was my choice. Didn't you say I was to be the seductress?" She wasn't angry but she needed Nova to believe her vehemence was sincere. A last bastion of self respect before refusing the contract she'd accepted so carelessly.

Nova looked away. "If you fail, he'll be expelled

and I will lose him forever. My heart will be cut from my chest. A loss I will not survive."

The stakes were too high. Too much pressure. "Survive? I thought you were immortal or—"

"Even immortals can experience too much pain. When our minds break, we wander for eternity. Broken souls that can no longer be repaired."

Sam's eyes burned. Warm tears dripped down her cheeks. She wiped them away and sniffed, trying not to blubber in front of Nova. "You ask too much."

Nova wrapped Sam in a warm embrace and hugged. "Perhaps, but I have no choice. You must succeed or I will perish."

Sam pulled her shift tight and stared at Gage's perfect form, resigned to try in the face of inevitable failure. "Where do I start?"

Nova kissed her cheek. Pure affection. Relief. She laid her head on Sam's shoulder. "Tend to him. Show him the Samantha I know you can be."

"Tend to him?"

"Bathe him. Clothe him. Let him learn your touch."

"Do I...you know...give myself to him if he...I mean he wouldn't but if he asks?" It didn't make sense but Sam wanted Gage even after the way he'd treated her. *Why am I drawn to those who want to hurt me?*

"No. That you cannot do. Seduction is the promise of things to come. Not the thing itself. You must bring him to the edge. Hold him there and refuse him release. His lust will grow until he has no choice but submit. His entire being will crave you more than water. He will give anything just to have you. Submission is just the beginning."

***

Sam took a deep breath and stepped toward the moaning hulk that had once been Gage. She wondered where to begin. His hot hands found her ankles, gripping with entreaty before he gazed upward, begging for leniency. His black eyes swam in pain. His cheeks turned crimson and dripped with tears.

Sympathy rose within Sam's heart. She embraced it. Kneeling with grace, she placed her hands on Gage's back. "Shhhh." She rubbed with an Angel's touch. "I'm here."

His cheek found her knee with gentle pressure as he continued to gasp.

Sam pulled her fingertips across his back, tracing the impossible musculature. "Come." She placed her tiny hand beneath his bicep and pulled. "Stand with me. Please."

Using her body for support, he bent his knee and pushed himself to standing. On shaking limbs, he shuffled forward and let her lead him toward the pool. His massive cock, not yet awake, brushed against her thigh. She'd tried not to think about the size as she shifted her hand to his lower back and brushed his abs with the other. Hard. Cut. Perfect.

They waded into the pool together. The warm water lapped at her ankles. Gage wobbled like a newborn kitten, placing more of his weight on Sam every time he stumbled. As the depth increased, Sam lowered the Adonis. The buoyancy took over from her aching muscles. He half floated, half sat in waist deep water before splashing water on his face.

Soaked through, Sam's shift had become even more see-through. She turned to Nova, wanting her approval before she removed her clothing but the sprite had gone without at sound. With blushing cheeks, Sam pulled the shift from her body and tossed it to the side. Water rushed against her soaking cleft as she knelt behind Gage. A sensual massage between her legs. She lifted her hands to his shoulders. Trepidation tempered by her need to touch him. Kneading his hard muscles, softly at first, increasing her pressure only when he relaxed beneath her fingertips. Her nipples brushed against his back and flooded with lust. An electric tingle she encouraged, leaning against him, sliding the swollen buds across his water-slicked skin. Her heart galloped like a frightened doe. She inhaled the musky scent of his neck and embraced the tickle of his long hair against her cheek.

Gage lifted his hand and placed it on hers. He turned and stared through her with his black eyes. She licked her lips and pulled her fingers lower, caressing his bulging pectoral muscles and circling his nipples gently until they rose as hardened kernels. His hand moved through the water and cupped her breast. Massaging. Lifting. Stroking. He pinched her nipples with tenderness. Turning. Pulling. Her breath came in short puffs on the verge of moaning. She moved closer and let her fingertips find his knee. His thigh. Her knuckles brushed against his cock. Hard now. Massive power. She gripped his shaft and squeezed until he began to mewl in pleasure devoid of words. As she stroked him, his hand found the open folds between her thighs. His fingers probed, separating her labia with ease, slipping inward until she spread her legs to accept. Expert fingertips massaged her clit, entered, and found her clit again. Her back arched as she slid her hips forward.

He stood slowly. His balls lifted high and tight as

they tried to reign in the huge hard-on inches from her face. She looked up at him. Wanting to see the desire she felt for him reflected in his eyes. Only hunger greeted her. She ached to feed him. She rose on her knees and touched his balls, letting the water lap at her sensitive breasts. The sensation echoed between her thighs as she leaned in and pressed her tongue to the heated cock, which seemed to beckon beyond reason.

He placed his hands on her shoulders. His lust pulsed so close to her lips. Water dripped from the tense sides. Each drop bumped against veined flesh pursuing their own wayward journey downward. They joined in a succulent rivulet to roll across the massive base and play upon his balls pulled up snug in response to her hunger.

She clutched his hips and pressed her tongue to the swollen head. So soft. Teasing. With his hot flesh between her lips, she slid downward, a moving kiss across the unyielding surface. When his fingers tightened, or his hips inched forward, she lingered. Sucking. Tiny movements of her head allowed her tongue to worship the sensitive spots he wanted her to spoil with special attentions. She needed only listen to his body and respond to the requests meant for her alone.

Even beneath the still water of the pool, the heat inside her pussy grew. The way he'd approached her had been an aphrodisiac rather than anathema. *Maybe I'm a submissive after all.* She would've crawled to him with or without compulsion.

She moved her hands to the surface of his shaft. Just the fingertips between his hard abs and cock, pressing the luscious pleasure against her tongue. She slid upward, wanting to take him between her lips. To feel his length deep in her throat. She would kindle the flames inside him until his resistance crumbled and her touch became the only thing he craved.

Clear drops of pre-cum flowed from his tip. Perfection. A flavor she'd evoked from him. Squeezing her eyes closed, she pulled him into her mouth. Gently, her fingers closed around his hot sack just above his balls. She took him deep, sucked and withdrew with smacking lips before swallowing him again. Her free hand tightened, released and slid in counter-pose to her bobbing head. The more he moaned the deeper she took him, driven by the desire to make him hers. His fingers entwined in her hair as he pushed himself deeper. He wanted her and she could barely breathe.

Gage moaned and thrust deeper, choking her,

giving respite and choking again. He growled with animalistic vigor. "You feel the power of my cock as it slides down your throat, don't you? Strength you can't live without. You're a good little girl. You may have seen me broken but you will never see me beg."

Sam's heart burned on his words. Bubbling cinders of charred passion they never shared. Everything to this point had been her fantasy, not his. She tried to pull free but he only forced himself deeper. She tried to understand his abuse as her tears came, pleading with her mind and telling her she'd misunderstood.

He held the back of her head tighter. "You will beg for me to cum inside you. The number of women who've begged for my seed on their lips will pale in comparison to the ones who follow you. You can be their example."

Sorrow became anger. Hate floated in a sea of molten brimstone. *Motherfucker.* She tried to pull backwards but he held even tighter. The disgust and mistreatment she'd suffered at the hands of every lover she'd ever known burned her lust away in an instant. *I no longer kneel for anyone.* She tightened her hands on his sensitive balls and squeezed with all her strength. Gage screamed and ripped his cock free before splashing to his knees to writhe in pain again.

She stood over him with fury and spit in the water, forcing his seed from her mouth. She wiped her lips with the back of her hand. Her voice became acid. "You will never speak to me like that again. No one will ever speak to me like that again. Do you understand?" Like rapid dogs, years of self deprecation snapped at her consciousness and she refused to cower ever again. "You earn me, you son of a bitch, or I will take you apart myself." Intent on beating him senseless, she raised her fist with demonic ferocity she could no longer control,.

A light, twittering laughter skipped across the water from behind her and stayed Sam's hand. She turned as Nova placed her hand over her own mouth, seemingly unable to control her mirth but hoping to disguise it. Sam spun on her heel, determined to redirect her anger at the giggling woman. *Your council can bury him and I won't shed a fucking tear.*

With shaking shoulders, Nova lowered her hand and smiled before looking at the ground. "You see? Who would tolerate such behavior from any man?" She looked up, biting her lip with innocent mirth. "I thought I'd have to save you. Apparently he's the one who needs help."

Sam held her tongue and looked at Gage gasping for air in the water. Her anger faded in an instant, replaced by shock at her own actions. Without warning, Nova's delight pulled her own free, pinking her cheeks as she took in the scene. She stood naked in a pool of water, far from her own world between a gorgeous fairy and a writhing Adonis whose balls she'd just crushed with her own hand. *Nonsensical.* She laughed uncontrollably.

Nova laughed with her until neither of them could catch their breaths. "It appears I chose well after all. I think you'll do nicely."

Sam stepped from the water. Her mirth evaporated the moment she noticed the two hulking men standing behind Nova. She turned sideways and covered her breasts with her hands, blushing madly.

Gazing at the shirtless men standing by her side, Nova chuckled again. "Why do you cover that beautiful body, Samantha? You have nothing to be ashamed of." She held her arms wide. "Come."

The consolation Nova offered seemed misplaced after Sam's treatment of Gage. "You're not angry?" Sam walked toward the blonde nymph. Lowering her hand with trepidation, she tried to gain control of her self-consciousness. She pressed against Nova's chest and accepted the purity of the embrace. Truth. Hope.

"Angry?" Nova pressed her lips to Sam's and kissed deeply. Lingering. "Why would I be angry? He deserved it. You put him in his place. I'm not angry, precious girl. I'm wet."

Sam stepped back, flushed with embarrassment again. "I'm sorry. I should've thought. I didn't see a towel. I didn't think—"

"No, silly girl." Nova pulled Sam's hand beneath her negligee and placed it between her legs. "Not my clothes. My pussy." She motioned to the men behind her. "I brought toys. It's time you were rewarded for all your hard work."

Sam's mouth fell open in disbelief. The men were identical. Long blond hair fell behind their broad shoulders. Lit by starlight alone, their blazing blue eyes twinkled back at her. Strong chins jutted forward on unsmiling faces, clean shaven and young appearing but powerful. They held their massive arms crossed over bulging chests. Wicked abs, each muscle cut from granite, ran in a sharp V toward bulging loin cloths. Portraits of masculinity. "You want me too..."

"To play with me, Samantha." Nova's giggle could have brought angels to tears. "Take your pick or, better yet, we can share."

"Here? Now?" Sam glanced over her shoulder at Gage and the damage she'd inflicted.

He deserved worse.

"Forget him, my love. It's our turn. He can watch us take what he cannot have."

Nova raised her hand and curled her finger. Gage stood with a groan and shambled out of the pool, staring at them in pained disbelief. As he stepped from the water, Nova opened her hand and tuned it palm downward. Gage fell to his knees hard. The impact boomed through the soles of Sam's feet. He grunted. Racked with pain. Nova extended her finger and pointed at the ground. Gage cried out as he fell forward on his hands, clawing with white-tipped fingers. With a smile, Nova turned her hand upward and raised her fingertips. Her lover's chin turned toward the sky until his neck muscles strained with shaking tension. His black eyes fixated on them. "Do not avert your eyes, my love. We want you to watch us enjoy our evening." Nova directed her attention to Sam again and sucked her lower lips with a resounding pop. "Now, where were we?"

The kneeling form of Gage warmed Sam's heart. His treatment of her demanded immediate punishment and Nova's offer seemed the perfect way to start. Her coy demeanor slipped away as she imagined Gage watching her being fucked. A proper torture. She stepped toward the two men and reached toward the one on the left. She stopped before touching his skin. "May I?"

The gorgeous sculpture lowered his arms. "You may do as you please, Mistress."

"Oh, I do like your choice in toys, Nova." She traced his abs with her fingertip, letting it bounce across each muscle as she headed lower. The fabric at his waist rose with unprecedented speed. "Have you named them yet?"

The man on the left chuckled. "I'm Jace and this is my brother Joshua. We are here to serve your needs."

"My needs?" Sam looked at Gage's kneeling form again. "How delightful."

Nova stepped forward and kissed Joshua's chest. Licking across until she found his nipple. Nibbling. Sucking. His hands moved to her ass. A tight squeeze. His head lolled backward in ecstasy.

Blood rushed into Sam's clit. Her entire pussy felt hot. Indescribable need rose. An itch only Jace could scratch. She looked into his eyes and undid the pin at his waist. The loin cloth fell to the ground. His cock made his muscles seem insignificant. Rock hard and long. He would stretch her wide even if he chose to be kind. "Jesus. You're huge."

Nova undid Joshua's pin and let his wrap fall to the ground. She pulled her negligee off with grace.

"Wait until you see what he can do with it, baby girl." She reached high and touched Joshua's neck. "Lift me. I need a man inside me now."

Joshua stooped. He placed his hands below Nova's thighs and hoisted her like a feather. Nova let her arms snake behind his neck and wrapped her legs around his hips. She kissed him deep. Devouring his mouth as he positioned her vagina above his erection and pushed her hips downward. The head of his dick parted her wet opening. She moaned, digging her nails into his back as she accepted his offering.

Sam reached out and clutched Jace's cock. She pumped it hard as she stepped to his chest. His skin teased her tongue with hint of salt. Sweet scents rushed into her nostrils. Flavored oils. Cinnamon. Spice. The sound of Nova's mewling cries made Sam's pussy throb. She hadn't had sex in months and wanted this moment more than ever. She needed Gage to remember. Her voice dropped to a whisper. "Will you show Gage what he could've had?"

Jace kissed her hard while gripping her ass in one hand. He pulled her pelvis against his cock. "Your screams will haunt his dreams forever."

Sam smiled with wicked pleasure. She knelt on the closest divan's cushioned surface, opening her knees. Waiting. Joshua's cock slid in an out of Nova's wet pussy right before her eyes. The wet slap of flesh resounded in her ears. Passion mixed with the blonde's rising cries.

Sam turned her head to peer at Gage, still on his knees and held fast in Nova's spell. Fury pulsed across his scowling face. His teeth bared like a raging tiger. His anger only fueled her desire. Gasoline tossed upon an open flame. "Fuck me, Jace. Show Gage how a real man makes a woman come."

Jace stepped behind her. His fingers dug into her hip. The smooth head of his cock moved up and down between her soaking outer lips, teasing her open.

Sam pushed backward each time his tip parted her vulva and rose to her waiting entrance. Her gaze burned into Gage's eyes as she tried to capture Jace's lust and force him deep. She wanted Gage to see her taken apart. "Don't be gentle, Jace." She panted. His cock opened her up and slid back. Stroke after stroke. Deeper with every pass. "I'm done with gentle."

Jace drove in deep, forcing the air from Sam's lungs. She moved her knees farther apart to accept the pain, but the power of Jace's massive hard-on couldn't be lessened. She screamed. Both his hands gripped her hips. He slammed into her with thrust after thrust until she collapsed onto her forearms.

Domina

Joshua laid Nova back on the adjacent divan. He hooked his hands behind her knees and pushed them to her ears, holding her wide. He pulled his entire cum coated length back before every thrust and used his weight to ravage the gorgeous nymph again and again. Nova scratched angry marks into his chest and opened the sky with her howls. "Yes! Yes! Yes!"

Sam's orgasm rose. Pressure increased in her pelvis and spread between her thighs. Her body shook as her pussy clenched in spasmodic contractions. She screamed as undulating waves raced upward with each concussive shock of Jace's loins against her own. She closed her eyes and accepted, squeezing the edge of the settee with aching fingers and burning muscles. Jace continued his vicious onslaught until Sam's screams became continuous.

The contractions in Sam's pussy decreased after her release. A brief respite allowing her to gasp as another orgasm came closer. Unable to use her burning vocal cords, she could barely eek out blissful grunts to punctuate Jace's unrelenting ravishment.

On the edge of ecstasy, the familiar scent of Nova's cum filled Sam's nostrils. Liquid desire. Sam forced her eyelids open. Joshua's cock shined with Nova's essence inches from Sam's mouth. He wrapped his fingers in her black hair then pulled upward, arching her neck as he fed his cock into her mouth. She savored the blended flavors of wet pussy and thick seed on her tongue, sucked and swallowed, as Joshua forced himself deeper down her throat. Her lungs burned. Hot teardrops rolled down her cheeks but the brothers refused to relent.

Sam raised an aching arm and clawed at Joshua's stomach. Pushing him backward she gasped. Cum dripped in long strands from her lips. She shrieked as another orgasm took her. Molten fluid flooded into her throbbing pussy as Jace's howls echoed her own.

The pounding cadence in Sam's chest diminished as her climax receded again. Gage had been forgotten in a sea of lust. When Jace withdrew his cock from her dripping pussy, aftershocks raced across her flesh. She gasped and opened her eyes to find Nova's smiling face before her own.

The goddess smiled, swirling her hips back and forth like a little girl. "Come. Let's get you cleaned up and fed. You must be starving. Our night is just beginning and I'm looking forward to dessert."

Sam clasped hands with the goddess who'd chosen her. Wanting to please her. Wanting to grant her anything she desired. She stood up with aching muscles, admiring the sweaty bodies of the twins as they secured their wraps. "You two were magnificent. I thought you were going to break me."

Jace stepped forward and kissed her on the forehead. "There is always next time. Perhaps we should take turns."

Joshua wrapped her naked body in his arms and squeezed tight. "We are your servants. We search for who we are the same as you. Don't forget us on your journey."

"Impossible." Sam's happiness prevented her from questioning the cryptic message.

Nova pulled Sam along a few steps before she stopped. "I almost forgot." Turning toward Gage, she cut the air with her hand. He crumpled to the ground in a panting mess. She formed a cylinder with fingers touching her thumb. "You will remain engorged until the sun rises, my love. Your hands will not grant you respite and only increase your need. Release will be denied. The men and women of our home will not grant you abeyance. Let your mind wonder what we do in your absence. Sleep beneath the stars and wish for reprieve. The torture is of your own construction."

Nova pulled at Sam's hand, leading her onward. Sam's anger at Gage had evaporated. Not forgotten but bubbling beneath the surface far away. She raised her voice and hoped Nova would understand. "I can't wait to make her come, Gage. Perhaps I'll dream of your hard cock sliding into my ass. Perhaps not. Sleep well and wonder." Her cheeks warmed as they walked away.

Nova put her arm around Sam's waist, pulling her close. She chuckled. "You really are wicked, Samantha."

Chapter Five

A New Day

Sam woke on the supple mattress she'd shared with Nova for countless hours the night before. Sweat and strain. Orgasm upon orgasm. Fingers. Tongues. Passionate kisses. Flawless consummation.

She stretched with languid satiety, searching for the lover who'd already gone. The fragrance of their sex still lingered on the sheets, brightening the room with reminiscence. On two sides, the room opened on a small courtyard. Sunlight streamed in and warmed the simple room. A bed and little else.

Rolling free of the sheets, Sam searched for her missing clothes. Unable to locate her shift, she unfolded a pile of linen hoping to find something to dress in. A long bolt of soft cloth unfurled in her hands. Remembering forgotten modesty, she pulled it across her breasts and thighs, knowing she had to find the bathroom before continuing her search for proper attire.

Sam tiptoed across the ornate tile and into the courtyard searching desperately for anyone she could ask for directions. She crossed and uncrossed her ankles, bouncing in place as her bladder screamed for relief. When she turned back to the room, she unleashed a startled squeak. Gage stood against the wall just outside her room wrapped in nothing but his simple loin cloth. The sun ignited his bronze skin, pulling her into his black eyes before she shook her head to clear a flustered mind. No matter how gorgeous he seemed, his disrespect from the night before had charred her compassion and blunted her prurience. She wasn't ready to forgive but her bladder celebrated the finding of another human being. She pulled the wrap tighter and pulled it across her ass. "You waited for me?"

Gage held her gaze with a flat stare. Emotionless. "I was compelled. I am not here by choice. I'm required to take you to the baths before your first lessons."

"My lessons?" Sam didn't have time for confusion or further discussion. "Can you tell me where the... I need a bathroom." Her cheeks smoldered.

"A bathroom?" He narrowed his eyes in confusion.

"Yes." Her voice began to rise. "A bathroom. I have to pee." Her cheeks only grew hotter.

"You don't have a chamber pot?" His face twisted in disbelief. He stepped around her and walked into the room before pointing to the corner with annoyance. "There. What's wrong with it?"

Sam stepped inside. A large ornate vase with a formed neck sat in the corner. A basin of water sat beside it next to a small stack of dark linen. Her voice betrayed her surprise. "That's the bathroom?"

He looked at the half-wit before him with horror. "A chamber pot. You—"

"Yeah." She cut him off before he finished. "I got it. Thanks for nothing." She walked quickly to the vase with concern, knowing she couldn't wait any longer. She began to unwrap her cover and stopped as she noticed him still standing in her room. Her blush spread to encompass her entire body. She crossed her ankles again and leaned forward to relieve her pain. "Well?"

"Well what?" Gage looked even more concerned now.

"Get out," she screamed. "I have to pee."

His eyes scrunched in horror or disbelief before he turned and strode out of sight. Sam unwrapped the cover and sat, happy for the fitted seat but disappointed in the facilities. *Well... When in Rome.* When she'd finished, she searched for toilet paper finding only the small stack of clean linen to the side. She unfolded one and blotted, hoping she understood the procedure and embarrassed by her own ignorance at the same time. She tossed the used linen into a small bucket at her side. Standing, she washed her hands in the water basin and wrapped the bolt of cloth around her body again.

I don't even want to know what they do with periods.

She walked into the sunlight again and found Gage waiting to the side with a concerned look ground into his brow. She pulled the linen around her bottom again. "Okay. I threw the... Uhm...toilet paper thingy in the bucket. I hope that's all right." She looked at the ground, unable to meet his gaze. Chagrined.

He cleared his throat uncomfortably. "It's fine. It will be taken care of. Why are you wearing your wrap like that?"

Sam looked down. She'd circled it around her hips and over her shoulder, struggling to hold it in place. "My wrap? I couldn't find any clothes so I covered myself with this. If you could help me find something more appropriate, I'd appreciate it."

"I see." He walked forward and held his hands

outward. "May I?"

Sam looked down at his huge hands and before focusing on his black eyes with suspicion. "May you what?"

"Your wrap. It's like a...a toga. You're wearing it all wrong."

Sam's embarrassment couldn't get any worse. "Sure."

Gage pulled the cloth free, leaving Sam completely nude. Her blushing cheeks only heated more as she watched his loin cloth begin to tent. She pretended not to notice as he unraveled the cloth. He wrapped it about her hips and over her shoulder before handing her the free end. "You can drape this over your arm or pin it. Do you have a pin?"

Sam looked around the room. "A pin? I don't think so."

Gage walked to a small table and picked up an ornate pin. He moved to Sam's side and secured the end to her waist as she held her arms to the side. "There. Now it will stay in place without thinking about it. Are you ready?"

Sam liked the feel of the material. *Going without panties is becoming a habit.* "I think so. Where are we going?"

"I'm to bathe and feed you before your lessons.

This way." He motioned across the courtyard.

"Bathe me?" Sam had become aroused again but wasn't about to experience another disappointment. "Not likely."

"Yes. Bathe you. I can show you where the baths are and you can bathe yourself if you wish but Nova will be disappointed." He began walking across the courtyard toward another building.

The uncomfortable silence between them stretched on forever. Sam changed the subject. "Why don't you have running water? You have magical powers, couldn't you just, you know, whip up some water pressure?"

As if looking at a particularly slow child, Gage stared over his shoulder with raised eyebrows. "Whip some up? The use of magic is not free. It drains your energy. Moving water for comfort would be wasteful. We have running water. For baths. For fountains. For drinking. A Roman like aqueduct system. Low pressure only but sufficient for our needs."

"I know, but what about important things like, you know, toilets and showers."

He exhaled, irritated by the continued onslaught of questions. "We don't have electricity. No electricity means no pumps. No pumps means no high pressure water."

"So, why don't you get electricity? For comfort."

"Are you not comfortable?" He ran his hand across his forehead and down the back of his hair with a sigh. His biceps bulged. "I forgot. You're our guest. You don't understand because you weren't born here. What's the best way to explain this... Electricity interferes with magic. As more technology is used, the magic fades. Spells fail. As spells fail people lose faith. The lore and the old ways are eventually lost. That's what happened in your home. The place where I was born."

Sam could barely believe Gage had ever been mortal. His perfect body seemed beyond humanity even if his attitude could be nothing else. "Where were you born?"

Gage stopped at the end of a long hall and turned on her. His pursed lips suggested frustration, but he softened after a moment, as if considering what to tell her. "North Africa. Near Carthage. I was a slave. Nova freed me." His brows tightened as he spoke. Darkness spread across his face. "It's not a time I wish to remember."

A slave?

Gage turned and walked on at an increased pace. Sam struggled to keep up through the myriad twists and turns. The air became wet and humid as they approached an arched portico. The temperature rose. As they crossed an open courtyard, the sound of running water called to her from an ornate building embellished in sea themed frescoes.

Sufficient for our needs.

They entered a room with a low ceiling. Multi colored tiles formed intricate patterns beneath her feet on a floor sloping away to the right. The slope gave way to a pool. Steaming water fell from copper pipes emerging from the far wall above the deepest area. On either side of the pool, recessed shelves hung above long stone benches. Jars of soaps and oils ringed the sides of the pool, filling the sweltering room with magnificent scents.

"How's the water heated?" Sam marveled at the amount of work the construction must have required. "Magic?"

"No. I told you that would be wasteful. Geothermal. It has to be mixed with large quantities of cold as it comes out of the wall or it would scald." He unpinned his waistband and removed his waistcloth, folding it carefully before he placed it on a shelf above one of the benches.

Sam's mouth fell open as she spied his massive cock. *I must have repressed it.* She snapped her jaw shut before he noticed, fiddling with her hair as if unimpressed. The heat rising between her legs said otherwise.

Gage walked to her side. "Well?"

"Well what?" Sam tried not to blush.

"You have to get undressed if you're going to bathe."

"Of course." Sam struggled to undo the pin at her side. Her heart hammered in her throat. She had to concentrate just to breathe. She tried to make light of the situation. "I was just admiring the scenery." Her voice cracked as she motioned to his shaft. She spent extra time folding her wrap, wanting to compose herself and appear disinterested in his erection's steady upward rise. It wasn't working.

His lecherous gaze prowled across her flesh. "I'm enjoying the scenery myself."

"Well, admire at a distance. Your words from last night still sting." Her tongue became more facile with the memory. "I haven't forgiven you and I don't know if I ever will. Do we soap in the pool?"

"No," he muttered below his breath as if disappointed in her answer. "Enter the water and wet yourself thoroughly first and then return to the bench."

She walked into the water slowly, testing the temperature with her toes, knowing he watched. *I could get used to this.* "I'm quite wet already, but we'll do it your way for now. I'm still upset with you."

She waded deeper, soothing her exhausted muscles in encircling warmth. Relief from a night without sleep. She lowered herself and let the heat tickle her nipples. Closing her eyes, she dunked her head and surfaced again, pulling the hair from her face. She waded back up the slope with a ramrod straight back, presenting her breasts for full effect. Seeing his gaze trace her figure with pure lasciviousness, she smiled. "You may begin. We wouldn't want to upset Nova now would we?"

She sat on the bench primly, keeping her knees together. Aspirations of seducing someone so gorgeous, experienced and well equipped had chased the last of her modesty away.

Gage's desire could no longer be concealed. His erection dripped with truth.

This is what I was born for.

Gage lifted a small vase and filled it with water from the pool. In his other hand he retrieved a linen sponge and a tiny vial. He poured the vial's contents into the vase and wetted the sponge, wringing it until soapy bubbles floated across the water's surface.

Jasmine tinged with vanilla wafted to Sam's nose. As he reached toward her, she held up a hand to stop him. "Behave. Remember, Nova watches. You still need to earn my approval again and I have a long memory."

His mouth turned downwards. A frown dipped in dejection.

Sam wanted him to touch her but she craved control even more. "If you can't do this with a smile, I'll do it myself."

He hesitated. His frown deepened and then lifted into some semblance of sickly, forced musing.

Sam forced an exaggerated groan of displeasure. "I suppose that'll have to do for now. My feet. You may start there."

Maintaining self control became impossible when he followed her instructions without another word. He rubbed softly. Between her toes and across the soles of her feet before rinsing the sponge and moving up each of her calves in turn. *You've been a good boy, Gage.* She opened her legs as he reached her knees. He looked up and into her eyes. A silent question. Asking for permission. "Behave." She pointed her finger and used a commanding tone, hoping to disguise how much she wanted him to taste her.

His gaze fell again, absolute focus on the cleft between her thighs. *I'm even wetter inside.* The soft surface of the wash cloth tingled her wetted flesh as he stroked the top of her legs and moved between them. Sam bit her lip to keep from moaning as he rose higher, across her body in concentric soapy circles. Her eyes closed in luxury as steaming water dripped downward in delicious rivulets, coursing across her sensitive labia and swelling clit. A tickle begging her to offer more.

Her breath began to falter as his hands tore down the last of her resistance. "That feels wonderful. I'm assuming I'm not your first sponge bath."

"No, but not one I'm likely to forget either."

Sam couldn't stop the blush this time, but she wasn't about to forgive his vitriol from a few hours ago for a single compliment. *But I do need to have you.* Knowing she could lose control at any moment, she stood and turned to the wall. She opened her legs a little more than her balance required and placed her hands against the warm stone. Arching her back, she began to sway her ass enticingly. "My back needs attention too. If you'd be so kind."

She closed her eyes as the sponge touched her shoulders. His hard cock, hotter than the water rolling down her back, pressed against her ass as he rubbed. His erection slid between her ass cheeks. A lubricated piston machined for rapture. Her defenses began to fail. When he pressed the steaming cloth between her legs she nearly came. *I can't give in.* She stood before surrender became inevitable, moving in slow motion as if indifferent to his touch. "Do I rinse in the pool?"

"No. Move over to the side where the tile slopes away from the pool and place your hands against the wall. I'll rinse."

I can't hold on much longer.

She glanced where he indicated. A small section of flooring formed a natural funnel toward a drain and away from the clean water of the pool. She placed her hands against the tile and waited. He dipped another vase in the heated water and poured it across her shoulders, refilled and poured again.

Who needs running water?

His voice became soft. A gentle flutter on gossamer wings. "Turn around, beautiful."

She turned to him. His hard dick brushed her clit as he poured another bucket across her breasts, rinsing the last of the soap clean. She almost yielded. *How could anyone as gorgeous as he is, after the number of women he'd had... How could he find me attractive?* Her heart leaped. The air grew thin. She stepped around him and moved into the pool, walking forward until she could dunk her head again. *A little distance is all I need. He belongs to Nova.* "She loves you, you know?

I'm only here because she knows she can't live without you. Do you still love her?" The words came before she'd considered how they'd be received.

Deafening silence filled her ears. He hadn't joined her in the pool and he hadn't spoken. Newfound hope dissipated as she turned. His face twisted with an acidic snarl of pure fury. Tight cheek muscles. Pursed lips. Eyes of smoldering coal.

His words became the hiss of frozen water poured across a bed of coals. "Never confuse my anger at her treatment of me with an absence of love." His fists clenched and released as a molten growl oozed from his lips. "There are towels on the shelves. I'll meet you outside." Without another word, he snatched his waist wrap from the shelf and thundered from the bathhouse.

Sam's voice dropped in shame. "I didn't mean to..." Her apology came too late. Gage had already gone. *How could I have been so insensitive?* She moved from the pool, fighting back tears as she searched for a towel. After drying herself she secured her wrap as he'd taught her and pinned it into place. She walked into the blinding sunlight filled with regret.

***

Sam squinted in the bright rays, noticing the

details of the courtyard they'd crossed for the first time. Small olive trees adorned the four corners, each reaching for the light with graceful limbs. Water poured from the mouth of a marble cherub in the center of a tiny circular fountain with raised walls. Beside the fountain, a chiseled man with ebony skin stood beside a rectangular table filled with fruits, eggs, meats and dishes she didn't even recognize. His entire body danced with tattoos from his cut stomach to the dark lines drawn on his face. He held a white pitcher in his hand and motioned to a single chair with a smile. Sam searched the open space for Gage, but he'd left her alone with a stranger. She walked to the table and sat before realizing how famished the night of passion had left her.

The man helped her move the chair closer to the table and poured a glass of orange juice before moving to the side.

She lifted her glass and sipped. A perfect blend of tangy sweetness as if squeezed from the sun itself. "That's delicious. Thank you."

"You're welcome."

She couldn't place his thick accent and unfamiliar inflection.

"I'm Khanzani. I wish only to serve. Can I get something for you?" He moved to the side and lifted a dish of fruit.

"Some strawberries? Oooh. What is that, cantaloupe? A few pieces of that too." Her hunger grew. She began pointing at dish after dish. "And that. And that. And...Oh my god, do you have coffee?"

Khanzani moved to the end of the table and lifted a stone pitcher. He poured the thick brew in a cup by her hand. The powerful aroma caused her eyes to close as she inhaled the hints of bitter earth culled from far-off lands. Starting slow she tasted each dish before proceeding to devour everything in sight. Each bite more delicious than the last. A starving survivor of a forced march seeing food for the first time in months.

With cheeks full and near bursting, Sam looked up in near rapture to find Khanzani watching her eat. His grin stretched from ear to ear. Mortified by her complete lack of manners, she attempted to smile without opening her mouth and hoped it didn't look smug. With chipmunk cheeks, she held her hand in front of her full mouth and tried to speak. "I'm sorry. Will you join me?"

"No. Thank you. I've already eaten." He laughed. "Enjoy. Please."

Sam ate until her stomach threatened to rupture

with another bite. She sipped her coffee and searched for Gage surreptitiously again. *I guess I'll apologize later.* She refocused her thoughts on Khanzani. "Do you live here?"

"I do. For now. I have for a long time."

Sam had so many questions. She didn't know where to start. "And you...serve food and such? Is that your job?"

"My job is whatever you desire. I am here seeking fulfillment. The same as you."

"What kind of fulfillment?"

"I seek purpose. Pleasure. Something. I don't know. I still search." He crossed his arms over his massive chest.

She forced her gaze to her coffee. The question burned her tongue, begging her to spit it out. "And you...you know. Sleep with the women here."

"I do. If that is what they desire. They are searching too."

The next question died on her lips. Gage appeared from a building on the other side of the fountain. He held several coils of rope in his hands and walked with purpose.

Gage's expression tipped from one of distaste to a smile of wonder when he spotted Khanzani. "Khan." He jogged across the courtyard, clutched forearms with the giant, and then embraced him as if separated from a long lost friend. "Where've you been hiding? I haven't seen you in days."

The dark man laughed. "So many women. So little time. Have you met Katherine? She arrived a few days ago. Gorgeous red hair. A body to kill for. Right up your alley. We've been spending a lot of time together."

Gage glanced at Sam as he answered. "I'm afraid I'm...preoccupied. You'll have to introduce me. I'm in the middle of training our newest guest."

His deprecation made Sam's anger rise again. She cast her apology aside with no intention of offering it again. "Don't miss your newest conquest on my account."

Khanzani looked at the ground. "I'm sorry. I forget myself."

Acid dripped from Sam's tongue, bathing her lips in hate. "No problem. You two seem to have a lot of pussy to catch up on. Just point me back toward my room and you two can go play with whomever you choose."

Gage scowled, raising his lip as if scenting rancid meat. "We have lessons."

"Do we?" She sipped her coffee as she met his gaze. *Fucking asshole.* "I disagree. Go play with your toys." *Dickhead.*

Khanzani bowed. He scurried toward an open door without another word.

Gage held out a thick coil of silk rope.

With a harrumph, Sam took the coil of rope as if accepting soiled linen from a cholera ward. She let it uncoil in her hands until one end bounced across the ground. Silk windings half an inch wide. "What would you have me do with this?"

"Learn." Gage unrolled an identical coil, holding one end in each hand. "If you are so inclined. It makes no difference to me. I can teach. I can't make you understand."

Any kind words she might have had stuck in her throat, jagged pills edged with pride. *Unfounded pride.* Her thoughts of apology threatened again but she refused to utter any kindness now. The hurtful words had been hers this time, not his, but his tone irked her more than anything else. She tried to sound haughty, matching his disrespect word for word. "What do you intend to teach me? Perhaps I don't give a shit."

His jaw twitched as if she'd slapped him. "To bind."

"How do you know my binding skills aren't sufficient already?"

His jaw tightened further. He ground his teeth

and hissed again. "Show me." Stepping closer, he dropped his rope and crossed his wrists.

Sam had never tied anything more complex than a shoelace in her life, but she wasn't about to let him know that. She coiled the rope around his wrists and pulled tight, deliberately trying to hurt him. She tied a quick knot and swatted his hands away. "There. Satisfied?"

Gage looked at his wrists briefly and then connected his gaze with hers. "No. I have my work cut out for me. Neither secure nor sensual." He twisted his hands once. The rope uncoiled before falling to the ground.

Sam growled at her shoddy job. Disappointed in herself. Singed by his words. "Knots aren't sexy. They're meant to hold."

"They're meant to bind. Tied correctly, they can be an aphrodisiac." He exhaled and retrieved his own coil. Rolling his shoulders, he softened his voice. "Listen. Please. I'm sorry for my behavior. I just wasn't ready to talk about my love for Nova. She is my heart. My all. I miss her. Can you understand that? Let's start again, okay? I'll make you a deal. Give me a chance and perhaps my tongue will loosen."

Sam couldn't believe *he* apologized to *her*. Guilt tightened around her heart. Barbed wire digging deep. She picked up her own coil with something less than reverence and whispered, hoping he'd grant forgiveness before she changed her mind. "I'm sorry too. I shouldn't have asked about...that. It's a deal. Where do we begin?"

"I shouldn't have gotten angry. Your question was innocent enough." He took an end of the rope in each hand. "There are innumerable knots. Some are useful, others less so. Hold an end in each hand and let the loop fall to the ground. Like this." He held the free ends pointing upward to demonstrate. The U shaped bend fell at his feet.

Sam replicated his actions. Intrigued. "How's that?"

"Yes. When I say 'right' I mean the end in the right hand. When I say 'left' I mean the end in the left hand. Got it?"

"Sure."

"Cross the right end over the left and change hands. The left hand now holds the end the right held and vice versa. Like this."

Sam followed his instructions, crossing the rope in the middle as if starting a shoelace.

"Now. Cross the right over the left again. Change hands again."

Sam smiled at the result. Her first knot. "Like

this?"

"Exactly. Look at it. See how the ends don't move? This is a maiden's knot. A grandmother's knot and countless other names. The point is this, it's useless. Remember it. Untie."

Sam's elation evaporated. *Then why show me? Jerk.* She untied the knot, holding one end in each hand again.

"Now a little different. Cross the right over the left and change hands. The end from your left is now in your right. The end from your right hand is now in your left. Good. Now, this time, cross the left over the right and change hands again. Do you see how it is different? How it lays flat now?"

Sam repeated his actions and replicated the result. Excited by her success once again she bounced in place. "I do."

"Do you see how it forms two loops that slide on each other? With a little imagination you'll see the loops form a square. Thus, a square knot. Hold the rope and both ends in opposite hands. Pull the rope. It doesn't slip but..." He pushed her hands together and the loops unraveled, the short ends slipping through the loops. "It's only strong in one direction. Remember it."

Sam played with it for a second. *Easy enough.* "I

guess I'm a good student."

"Or I'm a good teacher." Gage smiled. His face seemed pacified. "Either way, a beginning."

Sam didn't know why his smile and praise over such a little thing meant so much to her, but it did.

"Now the hitches. These require something to tie around." He sat in a chair and ran one end of his rope under his thigh. He held one free end in each hand again, the loop pulled tightly against the back of his thigh. "Start like this."

Sam pulled the rope behind her knee and extended her leg, delighted he stared as she hiked her toga higher.

"Right over left. Switch hands. This is only half a hitch, hence, a half hitch. Pull the ends tight. You see how it tightens and slips?"

Sam repeated his motions. "Yes. It tightens the harder you pull."

"Exactly. But, if you release the tension." He demonstrated before continuing. "It falls apart. Useless by itself but it's the start of an infinite number of ties."

Sam tied it without effort, proud of the result. Seeking his praise, she looked into his dark eyes again.

"Good. Now show me a maiden's knot. A square

knot and a half hitch on your own."

With minimal struggle, Sam demonstrated each of the knots he'd taught her. Almost giggling with the ease she'd accomplished them, she realized her delight stemmed more from his approval than anything else.

"Good. Now, run it under your leg again. Right over left. Switch hands. A half hitch. Tie another half hitch above it. Two half hitches. Now, if you pull it doesn't tighten and it stays when I release the tension. Do you see?"

Sam made the proper turns and achieved the correct result. She squealed. "I did it."

"You did. Now untie. Tie me a maiden's knot. A square knot. A half hitch and two half hitches."

"Again?" She exhaled but untied as instructed. "We already did those."

"We haven't even started."

Sam followed Gage's instructions again and again. Knot after knot. Hitch after hitch. The sun rose high overhead and began its descent. Clove hitch, timber hitch, taut line hitch...

Khanzani brought them refreshment from time to time and they even picked over a light lunch as the instruction continued. Knots to tie ropes together. Knots that slipped. Knots that didn't slip. Figure eights, bends and shanks. The terminology began to run together. Running lines. Standing lines. Bowlines, double bowlines, triple bowlines, bowlines on bights and off bights. Each time he taught her a new knot, she had to retie all the knots they'd done before, again. They paced and tied. Laughed. Sat and paced again.

Sam began to feel dizzy. Her numb fingers bubbled with tiny blisters. "We have to stop, Gage. I can't process anymore. I can't tie anymore. What's the point anyway? This is exhausting."

"The point?" Gage looked hurt. With sagging shoulders, he stared at the ground. When he looked up again, his brows furrowed. "You cannot see..."

"I'm just tired. Tomorrow. We can start again." She watched him rub his chin, mind working overtime. *I'll never be good enough for you, will I?* "Please, Gage. No more knots today." She rose from the chair on shaky legs.

Gage lifted a hand. He touched her arm with softness, not strength. "One more lesson. Please. Sit."

Sam sat in down with a groan.

"Cross your hands behind your back."

Wary, Sam crossed her hands behind the chair. "I'm too exhausted to argue anymore."

"I don't want to argue. I want you to see. To

understand."

Gage looped one coil of the rope with skill bordering on instinct. He slipped two ends of a figure eight around her wrist and eased it tight. No burns. No discomfort but snug just the same. He ran the free end beneath the leg of the chair and looped it once in what looked like a half hitch or, something. She didn't care anymore. He moved to the other leg and repeated the knot, securing her other wrist. As he reached for the other coil she pulled at her wrists, surprised when they couldn't move at all. Realizing her predicament too late, her heart began to pound. *Well, I'm awake now.*

He ran the other ropes behind her elbows with a knot she couldn't see but it tightened as he removed the slack, forcing her shoulders against the back of her chair. Her breathing quickened as she tried to follow his hands, but he moved too fast. The free end of the rope snaked beneath her chair. With two quick loops her right ankle pulled tight to the leg of the chair. She began to protest, struggling against the tension as her other ankle became immobilized in the flash of an eyelid. He pulled the rope beneath her knee, wrapped it beneath the chair and tied it to her other knee before moving in front of her.

Sam couldn't move her arms. She couldn't move

her legs. Her knees were held open and her shoulders pressed against the back of her chair. Wherever she found slack, pulling only tightened the lines somewhere else. Her chest heaved as she stared at him. Black eyes. A wicked smile. Less than five minutes and she couldn't move. Complete and total immobility.

"Ten knots, Samantha. Ten knots and now, you are mine." He leaned in close and sniffed her neck. His hands rested lightly on her thighs. His breath fell upon her ear. "What are you going to do, Samantha?"

Sam couldn't speak. Her mouth had become barren. She'd never become so wet, so fast. She searched for breath in rarefied air. The erotic bonds fueled her ardor. He could do anything to her and she could do nothing but submit. All she could do was give him what he wanted. *What we both want.*

He knelt and slid her wrap upwards across her thighs. Tied in place with open legs, she could only consent. She dripped. The heat between her legs had become sweltering. Need beyond need. Understanding obliterated by a rope. His breath stirred the tight curls between her thighs. A maelstrom hidden within a gentle breeze.

A scent of vanilla purity attacked her senses. A breeze of fresh air rushing through her hair, tickling her scalp. *Nova*. Gage raised his head before he could taste Sam's desire. Sharing the sensations with her. A call.

The angel spoke. Nova's voice had power to draw attention without effort. "That succulent pussy is mine, lover. Behave and perhaps I'll share a drop with you. But not today. I have need of our pupil. A different kind of lesson."

Gage stared into Sam's eyes with both pain and disappointment. His mouth twisted as he stood. Nova kissed him on the cheek with a disarming smile. She stared at Sam while wrapping her hands tightly around Gage's waist. "We've been having fun today, haven't we? It seems I arrived just in time."

He looked down and growled just above a whisper. "Knots. Nothing more."

Nova ran the backs of her fingers against Sam's cheek. "I see. And I thought you were about to taste her dripping slit. Too bad. I would liked to have seen that."

Pressing her ass against Gage's hips, Nova bent at the waist. With a few pulls she untied Sam, freeing both her arms and legs. Sam stood and massaged her wrists even though they weren't sore. She looked at the ground and twirled a finger in her hair. Guilt flushed her skin with unexpected fervor. They hadn't done anything. *Yet. A few more minutes would have told a different story.*

Nova interlaced her fingers with Sam's. "Are you ready, Samantha? Or do you wish to stay and play with my husband?"

Sam looked up at Gage's pained face before turning to Nova again. *I do. But does he wish to play with me?* She cleared her throat and tried to push her dreams of Gage away. "Ready for what?"

"A field trip." Nova reached out a hand and touched Sam's arm.

Before Sam could answer, the world spun. Lights pulsed behind her eyes. Roaring air slammed against her ear drums. Her stomach churned.

Chapter Six
Playtime

The world stopped spinning but Sam's stomach didn't. Acid rose into her chest. Her lunch rebelled. As her vision cleared, a swirl of people solidified around her. She retched. The busy sea parted like the waters before Moses. She gasped for air again and again. Pleading for mercy as her last meal emptied onto the sidewalk.

An eternity passed. The shaking ground stopped its horrid movement beneath her feet. Sam wiped her mouth with the back of her arm, happy to be alive. With horror, her surroundings came into focus. Buildings rose up from the ground on all sides, threatening to pierce the sky. The honking horns of a thousand taxi cabs echoed off the concrete and merged again into a single smog-filled cacophony.

Sam stood with aching abdominals. Her cheeks reddened as the lines of people continued to part around her like a leper cast into the middle of a beauty pageant.

Unable to fathom her new surroundings, Sam turned to Nova for understanding. The goddess's skin glowed in the sunlight. The simple wrap she'd worn minutes before had been replaced by a short pink dress that dove between her small breasts. Spaghetti straps pointed toward hard nipples, lifting the soft fabric in a delicious tease. The garment ended mid thigh, unveiling long perfect legs flowing into six-inch heels. The promise of sex without limits. Without boundaries.

The succulent nymph in dark sunglasses stood by Sam's side, grinning despite Sam's discomfort. "Sorry about the trip, Samantha. I forget how disorienting it can be."

Sam looked at her own simple wrap with self conscious agony. "You changed your clothes. I suddenly feel underdressed."

Nova giggled softly. "This is New York, Samantha. You look fabulous." She leaned forward and kissed Sam on the cheek then waved her hand before her face and stepped back. "However, you do need a mint."

Before Sam could blush, Nova offered a small wet towel in one hand and a wrapped mint in the other. Sam reached for the towel and wiped her face thoroughly before tossing it in the nearby trashcan. She opened the mint and popped it in her mouth. "You look stunning, Nova. Everything you wear is seductive. You'll have to teach me how to dress like that if you want me to...succeed."

"I'll tell you a secret, beautiful." She leaned forward and whispered in Sam's ear. "I am not actually wearing anything. You only perceive me the way you wish to see me." She kissed her cheek again. "So, technically, *you* picked this outfit. I don't have to teach you anything about dressing." She rocked her hips left and right as she examined herself with a flourish. "You have very good taste in clothes."

Sam looked at her own outfit again wishing she felt as sexy as Nova looked. "Bare feet wouldn't have been my first choice."

"You aren't happy?" Nova stuck out her lower lip in a sexy pout. "How about now?"

"What?" Sam's mouth twisted in confusion. Startled, she looked down at herself again. She gasped at the tight, strapless yellow dress that had appeared from nowhere, hugging her own hips and showing off her ample breasts. Her own nipples pushed outward in a sultry call. *Bras don't seem to be a priority today.* She lifted her foot, smiling at the high heels tied to her ankle in a complex web of beautiful straps.

Nova giggled. "I have a secret, my love." She leaned in close and whispered. "You aren't wearing anything either."

Sam ran her hands across her hips, knowing she didn't wear any panties. "I love it." She whispered as softly as she could over the honking horns. "Aren't you worried someone will notice our changing outfits?"

"Are you kidding?" Nova wrapped her arm around Sam's, linking elbows with her. She pressed her head to Sam's shoulder. "In this city? If you aren't firing a gun directly at someone, you don't even exist."

Sam scanned the crowd parting around them like rocks in a stream. Eyes straight ahead. Fixed expressions. Everyone going or coming from somewhere. Destination unknown. "What're we doing here?"

Nova tugged Sam as she walked across the crowded sidewalk toward tall glass doors at the base of the nearest building. "Training, my heart. Training."

Two doormen in long coats and hats pulled the doors open and stepped aside as the women approached. Sam's heart fluttered with nervousness. "What kind of...training?"

The palatial lobby's vaulted ceilings towered above them. Polished marble clicked beneath their heels. Nova continued to lead the way, holding Sam's arm tight. "Seduction. The most important tool in a woman's armament."

Sam's mouth went dry as they approached a small café filled with people. Everyone seemed to be wearing suits or expensive dresses. Each sat in groups of two or three, chatting in hushed tones. A waiter intercepted them mid stride. "Table for two?"

Nova touched his arm with her fingertips and dragged them toward his wrist. "Yes, my dear."

The flustered young man led them through the busy room without further delay. Unlike the streets outside, several heads turned their way as they weaved between the circular tables. After being seated, the waiter handed them each a black leather-clad menu. "Enjoy your lunch." With a half bow, he moved off toward the entrance again.

Sam's hands shook as she perused the fare. Nova seemed to be studying the crowd without interest in either food or drink. "Aren't you going to order?"

"We aren't here to eat, Samantha. You're looking at the wrong menu."

Domina

Sam closed the binding. Perplexed. "What? Then..."

"Seduction." Nova reached a hand across the table to steady Sam's own. "Who do you think the hottest guy or, if you're really motivated, girl in here is?"

Sam followed Nova's gaze around the restaurant in spite of her confusion. Her voice dropped to a low mutter. "What do you mean?"

Nova reached her other hand across the table and took both of Sam's palms in hers with reassurance. Her piercing gaze pinned Sam's attention without the possibility of discussion. "A simple question, Samantha. Choose. The most desirable man here."

Sam clutched Nova's hands tighter and gazed around the room again. "But why?"

"Because I asked. Tell me, Samantha."

Sam finally spotted a man in a dark blue Armani suit sitting alone three tables away. He seemed focused on the New York Times folded in his hands. Clean shaven with blond hair and blue eyes, he positively oozed gorgeous. His face looked rough but his deep eyes screamed intelligence. Worn features hid his age and exuded sexuality like musk.

Sam leaned forward and whispered from the

corner of her mouth. "Three tables over. Blue suit."

Nova grinned without turning around. "Ooh. Good choice. He's single. Recently divorced. He hasn't been laid in a very long time despite what he may tell you."

Sam didn't have to ask how she knew the details anymore. "And?" She chuckled on the edge of nervousness. "We care why?"

"Because you are going to sit at his table and seduce him. You're going to make him so hard that the only thing he can think about is crawling between your luscious thighs and fucking you into unconsciousness."

Sam's mouth dropped open. She started to protest but a young waiter stepped up to their table. "Are you ready to order?"

Sam's face heated, as if the man could see her thoughts. She looked away and tried to appear innocent despite the guilt burning between her ears.

Nova placed her chin on the back of her hand and batted her eyes. "A glass of Chardonnay, please. Food isn't what I'm hungry for."

The waiter wrote her order with shaking hands and turned to Sam with an uncomfortable blush. His voice cracked. "And you, ma'am?"

"Uhm..." Sam couldn't think, let alone form

words. "I-I'll have the same. Thank you."

The waiter's pencil lead broke as he tried to write their order. With obvious frustration, he closed his note pad and collected the menus. "I'll...I'll be..."

Nova circled her fingernail on the back of his hand. "You'll be right back with our drinks?"

"Yes. Exactly... That's what I was going to say."

Nova placed the tip of her fingernail on her lower teeth and stared up submissively. "And...if we need anything else... We should simply ask? Will you be taking care of all our needs?"

"Uhm... Yes, ma'am. I'll be... I'll be right back. With your...orders." The waiter scurried away, covering the front of his pants with the leather-bound books.

Sam leaned across the table and whispered in disbelief. "You're amazing. There's no way I could ever do that."

Nova only smiled. "Of course you can. You're a beautiful woman. An experienced woman. He's a man. Simple."

Sam shook her head. "For you maybe. Not for me."

Nova's face turned dark. A touch of wicked in an ocean of purity. "Don't say that. You have to. If not, your training is done already. I can't take you further and my husband is lost."

The waiter brought their drinks. Nova sipped hers with disappointed and downcast eyes, no longer wanting to play. Sam watched her companion for a time and realized she could never disappoint her. Resolved, she sipped from her glass and then, as an afterthought, downed the rest in a single gulp. She hoped the alcohol would bolster her courage. "Okay. I'll try." She watched Nova raise her eyes and smile with lips that almost made her heart burst with desire. "It won't work but I'll try."

Nova leaned forward and kissed Sam lightly on the lips. She squeaked out, "Thank you. I'll teach you. This part is easy. I promise."

With a long exhalation, Sam stood and smoothed her skirt with both hands. She kept glancing over at the gorgeous hunk's table. Her chest hurt as she tried to think of something to say. She coaxed her feet into slow motion, concentrating on every step. The closer she got, the harder her heart beat. It threatened to bounce out of her chest. She licked her lips and glanced back more than once at Nova's smiling face, but Sam couldn't find any confidence at all. She reached the edge of the stranger's table before she could change her mind.

The man looked up just as he started another sip

of coffee. His deep blue eyes found her before he lowered his cup to the table. Brows tight, he looked over his shoulder before returning his gaze to hers. "Can I help you with something?" His voice held deep and soothing tones mixed with the honeyed glaze of allure.

Sam licked her lips and looked back at Nova one last time. The seductress raised her glass and winked. Sam turned her regard to the delicious subject of their doomed experiment and searched for words again. Any words. "I... Uhm..." She shifted her weight from one foot to the other.

The man placed his newspaper on the table and pursed his lips. "Do we know each other? I can't believe I would forget someone who looked like you but..."

Sam took a deep breath. *I can do this. I can do this.* "Can I-Can I sit down? For a moment I mean?"

"Sure." He pulled his suit jacket downward and sat up a little straighter.

Sam swallowed hard and pulled the chair directly across from him free. Even without a bra and underwear she didn't feel sexy. She'd invited herself to a stranger's table with the intention of seducing him and didn't know where to begin. "Thanks. So, do you come here often?" Heat coursed across Sam's cheeks again. *Nice one. Do you come here often? What the hell am I doing?*

"I eat here a lot. I work in the building. You?"

"Uhm..." Sam shifted her weight, crossed and uncrossed her legs. She leaned forward, hoping her cleavage would do the talking for her. "No. This is my first time. My friend and I," she pointed to Nova, "decided to come here today to..."

The man leaned to the side, looked at Nova and then straightened again. The corner of his mouth rose in a half smile. His eyes tightened as if amused. "The cute blonde?"

Sam nodded and tried to smile brighter. "Yes. That's my friend. Nova."

"I see." He lifted his cup and sipped, never taking the oceans of blue off of Sam or her cleavage. "Is there something I can help you with?"

Why can't I talk? "You see I really like you..." *Oh my god. I'm an idiot.*

His smile lit up his entire face and his posture relaxed. "Me? I'm flattered." He held out a hand. "I'm Michael."

Sam let him take her fingertips in his hand. A gentlewoman's greeting. "Hi." *Jesus! Say something, you dolt.* She tried to appear more relaxed but couldn't find the right combination of both comfort and openness.

"And you are?"

Her cheeks had become molten embers. "Sorry. I'm Sam. Sam Keating." *Great. I can barely remember my own name.*

Michael chuckled softly. "Pleased to meet you, Sam. So you just decided to come over and say hi? Not that I'm complaining." He sipped his coffee again.

Knowing her pathetic seduction attempts had no hope of success, Sam looked over at Nova with rising nervousness. "I just thought, you know, you're so attractive and all... My friend dared me to come over. So, here I am."

"I see that. Do you work around here?"

Who's seducing who here? "No. We're just visiting."

"Can I buy you a drink or something? You look really nervous, Sam."

"Sure. That would be great. It's just that...I don't normally do this."

"Do what, Sam? We're just talking, unless you had something else in mind?" His posture continued to relax. His blue eyes roved over her body.

Sam could feel the wet heat rise between her legs. *I'm supposed to be seducing him and he's making me hot. This is never going to work.* "I mean, talking to strangers."

"I see. Do you have a boyfriend? A girlfriend?" He looked over her shoulder in Nova's direction.

She'd initiated the conversation and he'd turned the tables on her before she even got her bearings. *When did I lose control of this situation?* "No. Do you have a girlfriend?" Nova's words screamed in her head: *You're a beautiful woman. An experienced woman.* An iniquitous smile crept across her face on cloven hooves. "A boyfriend?"

Michael drank hurriedly as his face tightened. The waiter stepped up to the table and looked at Sam in confusion before he glanced over at Nova with nervous eyes. The blonde simply smiled again and gave a tiny wave with her fingertips. "Can I get either of you anything?"

Michael broke the silence hanging in the air. "Whatever my gorgeous companion is drinking. I'll have another coffee."

Gorgeous? Sam considered her options. *He's a man. Simple. What am I so afraid of?* She stared into Michael's infinitely blue eyes as she answered the waiter with calm, husky tones. *Now or never.* "How about...a blowjob?"

Michael choked on his coffee, spilling some on his tie.

"Excuse me?" The waiter's jaw dropped, hanging

open like a trap just sprung.

Easy. "Don't you two like blowjobs?" She smiled at Michael's obvious discomfort. *The shoe is on the other foot now, my friend.* "I'm surprised. I never had a man turn one down." She turned to the waiter. "Bailey's Irish cream, Kahlua and Amaretto. Don't mix it. Then top it with whipped cream."

"Oh." The waiter blushed. "The drink. I'm sure they can make you one. At the bar, I mean."

"Of course the drink, silly. You're just adorable, aren't you?" She turned back to Michael. "I love fresh cream. Don't you?"

"I... Ahh..." Michael straightened his tie and blotted it with a napkin. "I'll just have another coffee."

"I'll go get those drinks then." The waiter sped off in the direction of the bar.

Sam reached across the table and touched the back of Michael's hand with her finger, mimicking Nova's movements to the best of her ability. She purred. "Not drinking today?"

Michael forced a laugh. "This is my lunch break, honey. I still have to work."

"I understand completely." Sam smiled with lecherous victory, knowing he belonged to her now. "My friend and I are sort of taking a break today. We haven't decided exactly what we're going to do." She leaned forward, bearing more of her cleavage than before and whispered as if someone might hear. "I just hope it's going to be very naughty."

This is more fun than I thought.

Michael touched his collar and tugged, trying to swallow as he loosened his tie.

The skin on the back of Sam's neck warmed. Nova's light fingers brushed her neck gently before the teacher's soft lips pressed against her cheek. Sam's nipples hardened in a rush of heated blood.

"Oh you were so right." Nova's voice sent a tingle up Sam's thighs. "He is delicious." She held out a hand. "I'm Nova."

Michael almost knocked over his chair as he stood and took the tiny palm in his own. He stuttered. "I'm... I'm..."

"Delicious." Sam laughed. "We already know, remember?"

Michael's cheeks tinged with a tiny drop of crimson before he sat down again, obviously distressed.

Nova pulled up a chair and placed a hand on Sam's thigh. Her nails slid upward as she rested her chin on the back of her other hand and fluttered her eyes. "So. Delicious. What're you doing this fine afternoon?"

Before he could answer, the waiter brought the drinks to the table. "Your coffee, sir, and your drink, madame."

"What was it again?" Sam held her lip between her teeth and tried to look innocent.

"A..." The waiter looked around and then dropped his voice. "A blowjob, ma'am."

Sam touched his arm and left it there. *Prey.* "You should learn to say the word. In case you ever want one. The drink I mean." She lifted the glass and pressed her tongue into the whipped cream before licking her lips and releasing a subtle moan. "I do love a good blowjob." As the red-faced waiter walked away, Nova's fingers slid higher on Sam's thigh. "Don't you, Michael?"

Sam realized she liked teasing him and no longer cared who watched. She opened her knees until Nova's fingers could dance in the moisture between her legs.

The blue eyed hunk tried to recover. Unable to focus on Nova's hand or Sam's breasts without distress. "I-I do." He swallowed as if his throat had begun to close around his airway.

Sam tongued the sweet cream from her glass again. "You do what, Michael?" Nova's fingers slipped higher and brushed against her clit, bolstering her courage as no drink ever could.

Michael cleared his throat and spoke in a low voice. "Blow jobs."

Nova kissed Sam's cheek. "A man who knows what he wants. It makes me wet just thinking about it."

Sam almost moaned as Nova slid her fingers downward and back up again. She refused to be outshone in front of her teacher. "That's why we don't bother with panties. Who wants to walk around in wet silk all day?" She leaned forward and kissed Nova's neck, before dragging her tongue toward her shoulder.

Nova moaned. "So, have you decided what you are going to do today, Michael?"

"I have to go back to work." He checked his watch. "I have a meeting in thirty minutes."

"Such a shame." Sam stuck out her lower lip and opened her thighs farther. "Thirty minutes would never be enough time. Who wants to fuck without a little playtime? Right, Michael?"

Nova removed her hand from between Sam's legs and sucked her wet fingers. She stood slowly and then leaned over to whisper in Sam's ear. Her dress opened enough for Michael to see her breasts. She spoke loud enough so he couldn't help but over hear.

"Come, Samantha. I want to taste that sweet pussy before I get any hotter." She turned her attention back to their blue-eyed companion. "How much do we owe you for the drinks, Delicious?"

Michael's mouth hung wide in awe. He snapped it closed as Sam took Nova's hand in her own and stood.

"The drinks?" he asked before glancing at the table. "Oh. Nothing. It's on me."

"Are you sure? I love to pay my debts. I'm an excellent tipper." Sam licked her upper lip with all the sexy she could muster.

"No. Really. I got this." He motioned to their table. "I'll get your wine too. Don't worry about it."

"Are you sure?" Sam shuffled over to his side and pecked his cheek. "Thank you, Delicious."

Nova blew him a kiss as they turned to leave.

"Wait!" Michael began to stand with obvious discomfort. When he realized the huge bulge in his pants couldn't be covered surreptitiously, he sat down with crimson cheeks.

Sam smiled. "Did you forget something, Michael?"

"What're you two doing tonight?" His voice warbled. "At say, five?"

Nova stuck out her lower lip. "We have to head

back home soon. Maybe we'll see you again?"

"I'd love that." His voice held awe of things unknown. Untasted. "Really."

"It's a date then. Thanks for the blowjob, Delicious." Sam waved her fingertips and left the restaurant with Nova's arm hooked around her own.

***

Once they pushed through the glass doors and reached the street, Sam pressed her head to Nova's shoulder and laughed out loud. "Oh my god. That was beyond fun."

Nova held her hand and continued walking down the street. "You did quite well for your first seduction. He'll be hard for a week straight. Every day for the next year he'll sit in that same chair hoping we'll return."

"Damn. It made me so hot, Nova. I can't even tell you how wet I am."

"Trust me. I know." Nova licked her finger again.

Sam smiled. "I guess you do at that."

"Men are easy. You just have to approach them with more confidence. Let them talk about themselves. Everything they say is important. They tell you exactly what they want. What they're looking for. You simply listen and then, give it to them."

Sam grinned so hard her face began to ache. "I never thought of it that way. I was nervous at first, but when I realized how much he wanted me, it got easier. Just as I started to enjoy myself you came to the table and made me too wet for thinking. It just flowed after that. Incredible."

"Wait until you seduce your first woman. We're much more complicated and so much more fun."

Nova stopped in front of a small boutique. Through the large plate-glass windows, several mannequins dressed in everything from slinky negligees to solid leather came into view. Sam leaned in and cupped her hands against the glass to get closer look. "What're we doing here?"

"Shopping. You need a slightly different wardrobe for your...task."

Nova opened the door for Sam and followed behind her. The walls were filled with salacious displays. Vibrators. Dildos. Anal Plugs. Every toy from petite to over ten inches long and five inches across. Another wall held floggers, canes, whips and devices of pain Sam couldn't imagine how to use. On the showroom floor, racks of clothes filled every inch of the cluttered space. Each outfit seemed more sexy or revealing than the last. Corsets. Miniskirts. Leather pants. High heels with spikes so long Sam couldn't have walked in them without breaking her neck. "A playground for the kinky."

A woman with spiky pink hair and multiple nasal piercings walked up to them. Her tank-top couldn't hope to contain her enormous breasts. Large nipple rings pressed outward, outlined against the thin material and unimpeded by a bra. Multicolored tattoos twisted around her neck, across her chest and down her arms. They morphed into long thorn covered stems and wrapped around every finger. Her pants seemed painted on. Black spandex split the cleft between her thighs, inviting eyes to linger there. She looked Sam and Nova over with obvious delight before she spoke. "Can I help you ladies?"

Nova pressed a finger to her lips as she gazed across the displays. "Tight leather corsets. Lots of buckles. Thigh high boots with towering heels. I want this beautiful woman dressed like a high-class dominatrix from top to bottom."

The woman's face lit with excitement. "Sounds like my kind of party." She reached without hesitation and took Sam's hand in hers. "Come on, princess. Let's get you vamped up."

Sam had no choice except to follow. The woman pulled outfit after outfit off the racks and held them up against Sam's frame. She'd drape one over her arm with rising glee or hang a rejected garment back on the racks with a scowl. Encumbered with a dizzying array of selections, she pulled Sam back toward a small changing room and hung up the clothes on a solitary peg. "There you are, sweetie. Try them on. We'll be sitting outside."

Sam looked at the outfits with rising discomfort. "I don't think most of these are really me." She looked up for support only to find Nova holding hands with the pink-haired girl.

"We'll decide that, Samantha." Nova let her arm snake around the young woman's back. "All you have to do is change."

Their lustful expressions suggested they weren't about to take no for an answer. Sighing with resignation, Sam closed the door and stripped her dress before selecting the first outfit. A black leather corset with more ties than a pair of high top shoes. As she tried it on she realized it didn't cover her lower half. "I need a pair of panties," she called with an abashed squeak.

In less than a minute, the pink-haired girl opened the door and handed Sam French cut black panties with white lace. She paused, staring at Sam's uncovered pussy and licked her lips before Sam turned to the side. "Holy shit you're hot." She looked into Sam's eyes and handed her the panties dangling from a single finger. "Here you go." She shook her head as she closed the door. "Damn. I would be all over that in a heartbeat."

Sam slipped on the tiny piece of fabric and began fastening an astronomical number of hooks on one side of the corset. Holding it in place, she turned in front of the mirror, surprised at how aroused she'd become just putting it on. *Maybe I am kinda hot.* With apprehension, she opened the changing room door and peeked her head outside. The two women consumed each other's passion. Nova's dress floated above her hips as she straddled the pink-haired woman's legs and rocked her hips.

Is she always horny?

Sam cleared her throat noisily. "If one of you could spare the time to tie me up, I'd appreciate it." Her voice betrayed more than a tinge of jealousy.

Nova finished her kiss and stood before facing Sam. "Wow. Simply stunning."

Sam looked down at the outfit. "You really think so?"

The clerk stood with wide eyes. "Jesus, baby. Tie you up? I'd rather tie you down and own you for days." She smiled at Nova. "Are you thinking what I'm thinking?"

The blond-haired beauty nodded seriously. "Fishnet stockings."

"With lace garters." The woman grinned. "Oooh. And six-inch black pumps."

Nova tilted her head and tapped her cheek with a bright fingernail. "Long black gloves?"

Their host almost ran toward a set of shelves before pawing through stacks of boxes with cryptic labels. "Yes. Yes. Oh my god, yes." She dashed toward Sam with a pair of gloves in one hand and a pair of black heels in the other. "You can whip me any time, sweetheart. You're fucking succulent."

Sam stared at the floor. Unable to meet their praise head on. "I have no idea when I'd wear something like this." *Gage would melt if he saw me in this.*

"Trust me." Nova chuckled with delight. "Soon, Samantha. Very soon. Try on the next one."

Sam held her thoughts of Gage in silence. She changed again and again, modeling every outfit for Nova and the pink-haired woman. Each time she emerged from the changing stall, the heat between her legs rose higher. The new panties became even more damp. *I guess I'm keeping these.* If the two women weren't sucking each other's nipples, they had their fingers pressed into each other's pussies. As if they hadn't been interrupted, they'd stop and complement her new attire before piling on more accessories with sheer delight.

When Sam had finally tried on and modeled everything, she pulled her original dress on and loaded her arms with the piles of clothes before pushing the door open again. As expected, Nova had her legs up on the arms of the chair with the tattooed woman's face buried between her thighs. Sam didn't disturb them. Instead, she watched and dreamed of Gage doing the same to her.

Nova came with trembling legs and moans of carnal pleasure. With a gratified sigh she tasted herself on the woman's lips. "Thank you, Chloe."

Chloe bubbled. "Don't thank me. I could eat you forever." She licked her lips and devoured Sam with her eyes. "We should have a three way. I'd love to get into your panties. Hell, I'd pay to get into your panties."

A surge of confidence ran through Sam's veins like molten courage. "Thanks. I think." *Gage is going to crawl and then I will reward him.*

"Sorry, Chloe. We have a prior engagement." Nova helped Sam pile her clothes on the counter as the clerk began to scan each of the items. "But, we'll be back. I promise. Are you ready, Samantha?"

As the numbers climbed on the register, Sam realized she didn't have her purse. "Oh shit. I—"

Nova held up a small clutch she hadn't had a minute ago. "This one's on me, Samantha. You have better ways of paying people. Money is much too banal for a woman of your charms."

Sam couldn't help but heave a sigh of relief at Nova's offer. The cost seemed staggering. She would've had to sell her car. *Hell, I would've been walking the streets. At least I'd be dressed for the part.*

When everything had been bagged or boxed, they said their final goodbyes. Sam couldn't recall another time her own confidence had been more palpable or real. In a single day, the world had become hers to do with as she pleased.

Nova stopped on the sidewalk outside and let the people part around them again. "Take a deep breath, Samantha. Just stare straight ahead."

Sam shifted her boxes and glanced at Nova with confusion. "What?"

"Take a breath. Look at me."

"Okaaay..." Sam inhaled deeply and stared into Nova's eyes.

The blonde nymph touched her arm and shifted the world around them.

Chapter Seven
Misplaced Desire

*T*he deep breath helped. The Place In-Between warped into solidity while Sam still had air in her lungs, but it didn't stop the earth from moving. She fell forward, dropping her packages as she reached out and clung to Nova for dear life. The nausea ended quicker this time, but her stomach continued to boil long after the ground had steadied.

As the world came into focus, she watched Khanzani scramble to collect her packages. "I can take them, Khan." She spoke the words but stumbled when she bent to help.

He placed a hand on Sam's and pulled her to her feet. "Take a minute, Samantha. I'll carry them to your room."

"Thank you, Khan. I just need to get my bearings again." She steadied herself slowly, wishing Gage had run to her side with as much concern.

They'd returned to the pool where Sam had first bathed with Gage. The sun had begun its descent beyond the building. Twilight settled over the crystal clear water. At the edge of her vision, Sam recognized Gage's muscular back. Her heart pounded with excitement. She couldn't think about anything except Gage. Holding him in her arms. Giving herself to him.

Sam's smile faded faster than it formed. She watched Gage's hand come to rest on the ass of a gorgeous redhead as he laughed at something she'd said. Her brick-red hair shined in the fading sunlight, falling over her shoulders to end in the middle of her back. A simple wrap, identical to the one Sam had worn hours earlier, tightened on the woman's hourglass figure. It displayed her sculpted hips and enormous breasts as if cut for her alone. Her mouth seemed full and made for kissing. Without question, one of the most beautiful women Sam had ever seen.

Unbidden anger rose in Sam's chest. An unwanted warmth rising from the pit of her stomach. *Why should I be jealous? It's not like I own him.* She shook off the ugly feeling when Nova touched her arm. The sprite tugged her toward the happy pair with slow, purposeful steps.

Nova sashayed close to the redhead before sucking her bottom lip with a pop to grab their attention. "Aren't you a treat? I see you've met my husband. He's quite a catch, don't you think?"

The woman looked startled. "I'm sorry, mistress. I didn't know." She clutched the hem of her dress with shaking hands and lowered her head as she tried to scurry away.

Gage removed his hand from the woman's ass and glanced at Sam with pursed lips before shifting his gaze to his feet.

Nova reached out and stopped the woman's retreat in midstride. With her other hand, she raised the woman's chin with her fingertips. "You're too beautiful to be sorry. I'm not complaining. Merely stating a fact. I'm Nova and this lovely creature is Samantha."

The woman looked up with wide eyes before lowering her chin again. Nearly lost on the light breeze around them, she mumbled in a key just above the limits of hearing. "I'm Katherine."

"You're unbelievably gorgeous, Katherine." Nova stepped closer, until their chests almost touched. "The men are veritably singing your praises. I've been dying to meet you."

The corner of Katherine's mouth turned upward as she lifted her eyes. "Really? What have they been saying?"

Nova leaned in and brushed the hair back from her ear before whispering with honey sweet tones. "That you are even more beautiful with your clothes off than on. I'd love the chance to find out for myself."

Katherine giggled. "I'd like that."

"Perfect." Nova moved her hand to Katherine's hip and nudged her toward a divan a few steps away. Without pause she turned her head and spoke to Gage. "You don't mind, my love. Do you?"

Gage raised his chin and tensed his jaw. Filled with an expression of pure fury, he said nothing.

Nova swayed to Katherine's side and unclipped the pin holding her wrap. Gravity pulled the fabric to the ground. Nova drew circles around the toned muscles in Katherine's abdomen with one hand and clutched her ass with the other. The tight red curly hair between the woman's legs reminded Sam of a burning ember, cradled by her milky skin and framed by buxom hips. Without clothes, Katherine had become nothing less than Venus.

Sam considered Gage's reaction as Nova kissed Katherine a few steps away. She glanced at his clenching fists and rippling arms surreptitiously, trying to picture what ran through his mind as he watched his wife devour an Aphrodite bound to earth. *Seduction.*

Sam realized Nova had given her this opportunity on purpose. All she had to do is take it. "I need a bath." She waited until Gage's attention returned to her and pretended she hadn't noticed. Controlling her excitement, she walked slowly to the water's edge and kicked her shoes off. "While I was trying on lingerie, I watched a beautiful young woman suck Nova's clit until she came. Your wife is every woman's dream. I haven't been this wet in a long time."

Hoping he still watched her, Sam tested the water with her toe. With all the sultry smoothness she could muster, she rolled her skirt above her hips and pulled it over her head. Dropping it to the side, she looked over her shoulder, ecstatic her body held his attention despite Katherine's moans a few steps behind him. "Will you rinse my back?"

Gage's jaw seemed to loosen before he walked toward her, but she didn't stare long enough to make sure. Concentrating, she tried to appear indifferent to his approach even though her heart raced. As he came close enough to touch her, she could almost feel his black eyes burning into her flesh.

His voice dropped low. The tone he used when he wished to be in control. "Is that all you want me to wash?"

Not this time Gage. This is my show.

Knowing she had his full attention now, Sam forced a lighthearted laugh. Her thumbs hooked above the waistband of her tiny black lace panties as she stared across the placid pool. Katherine's moans had changed to high pitched cries of 'Yes!" Sam pushed the fabric downward, moving her hips left to right. Instead of letting them fall to the ground she stepped clear and held them dangling from her index finger. She offered them to Gage and held back her smile as he accepted them like precious jewels. "Is that wet enough for you? They were going to start dripping if I didn't get them off. I'd much rather go without."

Her mouth became parched as Gage raised the black lace to his nose and inhaled deeply. Sam hoped her voice wouldn't crack. "I must say your wife is having quite the effect on me. I adore the scent of a properly wetted pussy now." Sam swallowed hard and waded into the warm water. She could feel her hot juices begin their slow trickle down her leg as the water covered her swollen lips. "Almost as much as the taste of a hard cock pumping hot cum down my throat." As she splashed the water onto her neck and pressed her breasts together, waiting for his touch.

His hands found her shoulders first. Relentless

pressure softened her muscles beneath his palms. When his hot breath caressed the hairs on her neck, she pushed her hips backward until his hard cock pressed against her ass. Swollen. Solid. *Perhaps you will kneel after all.* His hands moved beneath her arms and caressed her breasts. He pulled her tightly against him.

Sam bared her neck to his lips, trying to control her breathing as she stared at Nova. The blonde temptress knelt on the divan with her face buried between Katherine's legs, devouring her wet heat. The redhead's legs draped over Nova's shoulders digging her heels in deep. Nova's dress had become bunched above her hips, clutched in Katherine's trembling hands as the redheaded beauty screamed in pleasured release. Just the outline of Nova's lips as she worked between another's thighs made Sam want to taste her or, even better, share her with Katherine.

Sam choked back a moan as Gage's fingers rolled across her swollen clit and slid lower, parting her outer lips. Sam panted. "Your lover is gorgeous. Everything about her is desire." His fingers pushed in deeply, touched her G-spot and then slid back up to circle her clit again. Sam bit her lip, wanting to suppress the moan rising from her throat.

"She is seduction." Gage's breathing had become

ragged. Weathered paper blown across a barren desert. "I'm not thinking about her. I want to concentrate on pleasuring you."

His cock sipped against her skin. With every touch, she craved his submission more. A groan escaped her lips. "I want you to fuck me hard, Gage. Can you take me to the edge or will you leave me unfulfilled?"

With her words, his hands entwined in her hair, pulling her head back with raw power. He licked her neck and bit her shoulder. He wrapped his arm around her waist and pushed his fingers deep inside her cleft, pulling upward as his palm pressed against her hardened clit.

Sam groaned. *You're mine already. You simply fail to see.* A whisper escaped her lips. "Submit and I become your plaything."

His pull lessened, allowing her to relax her neck. His fingers slipped free, making her gasp.

Gage growled. A grizzly wakened from his winter sleep, starved and prepared to kill anything in its path. "It's not in my nature to bow."

No. No. No! It's not supposed to happen like this.

Sam took a deep breath and tried to control herself as she moved toward the edge of the pool. Her emotions tangled and became confused. *Am I angry?*

Disappointed? She whispered, unwilling to let him see her break. "That's too bad."

As Sam left the pool, Khanzani stepped from the closest building and stared at her naked body with an open mouth. His muscles bulged. His chest rippled. The fabric covering his cock began to tent. *You will bow Gage or you will suffer.* Knowing Gage stared at her back, she didn't shy away from Khan's hungry look. Instead, she met his gaze with her own. She understood what she had to do.

I will make you beg, Gage.

Sam turned her head toward Gage still waist deep in the pool. Her tongue traced the shape of her mouth. "I'm going to come tonight, Gage. With or without you."

She moved toward Khanzani with slow steps, no longer caring she wore nothing but a smile. His rapt expression gave her all the confidence she needed. "Will you submit, Khan?"

The dark man's eyes narrowed. He raised a tattooed arm and rubbed his chin. "If that is what you wish, mistress."

Sam tried to focus on her words instead of his muscular chest. The multicolored tattoos seemed unfathomably complex. A million stories or a thousand dreams written upon ebony skin bronzed by an unknowable number of days. "It is." Gage's unwillingness to bend hurt. Her task had become more personal than she'd expected. "Like you, I still search."

Khan stepped closer. "Then we follow the same path. I am yours to command, mistress."

His scent had become palpable. Lust frosted in desire. "I need rope, Khan."

He touched his forehead and bowed slightly. "As you wish, mistress."

Sam watched Nova as Khan sped off toward the nearest building. The blonde nymph sat upright on the edge of the divan and stared intently at Sam. Her lips and chin still shined with fresh cum. Katherine lounged behind her, chin resting on Nova's shoulder, arms around her waist.

Nova's voice seemed thick. Filled with curiosity. "What is it you have in mind, my sweet Samantha?"

Khan returned at a run. He held out the soft coils of rope to Sam. She took them in her hand before she answered. "A demonstration for your loving husband. Punishment for sins not realized. Kneel for me, Khan."

The huge man knelt without another word. Sam walked toward him, stopping with her belly button inches from his lips. She lifted his chin until his eyes met her own. "Lick the water from my skin."

He reached for her hips only to be stopped by her finger pressed against his lips. "I didn't tell you to use your hands. You may touch my flesh with your tongue. I will tell you when hands are needed."

"Yes, mis—"

"I didn't tell you to speak," Sam cut him off with cold tones. "When talking, you're not pleasuring me." Her voice hardened as she enunciated each word with brutal clarity. "Lick. From. My. Skin."

Khan started with the tip of his tongue, one drop at a time. He kissed with tenderness, below her breasts, a butterfly alighting on naked flesh. Luxurious. His hunger grew with her own. He dragged the rough wetness across her abdomen until she coaxed his head lower, forcing him to circle her belly. She pushed his shoulders harder. Lower. Each time his tongue found the spots she wanted, she grabbed the tight course curls of his hair with her hands and pulled him closer. Suffering more than he did, she denied his advance if he moved without her direction.

Sam's eyes closed as Khan licked the tender skin between her outer lips and her inner thigh. She moved her feet apart, opening herself. Asking for more. He rose to suck her clit, kiss and descend down the other side of her pussy. He continued down her thigh to kiss her knee and ascend again. His tongue parted her lips before finding her clit again. Another passionate kiss.

"Such a good boy." The words stuttered in her throat. "Lie on the divan. It's my turn."

Khanzani stood.

Sam connected with Gage's eyes briefly before she barked her next command. He needed to know what she wanted. "No, Khan. I want you to crawl."

Khan didn't balk at her words. He lowered himself to his knees and crawled to the pillow-covered divan without complaint. He lay on his back. Waiting.

The wrap at Khan's waist bulged with impossible size. His massive balls lifted with every breath he took. Sam whispered. "Lift your hands above your head."

Khanzani raised his hands to the corners of the lounger. Even his triceps were cut and covered with colored ink. Sam did her best to appear confident as she stepped to his side and looped the rope around his wrist. She fumbled with a complex knot at first before giving up and switching to a simple double overhand as if it'd been her intention all along. It wouldn't look pretty, but it would hold. She wrapped the rope around the recliner's frame quickly and secured it with a slip knot.

Bending forward, she scented Khan's neck and licked his earlobe. She raised her eyes to stare at Gage who now glowered from only a few feet away. He wore a towel around his waist but showed no indication of leaving. *At least I still have your attention.* She reached forward and drew her fingernails across Khan's taught chest. Her eyes remained riveted on Gage as she moved to the other side of the chair, daring him to speak.

Sam didn't know if seeing Khan's cock or the idea of capturing Gage's jealousy excited her more. She savored the control she had over both of them. The power to make men ache to fuck her made her wet as hell.

This could become an addiction.

Hoping to make Gage even hotter, she turned her back to him and opened her legs. She bent at her waist when she tied Khan's other hand, sure her pussy lips would be prominently displayed between her open thighs. The knots came easier now. Her concentration soared in parallel with her arousal. The idea of manipulation and control with nothing more than her movement had become intoxicating. Irresistible.

She held the coil of rope in her hand and backed up slowly, dragging it across Khanzani's chest, his waist, and the bulge below his wrap. Opening his legs, she wrapped the fiber around his ankle and bound it to the recliner with a complex knot before repeating her efforts on the other side. Leaning forward, she undid the clip at his waist and addressed Gage with mock disdain. "I reward those who do as they're told."

Sam almost gasped as she pulled the wrap from Khanzani's hips. His dick throbbed with the beat of his heart. She hadn't seen many cocks in her lifetime, but at nine inches long and three inches across, this would be the biggest she'd ever taken. Hoping she hadn't bitten off more than she could chew, she stroked the hot shaft, milking warm pre-cum from his cock's head until it dripped on the back of her hand. She stood and licked the sugared seed from her skin. "I am going to fuck you slow. If you cum before I command it, you will never have me again. Understood?"

"As you wish, mistress."

Nova kissed Katherine again as they watched the play unfold before them. "A woman, who can ride a man well, deserves the pleasures she takes."

Sam watched Nova finger herself while

Katherine slathered her neck in kisses. Soaking wet herself, Sam stood and faced Gage. She climbed onto the divan and straddled Khanzani's massive chest. Leaning forward, she pushed her wet slit to his mouth. She took the massive cock in her hands and licked its tip, never taking her gaze off Gage's burning eyes. Her moans came on their own as Khan's hot tongue lapped with gusto. His chin bumped against her clit as he pushed deeper. Shockwaves raced up her body until her nipples tingled. With rhythmic contractions of her abdomen, she steered his hot mouth where it needed to be.

Gage's hard cock had risen as he watched her move. *I made you that hard, Gage. Remember that.* Sam sat up on her knees and crawled forward until Khan's massive dick pressed against her wet entrance. Gripping his cock in her hand, she moved his tip back and forth, spreading her lips apart and positioning him for penetration. She could feel the pressure of her outer lips against her thighs, bulging outward with his impossible girth. Watching Gage's breathing rate increase, she squeezed her tits together and closed her eyes, lowering herself as fast as she dared. With burning pleasure, her legs were forced wider, stretching her toward unbearable limits. Rising again with a moan, she dropped with more power, trying to make her pussy accept his size. She moaned as she rose and dropped again. "Oh my god! Too damn big. You're huge, Khan."

Khan moaned from behind her. "Don't stop, mistress. Please. I want to be all the way inside you."

She gasped, driving him deeper. "I'm going to take every inch of you." She breathed harder. "It's mine and I'm going to feel you come inside me."

Long slow stokes. Her thighs ached and trembled each time she lifted her hips. Her wet pussy took him deeper with every pass. She could feel the shape of her vagina, molded to his dick. Exquisite pain opened her beyond belief. Sliding. Every vessel in his shaft flashed across her mind as they coursed against the burning flesh of her pink core. Burning pain on the edge of tearing and still she wanted him deeper. Opening her eyes she gazed at Gage with profound longing. Wanting. Needing his touch. She spoke in painful gasps. "Don't just stare, Gage." She groaned. "Rub my clit so I can take the rest of him. I'm almost at my limit." *Please.*

Gage approached with cautious steps as she lifted and lowered herself again and again. Biting her lip, she swallowed the pain, accepting the pleasure as the man she wanted to dominate came closer. She placed her hands on Khan's legs, leaning forward to accept his length. Gage dropped his towel and brought his hard cock near her mouth. Rocking her hips forward and back, she accepted Khan in a passionate cadence of lust. She sucked Gage's tip once and panted again. She could barely talk, let alone take the hardened cock into her mouth no matter how badly she wanted him. "My clit. Rub my clit."

Gage sat and stroked her clit with his fingers. The sensitive nub had become caged. The immensity inside her stretched the thin restraining hood taught above it. Electric jolts shot across her body as Gage rubbed, pinched and flicked. Her legs shook with his touch. She wrapped her arms around his neck and leaned into him, pulling him tight as her own voice rose in ecstasy. "Yes. Oh god, yes."

She continued to work her hips. The orgasm rose. Her hand found Gage's cock. Pumping it hard, she bit into his shoulder until he screamed in pain. His cries pushed her over the edge. Taken by the moment, her pussy contracted on the massive dick deep inside her. Khan shuddered with a guttural growl, filling her with his hot seed in pounding pulse after pulse. She clawed her nails into Gage's back, refusing to let loose her teeth as she fought for breath and consciousness.

Her body's tremors subsided in retreating waves

of pleasure. Sam opened her mouth and gasped for air. The marks on Gage's shoulder already turned purple. Deep tooth marks remained and had all but broken his skin. *Don't expect apologies from me.* She raised her mouth to his ear. "A simple promise of more to come." Her lungs ached for air as she sat back again. "When you're man enough to take it."

She hoped she hadn't gone too far. Gage's seduction had become an obsession. She lifted her hips slowly, pain no longer tempered by pleasure. The withdrawal made her pussy throb again as another orgasm threatened. *The question is whether or not I can still walk.* On shaky legs, she cleared Khan's hips and stepped onto firmer ground. His face mirrored the pleasure pounding between her thighs and made the stream of his cum running down her legs even more sensuous. "Untie him, Gage. You two can compare notes. If you're lucky, he'll let you taste me on his cock."

She turned her back on the men and walked toward the closest building, hoping she could find her room again. Each step required intense concentration. Her legs threatened to fail with every step. Nova must have realized how weak she'd become. She slid between Sam's arms, providing support and comfort.

"You did so well, Samantha. I can't wait to

reward you myself. I'll get some food and join you in your room shortly."

Can I handle any more attention?

Still on the divan, Katherine licked her lips with desire. The excitement of having such a beautiful woman watch her, lifted the corner of Sam's mouth with unexpected lust.

This is what I've searched for, and now, I know how to take it.

Chapter Eight

Nothing but What is Given

The sun forced Sam to open her eyes with a squint. Nova had gone but her scent still lingered. A summer's breeze. The touch of a lover's hand. Sam pressed her face to the pillow and inhaled the strawberry flavor the blonde muse had left behind. Hours of tasting each other, holding, sucking and licking. Every minute of the night before flooded back to her. Passioned echoes of Nova's lithe body as she came in response to Sam's tongue. The size of Khanzani's cock. Gage's fingers upon her clit.

A beginning.

My beginning.

Sam moved to the side of the bed and stretched her aching muscles. The pain dwindled in shadows of the pleasure she'd been given. The breeze blowing into the room offset the discomfort of the sun's rays. The "facilities" were familiar now, but the open wall made their use uncomfortable just the same. As she scanned the courtyard, Sam made a mental note to ask for a dressing screen. She washed her face in the basin before pawing through the boxes of clothes she'd bought the day before with amusement. *When the time is right, I will break him.* With a sigh, she dressed in a simple light blue toga and stepped into the morning sunlight in search of her charge.

Gage leaned against the wall just outside her door. She jumped like a skittish kitten. "How long have you been here?"

He stood and looked at her as if studying some rare curiosity. "A while. I didn't want to disturb you. Are you ready?"

She squinted again. Too tired to think about anything but food. "For?"

"Lashings." He walked toward the next building.

Sam followed. She pursed her lips with concern. "Exactly who's lashing whom?"

He looked at her, lifting an eyebrow as if conversing with the insane. "What?"

"Who is hitting whom? Am I to receive or give the punishment?"

He laughed out loud as they passed through columned halls. "Lashings are advanced bindings. Tools of pleasure won't begin until tomorrow. Of course, if you would like me to flog your ass, I'm more than happy to oblige."

She blushed, wishing she hadn't tried to banter about something she didn't understand. *Two can play at this game.* "No thanks. Your wife deprived me of my beauty rest last night. I could use a proper bath though. My tender pussy is more than a little sore and I'm still covered in cum and sweat."

His jaw tightened. "Of course. This way."

He took two quick turns and then stepped into the courtyard leading to the bathhouse. She entered the semi darkness of the building and shucked her clothes without hesitation. She wanted him to think stripping for him came easy. The pool's perfect temperature helped her focus on keeping him aroused. Soft splashes in all the right places, her hands moved with single purpose, increasing his lust. She stepped to the drainage area and placed her hands against the wall, speaking without looking at him. "Wash me, please."

She moaned as he poured warm water across her shoulders. "Yummy."

He sponged her back in slow circles before focusing on her ass. She spread her legs wider as he worked on her thighs and legs, feeling his breath against her skin. "Work hard between my legs. I want my pussy clean enough to eat from. You never know who'll be dining."

It surprised her he didn't answer the quips with his own, but merely rinsed her vulva thoroughly. He spent extra time pressing the hot cloth against her clit and focused on the skin between her outer lips and thighs.

Sam turned to face him as he dipped the cloth in the scented soap again. His bitten shoulder had turned deep shades of black and blue ringed by a sickly yellow-green halo. Their eyes met as he stood. "Don't forget the front."

With coal black orbs held in an expressionless face, Gage pressed the hot sponge to her neck without taking his gaze from hers. Soft touches on the top of her breasts and across her nipples. Harder beneath them. Lifting. Rubbing. His hands moved lower with practiced certainty.

"Did you like watching me tie Khan to the divan?"

The pause seemed almost pregnant. He rinsed the sponge again and stepped closer as he worked it between her legs. "Your knots were sloppy. He could've gotten free if he'd chosen to. That's not control. It's lust."

She waited until he knelt to work on her legs. His

mouth inches from her clit. "And his cock driving into me? I thought you would've appreciated that."

Gage stood and dropped the sponge in the bucket. He filled another bucket with warm water and poured it across her, washing the soap away. "You can rinse in the pool again. We have a lot of ground to cover."

She smiled, knowing her words had the effect she desired. Stepping into the hot water, she splashed herself and then ducked beneath the wet embrace, soaking her hair before standing to walk from the pool. "Are you going to dry me or do I need to ask for Khan to help?"

Gage pulled a towel from the shelf and blotted the water from her body before pulling it across her skin. Slipping it behind her, he pulled her close and kissed her mouth. Hard. Passionate. "Do you think you can seduce me?" He didn't loosen his hold.

The kiss shocked her, but he wasn't ready to yield. Sam pushed against his chest until he released her and stepped from his arms. She met his gaze before she began wrapping the toga around her body. *It was a hell of kiss though.* "Perhaps. Your hard cock tells me what you want. I only have to convince your mind to follow what your shaft already knows. Are you ready?"

He grinned with lechery. "For?"

"Lashings of course. Were you hoping for something else?"

***

Gage guided them back to the pool courtyard from the night before. Cool air swirled around her despite the morning sun pounding down from above. Katherine stood by a small table covered with fruit and bread. She wore a simple blue pullover with thin shoulder straps. The contrast between her green eyes, red hair and nearly transparent fabric drew both her and Gage's gaze with ease.

Katherine bounced with excitement. "Good morning. I hope you don't mind. I asked Khanzani if I could serve you today." She looked down at the ground as if abashed by her presumption.

Watching the sparkle in Katherine's hair, Sam sat down in a chair. She tried to see through the thin fabric the redhead wore. A tease without revealing anything. Sam wondered what her demonstration from the night before had triggered in the young woman's mind. "I think both of us will enjoy your company." When Katherine raised her freckled face with a smile, Sam couldn't resist another comment. "Of course, I may not be able to pay attention to my lessons with a figure like yours distracting me."

Katherine giggled. She lifted a stone carafe of coffee and moved to Sam's side. She filled her cup with shaking hand, spilling a little on the tablecloth. "Sorry. I'm a little nervous."

Sam enjoyed the delicate skin of the redhead's arm, running her nails up and down. Steadying her hands. "Why on earth would you be nervous, beautiful?"

Gage sat at the table with a handful of rope and watched the women converse.

Are you watching me or Katherine?

Katherine set the coffee on the table. "Seeing you take Khan last night..." She looked at the ground and circled her toe. "It was incredible. I've never been more aroused. Now I just want to...learn a little more about you."

Gage tossed the coil of rope to Sam, emphasizing his impatience. "You two can *learn* about each other *after* we are done with our lessons."

Sam no longer cared if his response suggested real aggravation or simple sexual frustration, as long as his attention remained centered on her. She lifted the rope coil on a single finger before answering in her most sultry voice. "Such a vicious taskmaster. What would you have me do...Sir." She had no doubt the epithet would burn him to the core.

"A square knot and a simple slip."

Sam tied both knots with ease, tossed him the knotted line. She granted him a condescending smile before taking another bite of breakfast.

Gage examined the simple ties with disdain. He growled. "The hitches: half, two, taught line, timber, alpine, and clove." He slapped the silk line on the table.

One after another, Sam untied the rope and tied it again. She fumbled once with the cross over ends on the clove hitch but didn't need his help. "Ta da!" Smug satisfaction settled on her face. She twirled the loop on her finger and batted her eyelashes with childish exaggeration.

"Figure eight, eight on a bight, bowline, bowline on bight, double and triple bowlines."

Sam watched his face redden as she tied the knots he asked for. As the turns became more complex, she struggled more. She restarted more than once to get the harder ones right. As much as she loved getting the upper hand, a little helplessness never failed to fuel a man's desire. She fumbled with the next knot even though it wasn't complicated. "I-I forgot that one."

Almost smiling, he snatched the rope from her

hands and demonstrated the correct way to tie it. "You have to practice every day. You also have to dress the knots correctly or it will pinch skin. Not sexy. Show me how you would secure a wrist so you could tie it properly to something like...that divan over there."

His reference to the lounger she'd tied Khanzani to wasn't lost on her. *Bastard. Last time I give you an inch.* "Give me your hand, Katherine."

Katherine offered her thin wrist with excitement. Sam formed a quick loop, tied a slip knot and pulled it tight.

Gage guffawed as if he'd just seen her draw a circle with a crayon. "Effective but crude."

"Is that a fact?" His attitude started to grate on Sam's nerves.

Gage stood and walked around the table. He sat between the two women and took the free end of the rope from Sam's hand. "This knot's security is dependent on the bound person to maintain tension." He moved Katherine's wrist toward the main rope instead of away and the knot loosened. "You see? She slips free if she chooses. In addition, it's dangerous. If she pulls too hard," he pulled the rope sharply, tightening it on Katherine's wrist until she winced. "It cuts off the circulation and becomes difficult to untie.

In a fit of passion she could be seriously hurt."

Sam realized she hadn't even considered the subtleties involved. She watched Gage use two hands to untie Katherine and then massage her wrists with care she hadn't expected. Sam's shoulders slumped with disappointment. "There's too many to choose from."

"Pick a few that achieve your goals. Adapt them to different situations." Gage's hands flew as he fit a tiny loop over Katherine's wrist with a figure eight. He wrapped the rope around her wrist twice and made another loop with a second figure eight. "There. Secured by two points. She can't slip it off but it won't tighten either. In addition, it has this free loop you can tie other ropes to if you want a more complex pattern."

Sam ate as Gage untied Katherine, fascinated by the glee in the young woman's eyes.

When they finished eating, Katherine cleared the table while Gage recoiled the ropes. The redhead refilled her coffee cup. "I'd like to get together with you tonight, Samantha." She started staring at the ground again. "I mean...if you want to. We could...talk."

Sam stood and raised the girl's chin, kissing her gently on the mouth. "I'd like that, Katherine."

Katherine giggled like a little girl, blushing as she walked away.

"It looks like you've gained another admirer, Samantha."

"A date if nothing else." She looked over at Gage. "Jealous?"

Gage lifted two cylindrical wooden poles, each three feet long and three inches wide. "Perhaps."

Sam's pulse pounded in her neck. "Are you planning to make me a better offer?"

"Would you accept?"

"Perhaps. It depends on how wet your *lashings* make me."

Gage refused to take the bait. "Lashings. All of them start with one end of the rope secured to a wrist or ankle. These poles will serve as an example. You can tie any of several knots but the figure eight with the loops I showed you lies flat and doesn't cut into the skin." He tied the same knot he'd tied on Katherine's wrist around one of the poles. "Here." He handed her the other pole and another coil of rope. "Show me."

Sam secured the rope around the other pole. She struggled to make it perfect, wondering why she needed his approval. "How's that?"

Gage ran his fingers over the knot. He inspected

it from all angles before handing the pole back to her. "Good. We'll start with the square lashing." He placed the poles together in the shape of a cross. "This works best for crossed wrists or ankles. Use your imagination here. Start wrapping. Under the pole away from the knot. Over the pole with the knot. Under. Over. Under. I use three wraps." His hands turned the coils as he spoke. "Then wrap on the opposite sides using the opposite poles. Over. Under. Over. Under. Got it?"

Sam nodded.

"Now the most important part. Frapping. You wrap the coils you've already placed with more windings of rope but between the poles now. Like this." His hands moved with surety. "You have to be careful it doesn't bind. This tightens and secures. It can't be too tight and your sub must be comfortable. Understand?"

"I think so."

"Good. Ask them. Have them wiggle their fingers or feet. If you and your subject are satisfied with the result, simply tie it off again. I use another figure eight on a bight." He showed her the completed tie and then undid everything. "Your turn."

Sam began to tie. When she got confused, Gage stood behind her and guided her hands. His scent.

The touch of his skin against hers. Every movement he made only distracted and sent her thoughts tumbling.

Gage stood. "Excellent. I have to say, you have a gift for rope work."

Sam couldn't hold back the blush in her cheeks or the dampening between her thighs. "A compliment? I'm shocked."

Gage untied the knots while he moved back to the other side of the table. He sat in silence for a long time before he finally spoke with soft tones. "It's hard for me, you know?"

"Saying something nice about someone?" Sam furrowed her brow.

"No. About you."

"Wow." Sam couldn't disguise her facetious tone. "I'm glad I made your bottom five."

"No," Gage nearly shouted. "That's not what I meant at all. I mean it's hard with you because of the reason you're here. I feel as though you were forced on me unfairly. I don't know if I can do what they want even though..."

Sam shifted uncomfortably. Gage had never opened up to her before. She didn't want him to stop. "Even though?"

He looked at her for a moment as if choosing his

words. "Even though it seems I want you more than anything I've ever wanted in my life."

Sam couldn't breathe. Her heart hammered. Her skin became suffused with warmth flowing upward from the ready lips between her thighs. She looked down before she spoke, having no idea what she wanted to say or how to answer.

Is it possible? Or, do you just want to get laid?

Gage broke the uncomfortable silence. "Shear lashings." He held the two poles parallel to each other. "After the wrists or ankles are tied, you can use a shear lashing to bind the rest of the arm all the way to the shoulder. They also work to tie legs or arms to a pole, a bench or… the edge of a bed. Any two objects parallel to each other."

Sam watched in silence. She wanted to tell him her thoughts echoed his own but feared it would destroy the progress they'd already made.

Just agree, damn you. Once you submit. You can take anything you want. For as long as you want.

"Start on either side. Just like we did with the square lashing." He tied a figure eight with two wraps and formed a loop as he'd done before. "Then run the other end over the other pole, under the first, over the second." His hands made turn after turn. "After three or so, you frap again." He continued wrapping around the loops between the two poles. "Like the square, this is where the lashing is tightened. Make sure the coils set well across the skin. You have to communicate. Ask the sub. You can tease them so they don't realize you're adjusting to their comfort. Got it?"

Sam nodded as Gage untied everything again. Imagining him binding her. Pushing her own limits as she refused to use her safe word.

She began to replicate his actions. The knots came easier. Over. Under. Frap. Tie.

Gage examined her work. "That's good. You're amazing." He moved behind her again and touched her hands with his own. He whispered in her ear. "But you have to make sure the coils are straight. They can't overlap. Every turn must be beautiful."

She could feel his breath on her neck. His words tickled her earlobe, making it hard to swallow. When she reached for her glass of water, his hands slid up her arms, pausing at her neck. A shiver crackled across her skin, spreading outward until every inch of her body tingled.

Sam sipped her water as Gage untied her lashings with a self satisfied smile. "Are you all right, Samantha? You're uncharacteristically quiet."

Sam wanted him to squirm. "Don't flatter

yourself. I already have a date for tonight. Remember? I'll be eating pussy and you'll be stroking your own cock. That is...if Nova permits it."

His black eyes seemed to blaze. "How could I forget?" He crossed the poles again and began to tie. His voice had become stern. "Most of the other lashings are simply variations on the two you've already learned. The diagonal is a beautiful edition to your repertoire when binding wrists, but it can easily become too bulky."

Hours passed in practice, success and intermittent failure. Sam sighed as she followed his work. "I'm sure all of these will do the job but aren't they tedious? I mean, handcuffs would do the job just as well, wouldn't they? Don't you worry about losing the moment as you loop and tie. Loop and tie."

She watched the libidinous expression roll across his face. "Rope work is seduction. A promise of things to come. Each loop chips away another part of the sub's control until they lose even the hope of resistance. They become the Dom's toy. An object of pleasure. Complete and total submission reprieved only by the Dom or your safe word."

Sam swallowed, choking back her own desire. "Is that a fact?" She smiled, wondering if she should be more cautious. "Prove it."

Gage stood and lifted the multiple coils of rope. The muscles in his arms twitched until the tattoos danced upon his skin. His dark eyes came to life with the thoughts both of them shared.

"Kneel on the divan." His voice changed. Firm and demanding obedience.

She knelt as instructed on hands and knees. "How's this?" In an attempt to disarm him, she wiggled her hips back and forth seductively, daring him to question her intent. "Sir."

"Spread your legs wider. I want your knees and ankles in line with the frame."

Sam's control faded. She opened her knees, adjusting the folds of her toga so it fell between her legs. He wouldn't be able to see how wet she'd become. His hips remained in her peripheral vision. His hard cock, though covered, called to her from no more than a tongue away. His fingers pulled her hair over her ear. With a gentle tug he pulled backward, forcing her eyes forward. As she tried to control her breathing, smooth whorls of silk pressed lightly between her legs, bumping against her open lips before being dragged slowly across her ass and up her back. She bit her lip, holding her breath as Gage moved beside her, dragging the coil across her ass.

Sam tried not to flinch as the coil slipped down

her thighs toward her knee. As the back of his hand brushed against the wet lips between her legs, she bit her lip and closed her eyes, wanting him but unwilling to let him know.

Soft strands of rope wound around her calves with skill garnered over countless years. Gentle restriction. Immobilizing. Controlling. He sat between her legs as he bound her. So close she could feel his hot breath against her ass, inhaling her essence with every loop he turned.

He spoke before she could moan. "Is that too tight?"

Sam stretched her toes and wiggled them. From ankle to knee he'd lashed her legs to the lounger. Without pain he'd opened her completely and forbidden the movement of her lower legs or knees. She managed a whisper. "No."

His fingers moved across her outer lips. Barely touching. She could feel every bump, every fold, every curve as he continued his soft massage. Perfect awareness driven deep into the oldest recesses of her mind. Clarity.

The loss of his touch cast her into a barren desert without food or water. Pain. Loss. Before she could breathe again he laid a small pillow beneath her head.

"Put your head on the pillow and place your

hands behind your back."

Sam welcomed the position. "Do all your conquests receive such one-on-one attention?"

She didn't get words in response. His hot hands pressed her wrists together as his hard cock brushed against her side. A loop pulled tight before his palm rubbed her own cum up and down her outer lips. Fingers bumped across her clit. He moved between her legs and pressed his hips against hers, the fabric gone. Only hardened flesh, his sex slipping against her own. Loop after loop straightened her arms until she couldn't move, his erection slipped against her pussy. Circling. Offering. Sliding with slow strokes.

"Is it too tight?" His hands pulled her hips against his. He rocked and recoiled. "Or do you need it even tighter?"

Held in his hands, Sam couldn't move her arms or her hips. Only submit to anything he wanted. Anything he desired. She had no quips, even as she searched for one with desperation.

"I'll take your silence as approval."

He wrapped another rope around her elbow and tied to it the chair behind her knee. Her breathing soared as the other elbow tightened against the opposite side. She could barely lift her shoulders.

His hand cracked across her ass making her

squeak in surprise. Holding her hair, he lifted her head and held his rock hard cock at her mouth. She sampled the salty sweetness with the tip of her tongue. He slapped her ass again. Harder. His hand dropped across her ass. Two fingers slipped into her pussy. Pulling upward. Forcing her against the ropes.

"I'm going to fuck you for hours and there's nothing you can do about it except scream. Who's the master now, Samantha? Perhaps it's time for your submission. To me."

His presumption burned. Anger rose in place of lust. Her mind cleared in the blink of an eye. Seduction. Control. Passion. Separate ideas that could only be merged by someone with the skill and desire to understand. In a flash of clarity, she grasped the depths of Gage's disconnect with the world, and the reasons his lover no longer tolerated his insolence. The realization struck her like a bolt of lightning. Who he was. What she could become and what she wanted. Such simple a concept. She could only laugh at the fact it took so long for her to see.

As Sam nearly cried with mirth, Gage pulled his fingers out of her and released her hair. Her head dropped to the pillow as he stood.

With a reddened face and pursed lips, Gage screamed in booming tones. "I will flog your ass and fuck you until you can't walk. You'll be too busy begging for more to laugh again."

The more he spoke, the more ridiculous his words sounded. As her peals of laughter subsided, she permitted anger to fill the hole left behind. "You self-centered bastard. You never had control because I never gave it to you. I'm only wet because I want you to fuck me, you ass. You're only hard because I seduced you. I am bound because I allowed you to bind me." She chuckled again. "Even when you submit, you fail to understand that I am in control. Every movement you make. Every touch. Every taste. I allowed you to sample my pleasures and you're too stubborn to see the truth even as it drips from my wet cunt. So fuck me, you bastard. Fuck me as hard as you want for as long as you want because it's what I desire. You are my toy. My plaything and nothing more until I say you are, you self-centered, narcissistic prick!"

Gage's eyes grew to the size of dinner plates. He backed away in horror.

"What's the matter, Gage?" Sam continued, laughing nearly continuously now. "Get that luscious cock over her and fuck my mouth. I want your cum to coat the back of my throat until I gag. Perhaps I'll grant you release or I may just bite you in half. Either way it's up to me. Isn't it? You fucking asshole!"

In her fury, Sam failed to detect the scent of roses and the rising breeze. She nearly jumped as soft fingers entered her pussy, pumping hard and reaching deep. Nova walked between Sam's bound body and her husband. Gage continued to backpedal with an ever softening dick. Nova withdrew her fingers with a sly smile and sucked them clean, trading her gaze between the two of them. "Such discord in my house." She squatted, placing herself on eye level with Sam. "Delectable. We have somewhere to be, Samantha. If you would rather stay here while Gage continues to...*dominate* you..." She giggled. "We could reschedule."

Sam's fear of facing Nova's disappointment faded as she realized the words targeted Gage, not her. A continued taunting. Punishment. Praise for Sam's words. She screamed. "If he dominates me a minute more, I may just vomit. Untie me, please. Unless you would like to lick my pussy first. For that I would gladly remain bound, mistress."

Nova kissed her before whispering her reply. "You luscious tease. It's so sweet of you to offer while my poor husband torments you so. We'll have our time again." She stood and undid the bindings, never missing a chance to stroke between Sam's thighs.

Sam massaged her wrists. She found her feet again and glared at Gage's back. He stared at his feet, clenching and unclenching his fists. Even though his dick hung limp, her attraction for his perfect body hadn't wavered. She almost pitied him, but her rage still smoldered. Too recent to forget. She spoke loud enough to guarantee he heard every word. "I'm planning to enjoy Katherine's company tonight. Another submissive I plan to reward."

Gage lifted his head. His knuckles blanched white on solid fists. Sam could almost feel his teeth grind in anger or, perhaps, even hatred. She refused to drop her gaze from his. A stare down driven by an appetite for domination. *Test me, you asshole. I'll win every time.*

"Then we should go so I can get you home," Nova purred. "Her delights are not to be missed."

For the first time, Sam noticed Nova's attire. Far from her usual dress. She wore an almost see-through white blouse. Her nipples remained hidden from view by a dark leather jacket with long sleeves. Matching perfectly, her legs and hips stood out in tight black leggings, perched atop six-inch heels.

Nova answered her before she asked her own question. "Proper attire for our day, Samantha. Go change into the short leather skirt we bought and the black bustier with all the buckles. Top it off with those six-inch fuck-me heels I liked so much."

Sam could see Gage's interest begin to rise between his legs. "Perfect. Where are we going?"

Nova whispered in her ear. "It's a surprise, my sweet."

Sam wanted to complete the rise of Gage's cock and slap his ego at the same time. "Will I be getting fucked by someone who knows their place?"

Nova laughed. "More than one if you play your cards right."

"Yummy!" Sam grinned. She could see Gage's erection pound despite the fire remaining in his obsidian eyes. "I'm not wearing panties. I don't want to waste time if given the proper opportunity."

"Then I've taught you well." Nova wrapped her arm around Sam's waist before addressing her husband. "We'll be late, Gage. Don't wait up."

Chapter Nine
Control

Nova's transport had become easier to tolerate.

Other than a little dizziness mixed with temporary disorientation, Sam regained her bearings without nausea. They stood on a two-lane street at dusk. Bar after bar stretched into the distance on both sides of the pavement, broken only by the occasional pawn shop, bail bondsman, or strip club. The most striking aspect of their surroundings wasn't the shops offering sin for money but rather the number of Harley Davidsons. All models, years, styles, colors, and conditions stretched beyond the horizon in front and behind them. Each bike leaned inches from the next. Every front tire faced the street with the handlebars turned inward by the same amount, as if aligned by a master choreographer on the set of a post apocalyptic biker movie.

"Where are we?" Sam pulled her skirt

downward, suddenly uncomfortable.

"Daytona Beach. It's Bike Week." Nova clasped her hands together and bounced in place excitedly. "Isn't it wonderful?"

Sam didn't share her enthusiasm. In fact, the idea of wearing nothing but a short skirt and a revealing top in the middle of two hundred and fifty thousand bikers was downright terrifying. She moaned in horror. "Why?"

Nova answered with a smile. "Control."

"What do you mean?" Sam's voice shook as she tried to follow Nova's quick steps. Her day with Gage had been a revelation, but she wasn't sure she'd ever controlled anything in her life.

Men of every size and description filled the sidewalks. Tall and skinny. Short and fat. Clean shaven or with beards down to their knees. Earrings, nose rings, or no rings at all. Inked from head to toe or with pristine skin from pale to black. Unique leaves on a massive tree with a single exception, they all wore leather or jean jackets. The names of biker clubs adorned some of their backs, but Sam wasn't about to stare long enough to find out what the printing said. Fighting terror-inspired tunnel vision, she focused on the center of Nova's back and tried to stay upright on her own heels. With rare exception, each person stepped aside to stare in open-mouth silence as the women walked by. It didn't make any difference. Sam had become a piece of meat at the annual carnival of carnivores.

Nova stopped in front of a dilapidated two-story building of clapboard and faded green paint. Black iron security bars adorned windows that hadn't been washed since the turn of the century. Southern hard rock bumped and pounded through Sam's feet before boring into her bones. Above two solid wood doors, a barely legible sign hung at an angle due to a broken hanger. They had arrived at The Crunchy Frog.

Thinking again of how she'd dressed, Sam swallowed hard. "I don't think this is the best place for us, Nova."

"On the contrary, Samantha. This place was made for us. There's enough testosterone behind these doors to fulfill a hundred girls' fantasies. Male hormones will drip from your tongue like sugar before we're done."

Nova gripped the heavy door with her tiny hand and pulled it open. Sound wrapped in smoke blasted against them. Blaring music. Laughter. Cussing.

Sam moved closer to Nova's back. She wanted to reach for her and beg retreat. A long wooden bar on her left had padding with so many cigarette burns it looked more like a chewed strip of leather than a bar rail. Wooden planks creaked in pain beneath her feet as Sam searched the interior with terror-filled eyes and tried to allay her fears of the unfamiliar.

She wrapped her arms around herself tightly, covering her chest and avoiding eye contact with the men glaring at her with lecherous grins. She couldn't understand why Nova seemed so happy. Sam radiated discomfort while her teacher seemed to fit right in.

Nova stared at the bartender for a few seconds before Sam followed her gaze. Tall and well conditioned, the man wore a ragged jean jacket without sleeves. A blazing skull with the words Dead Already arching over the flames seemed to have been burnt into the fabric. He looked over sixty, but the expression he wore, the glint in his eyes, and the scars on his arms said he could handle anything the world threw at him and probably already had. A beard flowed from his chin like a grey waterfall from a weathered cliff. Lost in introspection as he cleared dust from mugs one by one, he turned and jerked to a stop, nearly dropping the glass he'd been working on. His crystalline blue eyes sparkled beneath thick wire rimmed glasses. He squinted as if lost in the past and turned his head to the side in confusion. "Nova?" His voice screamed quiet awe, as if disbelieving his own eyes.

"Yes, my love. I see you haven't forgotten me."

Tears brimmed in the old man's eyes even though his sun-worn face decreed he'd never cried over anything.

"An impossibility." He stepped to the edge of the bar with hesitation. "I'll take your memory to the grave and die a happy man. I promised. Remember?" He scratched his beard, thinking. "How long has it been? Twenty? Twenty-five years?"

"Thirty years, four months and fifteen days. But who's counting?" Nova giggled.

"Jesus Christ. I really am old." He removed his glasses and wiped the damp from his eyes with the dirty rag. "I've tried to keep my promises to you. All of them. I never hurt anyone again. I loved my family until my heart overflowed. I raised two wonderful children who hold the same values. I can never repay you for what you did for me. Even when my wife passed on, I've never taken another."

Sam listened with rapt attention. She wanted the beginning of the story that seemed to be ending before her eyes. *What could've happened to bring a man like that to his knees?* His pain had become hers.

Nova leaned across the bar and kissed the man

with palpable passion. "I know you have, baby. I cried when Darlene left us. I almost came to you but, you needed to mourn. I never lost sight of you. The world is better for your existence. For that, I am glad."

Before Sam's own tears formed, a huge man sitting next to them broke into raucous laughter. Tattoos of women in obscene poses danced across his bulging arms, rising upward until covered by his dirty white tee-shirt and short-sleeve leather jacket. A terrifying apparition had been silk-screened on the back in blazing color: A hand wrapped in barbed wire dripped blood above a naked woman bruised and bloody on a pile of other battered women. In large letters made of knives it declared him "Unrepentant" and Sam believed it.

The Unrepentant roared. "Shit, Frog. That's some sweet fucking cunt right there. Hey fuck toy, when you're done sucking tongue with a guy who can't get it up, I'll bend you over this chair and slam that pretty ass until you scream for mercy. You'll remember me forever and beg for more."

Sam shook in place. Nightmares manifested all around them in every direction. They had to get out while they still could.

The old bartender set the mug down on the bar and glared at Unrepentant. "Cool it, Animal. She's not one of your bitches. You don't know what you're doing."

"Fuck you, Frog." Animal drank the rest of his beer in a single guzzle before slamming the mug down on the bar. "This bitch knows a good thing when she sees it. Don't you, cunt? I'm gonna fuck her until she can't walk and then I'll have her little friend suck the cum off my cock." He started walking toward Sam with a lecherous smile. "On second thought, maybe I'll start with you, honey."

The crowd joined in on the impending disaster with loud chants. "Animal! Animal! Animal!" The women's retreat to the door had been closed off by a moving wave of leather and misogynist epithets. Sam's heart hammered in fear. Her hands dripped rivulets of terror-soaked sweat.

Raw, unmitigated power radiated from Nova. It pounded against Sam's chest like a sledgehammer. The tiny woman strode between Animal and Sam with a smile. A complete absence of fear. Nova placed a hand on her hip and sucked her thumb like a stripper in heat. "Ooooh. What a big boy you are. I like it rough."

The man behind the bar screamed over the music. "Stop it, Animal. You don't want this."

"Fuck you, Frog. You heard her. She likes it

rough. So do I." Unrepentant reached out his hands.

"Excellent." Nova took Animal's hands in hers. The man immediately began to shake as if electrocuted. His body bucked and contorted as he tried to pull away. His expression screamed for release from endless terrors. Sweat poured from his brow. A cry of bloodcurdling horror rose on his lips. Nova pulled him closer and kissed his mouth lightly. The man who'd been Animal crumpled to the ground in a writhing heap. Tears poured from his eyes. He cried as if his soul had been ripped from his body with a dull knife. Howls of angst drove the crowd backwards. The Unrepentant crawled to Nova's feet and clawed at her ankles, pressing his face to her shoes. "Please. Please," he shrieked like a wounded child.

"Awe..." Nova pressed the tip of her high heel against his forehead and rolled the crying mass of flesh onto his back. "I guess my big boy couldn't get it up after all. Pity." She touched the sole to his lips, rolling it across his tongue until the tip of her stiletto heel rested on his throat. "So disappointing. I'll just have to find someone worthy of my love to fuck me."

"Nova." The soft voice came from the man behind the bar. A plea for mercy. "Stop. Please."

The pressure waves thrown from the tiny blonde

shrunk until the music surrounding them became the only disturbance in the air again. The strength of Nova's power couldn't be denied. Sam had felt it. Tasted it. Craved it.

"For you, my heart." Nova lifted her foot and moved closer to the bartender. The crowd had parted in fear, allowing her to pass unimpeded. "For you."

Sam watched the people reform behind her. Hushed voices rose in timber again as Animal shuffled to the bathroom amidst jeers and laughter.

Now that is control.

Sam's nervousness began to fade as she walked to stand at Nova's side. "I need a drink. A strong drink."

Holding out his hand to Sam, the bartender chuckled. "I'm Jackson, but everyone here calls me Frog. I've owned this place for years. The clientele changes but I remain the same. Older, but constant."

"I'm Sam." She took his hand and shook it once. "I gather you two have known each other a while."

Nova kissed his cheek again. "We were lovers once."

"A long time ago." The bartender smiled at her touch despite the warble in his voice. A profound sadness.

"Only a breath, lover." Nova clutched his hand in

hers.

He squeezed Nova's fingers in a worn hand. "What can I get you, Sam?"

"Surprise me." Sam watched Jackson walk to the bottles before directing her attention on Nova again. "What did you do...to that man... Animal? His pain looked unbearable. The sound of his cries nearly tore my heart away even though I knew what a piece of shit he was. Even knowing he wanted to hurt me."

"I took all the pain he'd ever caused and drove it into his mind, releasing it all at once. Every person he ever assaulted. Every woman, girl, sister, and wife he'd ever tormented or abused. I gathered their pain and returned it to him forever. He will never forget. He will relive their pain until the day he dies."

Nova looked oddly satisfied as Sam tried to imagine the horrors Animal would experience and never be free of. It seemed cruel, even for someone who'd hurt so many others.

Mental note: Don't piss Nova off.

Jackson set four shots on the bar with a shaker of salt and several fresh cut limes. "Gran Patrón Platinum. Tequila to warm your soul."

Sam pulled her hair back behind her ears. "I'm not a big tequila drinker."

"Today you are." Nova held out her wrist to

Jackson. After he'd licked it, she sprinkled the wet spot with salt and lifted a shot glass in one hand while holding a slice of lime in the other.

Sam moved her hand to her mouth and stopped just before her lips. Changing her mind, she held out her wrist to Jackson. "Me too, Jackson."

Jackson licked her skin with tender care. She sprinkled it with salt and lifted her glass and a lime of her own. "To control."

Nova lifted her glass. "To the limits of passion."

The liquid seared Sam's throat, as if she'd swallowed hot coals. She pushed the lime between her lips and sucked as her eyes involuntarily closed. She shuddered, stomping her foot for relief. "Jesus."

Jackson nudged the other shot closer to her. "Good, right?"

Sam shook her head and scrunched her shoulders with a shiver before opening her eyes. The alcohol's warmth had already begun its spread throughout her body, flushing her skin. "Not the adjective I would use, but its effects are immediate and the burn is gone in an instant. Shit."

Nova lifted her wrist to Jackson's mouth again and Sam followed suit. They salted once more as Sam took in their surroundings. Everything seemed to have returned to normalcy.

As normal as this place can be.

Nova raised her glass and winked. "Your turn."

"For what?" Sam asked with confusion. Before she received her answer, Nova drank her shot and took a lime in her mouth. Sam exhaled and drank, twisting her face as the liquor began its unstoppable inferno within her chest. The lime helped a little but not much. The wave of warmth spread like wildfire, spinning her head like a top.

Nova set her shot glass on the bar. "To play."

When the singe of coals abated, Sam could finally swallow again. "I don't understand."

"Of course you do." Nova pointed her finger at Jackson and then crooked it, motioning for him to come. Nova continued as Jackson moved to the end of the bar and lifted the bridge exit. "Jackson and I wish to rekindle our spark, and you, my innocent little girl, need to seduce one of these men. Choose."

"What?" Sam nearly yelled in disbelief. "Here? By myself?"

"Yes. However, this time you must ask directly and he must agree to submit."

Sam's jaw fell open. "You must be kidding. I can't. What if they, you know, get rough?"

Jackson moved to Nova and took her in his arms.

Nova kissed him. "Simply call and I'll be there.

Confidence, beautiful. This is important."

Sam clenched her fists. She didn't know why the idea excited and terrified her at the same time. Whether the alcohol had emboldened her or because Nova would appear in an instant, Sam suddenly wanted to test her own abilities. *If I can do this, Gage will be a walk in the park.* She looked at the ground, took a deep breath and held it. "Okay. But you have to promise. You have to come if I need you. Instantly."

"Good girl. I promise." Nova took Jackson's hand and began leading him through the crowd toward the stairs. "We'll be upstairs. You still have a room up there don't you, Jackson?"

Jackson staggered behind her. "I do."

Nova laughed as she tugged faster. "It was a rhetorical question, lover. It's time to warm our bed again. I've missed you."

Sam watched the two ascend the stairs and leave her view. The lack of Nova's presence and protection made her mouth run dry. Her fortitude began to fail.

Maybe another drink will restore my courage.

Lynyrd Skynyrd pounded in her ears. The voices around drew together in a roar of indistinct white noise, muffling her thoughts and any hope of seduction. *I can't...*

"Evening." The deep voice roused her from confusion and startled her at the same time.

Sam whirled around and kept her back pressed against the bar for safety. The man stood over six feet tall. Brown eyes squinted from an oval face covered in dark whiskers. Long waves of black hair fell over his broad shoulders and blended into the black leather jacket of the same shade. His massive chest couldn't be hidden by the pristine white shirt he wore beneath the leather. It only covered. A tease. Well worn jeans secured with a silver buckle fit his hips tightly, diving down his legs before tucking into calf high black boots with silver buckles unfastened at the ankles.

He squinted, scratched the stubble on his cheek, and stared at her intently. "Didn't mean to startle you, ma'am." A deep, honeyed southern drawl. "Thought I'd offer to buy you a drink. Don't wanna intrude, but you're the most beautiful thing I've ever seen. I figured I'd be kickin' myself the rest of my life if I didn't try."

Sam reached behind her neck and looked away. *I can do this. I can do this.* "Uhm. Sure. I could use a drink."

The man stepped up to the bar by her side, almost touching her arm. Musk and leather assaulted her senses, weakening her resolve. The back of his jacket bore the dark silhouette of a man in front of a guard tower with the words POW-MIA above and You Are Not Forgotten below. "Joe!" he yelled above the din. "Gimme a couple more shots of whatever she's drinkin' and two Heinekens." He turned toward her. "I see you like the hard stuff. Beer okay with you? Don't buy ladies drinks much."

Sam could feel her face start to blush. She couldn't stop the grin forming at the corner of her mouth. Unexpected manners from a rugged little bear with a heart of daisies. "Sure. Beer is perfect."

Okay. Maybe he's all right. He's just a man. Simple.

He held out a weathered hand. "Name's Owen. Friend's call me Buzz Saw. You can call me anything you want."

"Sam. Sam Keating." She shook his hand and turned back to the bar, hoping he hadn't seen the red in her cheeks.

Looking in the same direction as her, he stared at the bottles of alcohol lined up behind the bar. "If you don't mind me sayin', Miss Sam. And, don't take this the wrong way...but what the hell are you doin' here?"

Sam turned her head toward him. "What do you mean?"

"Shit. Like I said, don't take this the wrong way

'cause, I couldn't be happier we met but dressed like you are... Here? What the hell were you thinkin'?"

Sam looked at her high skirt and fuck-me heels and realized just how crazy she must seem. "That's a long story, Owen. Let's just say...I'm looking for something."

The drinks arrived. Owen paid in cash from a leather wallet dangling from his belt on a thick silver chain. He hefted the four drinks in both hands and turned toward her with a wink. "Well, I got all night if you do. I'm always in the mood for a good story." He motioned to a table with four men in the same color leather jackets as his. Each of the men stared intently at Owen and his conquest. "Those bastards are still in shock that I got you to talk to me. They like a good story too. They ain't too pretty, but they're family. Do you mind sitting with us?"

Sam gazed at the expectant group. *Is it the danger or the seduction? Or, am I just too horny to think straight?* Hormones determined what she said next. "I can only think of one thing I'd rather be doing."

Owen looked at her with a sidelong glance. "Maybe you'll decide you like me enough to tell me what the other thing is."

I can't believe I'm doing this. She placed her hand in the crook of his elbow and moved a step closer.

"Perhaps. Will you keep me safe?" *Is this for me or Gage?*

"Miss Sam, you're about to sit at the safest table in this country or any other."

His excitement boosted Sam's confidence as they stepped up to his friends' table. Owen set the drinks down and placed his hand in the small of her back. He pointed from left right as he spoke. "Sam Keating, this here is Tom, Marcus, Coffey and David. My family in this world and the next."

Each of the men greeted her in turn. Owen pulled out a chair for her. She sat with as much sexiness as she could. She placed both elbows on the table before resting her chin on the backs of her hands. "So. You boys been riding together long?"

Marcus wore thick glasses, but his long red handlebar mustache and bleached goatee drew her attention more than anything else. He wasn't skinny, but thick veins rose on top of his arms like wound leather. "'Bout ten years now. We served together. Buzz and I met up...after." He sipped his beer and pulled a cigarette from his vest pocket. He paused before he lit it. "Do you mind if I smoke? I get nervous easy. It's the only thing that calms me down."

Sam's thighs slid against each other, slick with her own juices. *All in. You better come when I call, Nova.*

"Not at all. Sweet of you to ask though, considering I may be the only non-smoker in the bar." She pulled one of the shots of tequila closer, fingering it, and questioned her sanity. "I wrap my lips around all kinds of things to calm my...nerves."

Marcus lit his smoke and puffed with excited energy, staring at the table.

Tom sat up straighter. A full head shorter than his companions, his dark beard, cut off square, hung to the middle of his broad chest. The light reflected off his bald head. His green eyes twinkled. "I've only ridden with them about eight years. Somehow they found me even though I'd dropped off the grid. Wherever they go, I follow. No questions asked."

Sam placed her hand on Owen's thigh and gave her best pout. "Would you get me a salt shaker and a lime? I don't want to crawl through the crowd again without my...protection."

"Of course, Sam." Owen stood and walked toward the bar.

She couldn't help notice him adjusting his dick as he walked.

I could get used to this.

Coffey stared at Sam like a dirty glass. Bald and clean shaven, he had an old scar running from the corner of his mouth to his ear. His arms suggested he could bench press small cars if he wanted to, and his grey eyes drew her in like honeyed kisses.

She licked her lips. "See something you like, Coffey?"

"I haven't decided yet." His voice had become steel grinding on weathered stone.

Sam pushed out her lower lip as if offended. "Something you don't like?"

Owen returned with the lime and salt on a small saucer. He set them on the table and sat before lifting his own beer.

Coffey muttered, somewhere between a growl and a sneer. "I'm just wondering what it is you're looking for here. I don't care for women who use their looks to manipulate men."

"What the fuck, Coffey?" Owen asked. "Did I miss something? Isn't it enough that a gorgeous woman sits at our table? Half the bar is jealous as hell."

Coffey's comment took Sam off guard but failed to rile her. "Is that what you think I'm doing?" With a sly smile, she raised her hand to Owen's mouth. "Kiss please. It helps the salt stick."

Owen glared at Coffey before touching his lips to the back of her hand.

"Isn't it?" Coffey asked.

"It's more complicated than that." She sprinkled salt on the damp spot without taking her gaze from Coffey. She slammed back a shot of tequila and winced. Unable to hold her eyes open, she pressed the lime to her mouth and waited for the burn to subside.

When Sam opened her eyes and reached for a beer, she found five sets of eyes fixed on her with hang-dog expressions. More than a little uncomfortable, she tried to recover. "Let's just say, I'm discovering myself."

Coffey spoke after a long pause. "The only thing someone dressed like you is looking for is to get fucked. You just haven't decided how much you're going to charge yet."

Owen slammed his beer onto the table. "Enough of that shit, Coffey. I mean it."

Coffey held up his hands in mock surrender. Partially mollified, he smiled and took another drink.

Sam realized Coffey had given her the opening she needed. The most important interview of her life. Nova's hopes and Gage's life had been tossed in her lap whether she wanted it or not. If she froze now, she'd never be able to push the limits again.

Hell, I'll never be able to find the edge again, let alone walk it.

Sam could see the arousal in the men around her.

Anyone could. If these five couldn't take her where she wanted to go, no one could. *They just have to agree to my terms.* She took a deep breath and dove in. "My hero." She placed her hand on Owen's thigh, stroking up and down as she gazed at each of the men in turn. "It's a fair question. You see, I do want to be fucked. Hard." Her confidence soared as every one of the men tried to adjust their hard dicks with individualized covert skill. "However, with me, you can't just whip out your cock and drive it into my wet pussy. I have a few conditions."

Coffey glowered. "I don't pay for pussy."

This guy is going to be tough. Sam chuckled. "That's good. I don't pay either. I get all I want for free." Sam squeezed Owen's cock softly and tried not to be distracted by his impressive size.

David stared with an open mouth. He'd hung his jacket on the back of his chair, uncovering a worn and faded Black Sabbath concert tee with more holes than picture. His black skin and muscled arms could only be described as beautiful. His eyes reminded her of Gage and how badly he wanted her.

"What conditions?" David asked. "Getting me to agree won't be hard. I haven't been laid in over a year."

"A year," Sam exclaimed. "Have you been living

in a cave?"

"No. Dade County Jail. My wife and I had different ideas regarding fidelity. I put her boyfriend in the hospital. The state of Florida failed to understand."

Sam raised her eyebrows. "You're married?"

David smiled before taking a drink from his beer. "Not anymore."

Sam's heart pounded as she glimpsed the razor edge of passion in her mind's eye. *How far do I want go? Multiple men? One after another?* She stood and moved to David's side. Barely able to breathe, she straddled his hips and wrapped her arms around his neck. "That's good. I have limits. Not many. But some." She kissed him hard, sucking his tongue until the flavors belonged to both of them. The juices dripping down her legs would leave his jeans soaked. She looked over her shoulder. "To have me, you must relinquish control."

Marcus stubbed out his cigarette. "Meaning what?"

"I mean, I have particular tastes. If I want to tie you to the bed, the answer is yes, mistress." She focused on Coffey. "If I want you to kneel and lick my pussy without using your hands, the only response I desire is action without words."

Domina

Every eye focused on her with desire she'd never glimpsed in any man. *This is what I was born to do.* She kissed David on the cheek and rose again to straighten her skirt, and then with rocking hips sat on Owen's lap primly. She kept her hand on his chest and wiggled her ass against his erection. "When I place my hands on the bed and raise my skirt, you will watch quietly until I tell you how to touch me. Until I tell you how to fuck me."

Tom gasped. "Jesus Christ." He drained his beer in one swallow. "I don't think I've ever been this hard in my life."

Sam inhaled the musky scent of Owen's neck before she floated to Tom's side with airy steps. She pulled a chair closer to his and sat. Opening her knees, she placed his huge hands beneath her skirt until his fingertips touched the wetness there. "Oh, you can be so much harder." She lifted his hand and sucked the fingertip coated with her juices. "Don't you think?"

Her seduction had become all encompassing. An addiction she could no longer control. "When I want to be taken slow, you will obey. When I ask you to fuck me harder, you'll do as you are told. When I tell you to stop, there'll be no discussion."

"I'm in," Thomas whispered with shaking hands.

"Anything you ask. Anything."

David finished his beer in one swallow. "You already have me."

Marcus lit another cigarette and puffed madly. "What could I possibly say but hell yes?"

She walked to Owen's side and let him wrap an arm around her waist. She smiled as he pulled her tight and stared up at her.

Owen ran his hand over her ass, squeezed and released again. "Aren't you just a little bit worried here, Sam? It's a pretty dangerous game you're playing. What if we were the type of men who decided to leave you in a wet heap and take what we wanted?"

You better come when I call, Nova. She pushed her bottom lip out and gave her best pout. "But you promised to protect me."

"And I will," Owen almost shouted. "Nothing bad is going to happen when you're with me, but I worry about your judgment. Do you do this kind of thing all the time?"

Sam leaned forward and kissed his cheek. She could feel the truth in his words. She'd be safe with him. A warm drip fell from her pussy and began to slide down her inner thigh. She whispered, "This will be my first time but...you always remember your first.

Don't you?"

"You don't really think you can control a bunch of guys like us, do you?" Coffey laughed with disdain. "None of us would ever do anything to hurt a woman, but you couldn't do anything if we did."

"And I bet none of you would have thought Animal would be in the bathroom, blubbering like an infant, did you?" Coffey's arrogance had started to annoy her. She stood straighter and pulled from Owen's grasp even though she still held his hand. *All in.* "Listen up, Coffey, because I won't repeat myself again. It's all or nothing. Everyone or no one. My rules or you can all go home and jack off while thinking about what might have been. I already have a date waiting for me when I leave here. So what's it gonna be?" The anger had come unbidden. *Is this what Gage has done to me?*

Each of the men turned and glared at Coffey. Poison in their gaze, burning his flesh with something barely less than hate.

"Whoa!" Coffey held up his hands. "I want this as much as any of you. It just came out of left field, that's all. I'm sorry, Sam. I didn't mean disrespect. I disarmed bombs for a living. I have a hard time trusting anything that sounds too good to be true. Especially if it ain't ticking. I'm in if you'll have me."

He looked down at the table, properly in his place.

His words seemed heartfelt. Sam leaned across the table, knowing her skirt threatened to reveal everything behind her while her top gave the rest of the table a show. She lifted Coffey's chin and kissed his lips. "Then take care of me. I'll make you a deal. I run the show. If you say I've gone too far, we stop, no questions asked. As hard as it is to believe, I want this. Okay?" She kissed him again.

"Deal." Coffey looked around cautiously. "So where do we... You know?"

Sam sat on the chair, wondering the same thing. Before an answer came to her, the air seemed to move and clear. Her skin warmed. Comfort and security encompassed her entire body. *Nova.* "Oh, I think an opportunity will present itself."

Sam looked at the spiral stairs. The grinning form of Jackson descended, holding Nova's hand in his. His mussed hair stuck out like a disheveled porcupine. Sweat still beaded on his face. To Sam's surprise, Nova's glow stretched from ear to ear. Her ruddy cheeks radiated happiness. Satisfaction beyond measure. *You're going to have to tell me about you two someday.*

The couple walked over to the table. Nova straddled Sam's lap in a single movement. The fairy hugged Sam tight, kissing her as if she'd never touched another's lips. Breathless. "Hi, gorgeous. I see you've made some new friends." She moved her lips to Sam's ear and whispered in tones no one but Sam could hear. "Thank you."

I haven't done anything... Yet.

Sam held Nova's waist and stared into the infinite blue green depths of her eyes. "Unfortunately, we seem to be short a room."

"It just so happens, the one right above the bar is free at the moment." Nova grinned at Jackson with pure lechery. "Isn't it, my love?"

Jackson smiled back. "It is. Enjoy, Sam."

Nova lifted herself from Sam's lap. She stepped into Jackson's embrace before addressing the table. "Be good boys. I'll be watching."

As Jackson moved behind the bar and Nova took a seat on a barstool, Owen raised a questioning eyebrow. "What did she mean by that?"

Sam stood and held out an unexpectedly steady hand. "It's hard to explain and you wouldn't believe me anyway. Shall we?"

Patrick Khayler

Chapter Ten
Confidence

Sam didn't recognize the woman who led five bikers up the spiral stairs toward a bedroom rendezvous. She walked faster as they neared the top, her excitement building with every step. *Why do I want this so badly?* Seduction had become her drug of choice, and orgasm the promised rush that followed every dose.

Have I gone too far to return? Do I even want to anymore?

At the top of the stairs, a single wooden door left no confusion as to where she headed. The tiny apartment held a set of drawers, sink, refrigerator, oven and a queen-sized bed. Nothing more. Sam stood on her toes and tried to peer out the single window looking over the street below, but dust and grime made it blend in with the walls. Through a tiny door to her right, she could see a small bathroom with a toilet, sink and shower crammed into a space so small it shouldn't have been able to hold them. The bed's brass frame looked as if it barely supported its own weight. The rumpled sheets and disordered blankets proved it could hold at least two bodies joined in raucous pleasure. She intended to push its limits.

Sam turned to the men and watched them alternate their gazes between her, the bed, and the floor. *They are so adorable.* "So. First things first. Did anyone bring condoms?"

Five sets of hands dove into pockets and wallets with lightning speed before a plethora of small foil packets dangled from the hands of five men with hungry looks. Sam nearly burst out laughing. "That's my good little boys. Put them on the counter over there."

When they had set their packages down, Sam rubbed a finger across her lower lip looking at each of them in turn. She raised her finger and pointed. "Eenie. Meenie. Miney. Marcus..."

Marcus looked shocked. His exhalation of surprise blew the ends of his mustache upward. "Me?"

Sam winked once before whispering. "Unless there's another Marcus here, babe."

"Okay. What would you like me to do?" He took off his glasses and put them on the counter before walking toward her.

Sam held up a hand. "Stop right there. Take off your clothes and give me your belt. In fact, I want everyone's belts."

Marcus stripped. He had the build of an athlete. Lean and taught. Old scars crisscrossed his abdomen defining his twelve-pack with an unknown, painful history. He slipped his pants free but left his boxers in place. His cock pushed against the fabric, wet with pre-cum she'd called from his erection. He looked at his friends with nervous energy, trying to shield himself without appearing bashful.

Sam began to unsnap her corset. Loosening only. A tease without setting her breasts free. A hard pink nipple already peeked from the top. She made no effort to cover it. "I can't suck your cock through cotton, Marcus. Don't be shy. They'll all be undressed soon enough."

Marcus pushed the boxers down, unveiling his massive erection.

"Delicious. Lie down on the bed, Marcus. I want you on your back."

Thin strands of clear cum stretched between the head of Marcus's cock and his ripped abs as he lay on his back. Sam leaned forward and stroked him once. Hot in her hand. Filling it. She licked the clear sweets from his cock's head. Her heart pounded. *I want them all.* "Don't be nervous, baby. You're my centerpiece."

Sam stood. She pointed to Tom and Owen. "Take off your jackets and tie his hands to the headboard with these belts."

The nervousness in Marcus's eyes excited her, but watching the men do as she commanded made her drip. Her pussy throbbed. She could no longer tolerate the tension begging to be relieved. She sat on the edge of the bed, slowly stroking Marcus's hard-on. "Look at me, baby. I'll take good care of you."

The efficiency with which the men tied their friend suggested they'd used belts to secure wrists before. They stretched Marcus's arms tight. As his chest heaved, she squeezed harder, milking pre-cum onto her hand. She licked the clear fluid and turned to the men again. "Everyone take off your boots. I want David and Coffey to strip to bare chests. Pants on. Then all of you will stand over here behind me."

Following her instructions exactly, the men seemed to surge with excitement and urgency. She'd never seen clothes removed with such speed. Pure sex. Testosterone charged and waiting to pleasure her.

Patrick Khayler

They obey because of desire. Desire for me.

They stood side by side, dancing from foot to foot as they adjusted and re-adjusted hard cocks trying to pop free from restraining pants. She focused on the group as she undid the final straps on her leather top one by one. Slow. Calculating. Their mouths dropped in unison as she removed the glistening leather and set it on the bed. Pinching her long pink nipples. Pushing her tits together. She turned her back on them and faced Marcus. Keeping her feet wide, she bent at the waist, taking his throbbing cock in her hands before sucking hard. Taking him deep.

Marcus closed his eyes and moaned.

Without looking behind her, she held her position, lifting her lips only long enough to speak. "Roll my skirt up my hips, Coffey. Show the boys what they can have. *If* they behave."

Rough hands pulled her skirt up inch by inch. The air moving across her wet lips couldn't hope to cool her rising heat. Coffey held her ass, as if displaying a priceless portrait while she sucked Marcus hard. When he began to pulse inside her mouth, she popped her lips from his cock with a long slurp. "Don't come yet, Marcus. You get to have me first." She looked over her shoulder. "Owen. Move to

~254~

my other side. I want you to use your hands. Pull my inner lips wide and hold them. I want the boys to see how wet I am."

She swallowed Marcus as far as she could, searching for strength in ecstasy. Owen's fingers slid across her outer lips, jolting her with pleasure. As he peeled her open, her legs weakened. Indefinable clarity. She could picture her entrance by feel alone. Open. Inviting. The sensation continued downward and flowed across her clit in molten waves as he pinched and pulled her wide. Like a tongue splitting her pussy from top to bottom. "God yes." She panted. "Don't pinch too hard. I'm not a Harley, but I expect to be ridden like one. Push a finger into me, Tom. Just one."

Another hand in the small of her back. The gentle pressure at her pussy. Increasing. Relaxing. Deeper. Pulling back. "Concentrate, Tom. Find my G-spot and work it hard. If you can't find it, no one gets fucked."

He had no trouble finding her spot. None at all. His finger lit her up like an erotic pinball machine. The spot she'd never seen solidified in her mind. She became aware of her entire vagina. Waves of heated energy pulsed with each touch he granted her. Expanding at the speed of light to wash over her body from the inside out. Her knees collapsed until they pressed against the bed frame. Her toes drove into the front of her shoes as her heel spikes lifted from the floor. She pulled her mouth from Marcus's cock and groaned. Placing her cheek on his thigh. She dug her nails into his leg. "Oh! My! God!"

David chuckled. "I think she likes it."

"Get in there, David," she groaned. "Play with my clit. I'm going to come. I want all of your hands on me. Now!"

Another hand slipped between her legs with needed alacrity. Two fingers rubbed madly across her swollen nub. She screamed as her body shook. Pounding passion crashed over her and threatened to drop her to her knees. Her pussy contracted in spasmodic flurries as her heart raced.

"Stop," Coffey called. "Let her breathe, for godsake."

The hands left her pussy and leapt to her back and legs. Caressing. Comforting. The waves washed away as she searched for breath again. With their help, she stood on shaking legs and pressed her breasts together again. She'd glimpsed the edge and wanted it all. "Get undressed. All of you."

Clothes began to fly. She reached for a condom package and tore the foil open with her teeth. She desperately rolled the latex sleeve over Marcus's erection. Climbing on the bed, she threw a leg across him reverse cowboy and posed above his cock. Her heels and skirt remained in place. She guided the stiff cock between her thighs and lowered herself hard, gripping the brass footboard, enraptured by every new piece of flesh exposed before her eyes. Moaning. Searching for breath. She wanted them all.

Sam's hips slid forward and back, forcing Marcus's cock deep. Musk filled sex bathed her nostrils in the wanton depravity she craved. Worn leather slammed against the bedposts behind her. *Not this time. You're mine.* The air began to thin, punctuating her words as her moment of release climbed upward. "Owen. Coffey. By my side. Now. Kiss my neck. Hold me while I come. Hurry."

Her hips rose and fell faster as Marcus wailed in pleasure. Contractions started in the wet walls of her pussy, shaking her entire body. She reached for the cold brass footboard as the rock hard, gorgeous men climbed onto the bed beside her. Owen and Coffey's hands found her at the same time, but Owen's mouth found her neck first. The touch of his lips and the scratch of his whiskers almost made her come. Their coarse hands gripped her ass and squeezed her breasts. Coffey nipped into her shoulder before drawing his rough tongue against her skin.

Wanting more, Sam released the cold brass and sat upright, letting the men support her, groaning as the hard dick between her legs dove to its limit. As if synchronized machines, the two men lifted her and drove her back onto the hard cock again and again. High pitched screams of lust exploded from her burning lungs, urging them on like a whip.

Tom and David stood before her. They gripped their pulsing erections like drowning men reaching for a final lifeline. Their hands pumped harder as her screams shattered the air around them. She reached low, grabbing a massive cock in each hand. Hot flesh between her fingers, she stroked them hard, wanting their cum on her hands. Needing to feel their hot seed drip from her skin. Her hands tightened every time the men lifted her, holding on with pain tempered desire as they thrust her hips downward.

She forced herself to focus on the clear drips milked from Tom and David as they stepped closer and closer, fueled by the desire she'd infused within their beings. She'd become the only thing they needed. The only thing they could focus on. Their minds had become empty shells of lust only she could fulfill. She almost collapsed as Marcus's cock began to pulse inside her and he roared in trembling orgasm. The shuddering of his erection released her. No longer able to control her own body, her hands tightened on Tom and David's tools, forcing them to whimper and bite her shoulder as her pussy constricted around Marcus like a wet, pink vice. Every muscle contracted and relaxed in cyclic pleasure that seemed to last forever.

The world came back into focus with gasping breaths. Sam loosened her grip on Tom and David with regret, knowing she controlled them completely. They had set her on the edge of an infinite chasm of pleasure and all she had to do was jump. "Help me up." She searched for air between words. "Untie Marcus. I want you each to take me. One at a time. One after another. I want you to fuck me until I break. You won't stop until I tell you or...until I'm unconscious. That is, if you're men enough to take me that far."

On aching thighs, she raised her hips, gasping as Marcus slipped free. She leaned forward and held the cold footboard on unsteady arms, watching the hungry gazes of Tom and David fall on her heaving chest. She had no doubt she would allow them to take her any way they wanted, but she wasn't about to let them know that. She turned to face the headboard, remaining on her knees.

She looked at Owen before leaning on her

elbows. "I can't decide if I would rather taste you or feel you inside me. Why don't you surprise me?"

Owen smiled as he climbed on the bed in front of her. His erection glistened with pre-cum. "That's easy. I want to see your face when you come."

Sam stared up at him as she kissed the head of his cock. "Choose who it's going to be then, Owen. You're responsible for how hard I'm going to be fucked."

Owen held her face between his rough hands as she lapped at him. "David. You've gone the longest without. Are you ready?"

David ran to the counter, tearing a foil packet open and unrolling it on his cock as he nearly dove onto the bed behind her. "Jesus. I've never been more ready for anything in my life."

David's massive cock opened her with urgency. She gasped for breath as he split her in a single thrust. "Oh my god." She lifted her lips from Owen's cock, panting in frenzied moans until she could form words again. "Slow down, big boy. You don't want me to bite down suddenly. Owen would never forgive you."

Before Owen could retreat in horror, she sucked his dick into her mouth again. Savoring the salty sweet taste. She let David's rhythm guide her. Swallowing Owen as David pushed in hard. Sliding back and breathing as he withdrew.

Her thighs spread wide and still the sheer size of David's cock threatened to tear her open. She ignored the pain by concentrating on the salty musk rising from Owen's abs as she swallowed him again and again.

Breathless, she pulled free and looked at the men on her sides. "Everyone's hands or lips on me now. Now or we're done here."

The other men climbed on the bed as she took Owen into her mouth again. They kissed her back, pulled and twisted her nipples, caressed her ass or flicked her clit. She could no longer ascertain where one man began and another ended. Exactly the way she wanted it. Demanded it.

She closed her eyes as David powered into her harder and faster, clutching her hips in a deathlike grip. Stroke after stroke, his raw pistoning cock dragged a grinding orgasm upward. She took her mouth from Owen's dripping shaft and pushed her forehead against his stomach, gasping for air. His cock, wet with her saliva and mixed with pre-cum, slid inside her palm with ease. She pumped her hand furiously, clawing at Owen's ass as she tried to support herself on failing arms. David howled as his fingertips moved from her hips, digging into her shoulders to pull harder. He pulsed inside her with pumping waves, dragging her desire until she came in shudders of unbridled intensity. Her vision grayed, threatening her consciousness.

Coffey kissed her ear. "Are you okay, Sam?"

Sam let her eyes open into slits, amazed he'd treated her so softly. Making her want him more. "More than okay. That kiss earned you a special place, Coffey. I want you to finish me tonight. You."

David gasped and kissed her back, pulling out of her vagina with a powerful groan. "Oh my fucking god. I thought I was going to pass out."

Sam licked her lips. Her forehead still pressed against Owen's hot skin. She stroked him slow. "Fuck me hard, Thomas. I don't want to come down." She opened her mouth and took Owen into her throat again before pulling free slowly. Her gaze turned upwards. "Come in my mouth, Owen. I want to taste you."

Owen took her hair in his hands and pushed into her mouth, working her head back and forth. Forcing himself deep. Thomas entered her pussy with power. Not as long as David but wider. Hands found every inch of her skin as the new shaft tore into her and the memory of her own name began to slip away. She still rode the orgasm she'd just come off of. Thomas's pounding initiated a chain of release, one after another, each orgasm beginning as the last took her breath away again. The walls moved, falling out of her peripheral vision as she sucked air through her nose and Owen came in her mouth. She swallowed his seed like the elixir of life, refusing to waste a drop.

With her face pressed against the sheets and cum dripping from her lips, she felt Thomas release into her with a feral growl, making her scream. Nearly broken, her hips tried to collapse against the mattress. The men lifted her ass into the air, refusing her respite. Thomas pulled free. She could barely move from exhaustion. Chest heaving. She pressed her breasts together and rolled on her back then slid her ass to the edge of the bed with, what seemed like, superhuman effort before spreading her legs. "Are you going to show them how to finish a woman properly, Coffey? Take me to another place. I'm ready."

Coffey pulled a condom on and stepped between her legs. Standing, he fed the tip of his cock into her wet pussy and hooked her knees over his elbows. His golden eyes bored into her own as he lifted her ass and fucked her as she'd never been fucked before. Consecutive orgasm after orgasm. Her world faded and rematerialized only to be taken away again and given back to her in cum-filled ecstasy. Every man in the room devoured her as Coffey increased his power. Sucking her nipples. Tasting her mouth. Biting and licking her neck. Together, they pinned her arms down as the resounding slap of wet flesh between her thighs tried to compete with her own breathless screams for more. The world left her as she came. Her mind roamed unfettered in unending pleasure. Pleasure she'd taken on her terms. In her way.

Chapter Eleven

After

*L*ights *brighter than noonday sun.*

The walls warbled like a liquid mirage across sweltering sands.

Indistinct voices called her name.

Flickering echoes.

"Sam?" A man's voice. "Sam?"

Where have I heard that voice before?

A name on the tip of her tongue.

Somewhere. Anywhere.

Her eyes fluttered. A small room came into focus. She lay on a bed, her heart pounding. Unclothed men surrounded her, calling her name.

My men. The room I chose.

Sam found her groggy voice as she remembered. "What?"

Hands touched her and lifted her to a sitting position. Her head still swirled in confusion. Owen.

Thomas. David. Marcus. Coffey. Everything came back in a licentious flash. "Thank you."

"Are you all right, baby?" Coffey stroked her face before sitting on the bed next to her and wrapping his arm behind her back. "I stopped everything when you went out. Nothing else happened. I promise."

She tried to breathe. "I know, Coffey. I never had any doubt. This is what I wanted. Thank you for watching over me."

Marcus held out her corset. "Here you are, Sam. Do you need help putting it on?"

Sam shook her head and tried to stand. Ten hands supported her when she nearly fell. Her whole body ached, burned out by adrenalin. She reached for the corset but fumbled as she tried to wrap it around her chest. The men took over. Thomas pulled her skirt down sweetly, a princess doted upon by her men in waiting. Locked in heated discussion about how to keep one from popping open while another was secured, the others pulled clasps closed one at a time. She raised her hands high, letting the naked men care for her.

When they finished, she watched her courtesans dress before her, struggling into boots and jackets. She had to break the silence. "You were perfect gentlemen. I expected nothing less. You gave me everything I wanted. Everything I needed. Thank you."

Owen walked to her side and held out his elbow for her to take. He whispered with concern. "Did you find what you were looking for?"

She pushed her wrist through the crook in his arm. "For the time being. A beginning."

Owen crooked an eyebrow. "The beginning of what?"

"Something wonderful." She kissed his cheek.

Lighting a cigarette, Marcus opened the door. Coffey stepped to Sam's side and placed a firm hand in the small of her back. She moved out the door on wobbling legs but found her stride before they had to arrest her fall again. The others followed behind. In one night she'd made them hers. They'd shown her the edge she searched for and the control she craved remained in place. She could do it again. Any time she wanted.

The music, smoke and odor of spilled beer assaulted her senses as the door closed behind them with a noiseless click. The riotous voices from the bar rose to her ears. Indistinct laughter, yelling and cusswords blended in a barrage of noise she couldn't hope to comprehend.

As she descended into the maelstrom, she

spotted Nova at the bar. The blonde seductress leaned against the worn railing. Her elbows rested on the decayed padding, her smile perpetual and a single heel lifted and pushed against the wood paneling behind her. Twenty or more men in various club jackets formed a half circle around her, laughing as if she'd become their queen. The hazel gaze lifted to meet her own with a wink, warming Sam's heart as they shared each other's thoughts without words.

They met halfway across the floor and embraced with a loving kiss. The bar erupted in approving screams, catcalls, and applause. It didn't matter. They'd found ecstasy in each other's arms.

Nova purred. "Thank you, baby. You're ready now. Don't you think?"

Sam nodded. "I hope so."

"Then it's time for us to leave."

Jackson stood at Nova's side. A sad look graced his face. "I guess this is it."

Nova rose up on her tiptoes and kissed his mouth. "Until next time. No longer than that."

"Hell." Jackson looked down at the ground with wet eyes. "I'll be dead by the time you come back."

"Perhaps." Nova ran her fingernails down his chest. "Perhaps not."

Jackson's grey hair bounced as he laughed. No

longer hidden from the corners of his eyes, tears dripped down his grizzled cheeks. "I'll wait."

"I know. You always have." Nova let her other hand slip from the bartender's grip.

Sam entwined her fingers with Nova's. An airy brush of flesh against her neck forced her to turn with a questioning look.

"And us?" Owen looked as if someone had just run over his puppy.

Sam's heart raced like a cheetah's pounce. She'd never been happier. *They still want me.* She wrapped her arms around his neck and devoured his lips, pressing her tongue deep into his mouth. Searching for his. Telling him with her body the things her words could no longer find. She broke away and held both his hands with her own as she smiled at him. "I'll find you again. I will." She watched the other men look at the floor, scuffing their boots against the wood. "All of you. Get over here."

Her new lovers looked up and bounded to her side. Kissing. Hugging. Grabbing her ass. Boiling heat coursed through her skin as they worshiped her. She didn't want to leave. "Thank you all for helping me find my way. We have to do this again. Soon."

A mob of five answered as one. "Absolutely. Do we call? Are you coming here again? When?"

Nova took her hand again and tugged her toward the door. "She will find you. I promise."

Sam couldn't help but blush as she tottered on her heels behind the goddess. She stopped at the door and turned toward them, knowing what she wanted. The wetness between her legs had already begun its slow drip down her thighs again. Ideas spun through her head. Bright lights of dizzying fantasy. "Perhaps you could bring a few more friends next time?"

Her lovers erupted in accepting laughter as Nova pulled on her again. "Come on, my little Minx. I've created a monster."

Sam let the door close behind her, muffling the pounding music, drowning out the laughter, eliminating the scent of men and sex. Her confidence soared. Her need growing beyond bounds she didn't even know she had.

This is who I am. Who I was meant to be.

The darkness spun around her.

***

A fresh spring breeze wafted through her nostrils as the world steadied around and came into focus. Wobbling slightly, she reached for Nova's shoulder. The small courtyard solidified despite being lit by nothing but a glowing moon. Water fell from a winged cherub's stone pitcher before her. The calming pitter patter of droplets shattered a million stars reflected in the pool. She'd found heaven and never wanted to let it go. She wanted to linger in the afterglow of her night's accomplishment and the greatest night she'd ever shared with anyone. Hers to have and hold, forever.

"Samantha?" Gage's deep voice called from the darkness behind her.

She turned, excited to share her exploits. To finish what she'd started. Katherine, standing at his side, reminded her of the things he'd done. Of the things he'd said. *I am in control. Not you.* With anger stoked by undeserved jealousy, she reached out to Katherine, forcing her own expression into glaring anger even though she didn't really feel it anymore. "I don't have time for this, Gage. I don't want to fight anymore."

Katherine bounced to her side and clutched her arm, pulling it to her chest with a squeeze as she leaned her head against Sam's shoulder.

"What?" Gage's face twisted in confusion. "No. I don't want to fight either. I just... It's just that..."

Sam watched the corner of Nova's mouth lift in an expression that could have been interest or mirth. Approval either way. "I just fucked five gorgeous men and had the greatest orgasms of my life. Plural. You're not going to take that away from me. Right now I need a proper bath, food and a woman's touch." Sam began to walk away, hoping she'd played her hand with an experienced gambler's bluff.

Gage looked completely flustered. "Wait a minute. I just wanted to say you looked, well, radiant. That's all."

Once more into the breach. "Maybe I'll feel differently tomorrow but, then again, that's entirely up to you. Isn't it?" She pecked Nova on the cheek. Walking away from him, her heart ached even as the heat of Katherine's skin reminded her of the wetness between her legs. She resolved to make sure the redhead's mouth forced the thoughts of Gage's body from her mind or morning would never come.

Chapter Twelve

New Beginnings

*B*right sunlight roused Sam from passionate dreams. Despite her tired muscles, her eyes opened with eager anticipation. With infinite care, she untangled herself from Katherine's soft embrace and slipped quietly from the bed. The woman had been insatiable. She'd erased any thoughts of Gage from Sam's mind as they searched each other's bodies for the perfect connection again and again. Now, without pleasure to occupy her thoughts, she couldn't think about anything except him.

The breeze cooled her sweat-tinged skin as she gazed across the courtyard, searching for Gage's hard body. Empty.

Sam tipped the pitcher set next to the wash basin, sloshing water against the sides. She questioned her words from the night before for the hundredth time. The cold water invigorated her skin, rinsing the sleep from her eyes as it splashed over her tired face. Dampening a small washcloth, she gave herself a sponge bath and stared at Katherine's sleeping form, wishing she still slept in her arms.

With a sigh, Sam scanned the courtyard again before pulling a simple green shift over her head. Like smoke, her confidence dissipated with his continued absence.

I lost my chance. I should've played it differently.

With a last, lingering glance at Katherine, Sam stood up straight and walked into the morning warmth.

Gage stepped away from the wall outside her bedroom where he'd waited just out of sight. "Samantha."

The softness of his deep voice filled her heart with hope. She clutched her hands together so he wouldn't see them shake and did her best to look disinterested. *An impossibility. Breathing would be easier.* "So, the compulsion still drives you to fulfill your repugnant task?"

"What?" His eyes squinted as his lip lifted in confusion.

Just breathe. "My education. Your task. Without Nova's binding you'd still be trapped between some young woman's thighs. Don't deny it." She hoped he would follow her as she began the familiar walk toward the bathhouse.

His voice boomed between the buildings. "Wait. It's not compulsion this time. I'm here...on my own."

Her heart skipped a beat as she turned to look at him, searching his eyes for truth she couldn't accept. "What? What do you mean?"

"It's true. I woke this morning with a raging..." His face turned beet red before he looked away and dropped his voice even lower. "With my cock so hard I couldn't think straight. All I could think about was you."

"The compulsion." She sighed with exasperation.

He stepped toward her with caution. "No. That's just it. Nova lifted the spell. I didn't come here because I had to. I came because I wanted to. I can feel the difference whether you believe me or not."

She couldn't decide whether the possibility of the compulsion being lifted or his coming to her room without it excited her more. His powerful chest drew her attention for less than a second before her gaze drifted over his rippling abs and continued downward to the tented fabric of his waist wrap. *Seduction.* "I see. A different kind of compulsion then."

The initial shock of her statement fell from his face, replaced by a lascivious grin. "Perhaps. I believe you suggested your disposition was somehow dependent on me. Maybe I wanted to know if you saw things different today."

The echo of her own words stirred the wetness between her legs and made her pulse gallop like a prized racehorse. *He wants me but...will he submit?* She gave her best virginal smile. An attempt at innocence she hadn't possessed in a long time. "We'll see. A bath first then...perhaps. Let's see what your hands can do first."

They walked to the bathhouse in silence. Sam could feel his gaze boring into her back. She let her hips sway with purpose, trying to emulate Nova's walk without effort and hoping it had the same effect on him.

The steam seemed thicker as she stepped into the bath's semi dark. She turned in time to see Gage duck under the low archway and walk toward her. She contemplated her next words carefully. "Undress me."

He leered as he reached for the hem of her dress. His coal black eyes tightened with lust as he began to jerk it upwards.

"Slowly." She didn't want him to think her eager. "I want to feel the silk brush against my skin."

The fabric slipped higher. A tickle raced across her hips as it rose one delicious inch at a time. Her waist. Her breasts. His soft hands brushed against her hardened nipples, forcing her to bite her lips so she didn't gasp. He pressed against her chest as he pulled the dress over her head.

Needing to test his resolve, she stopped him before he tossed the shift onto the stone bench. "Fold it."

He hesitated. Just a hint of irritation crossed his lips.

She let her lip press outward in a tiny pout. "Please."

His face softened as he folded the pullover. He stepped toward her again, admiring her body from head to toe. "Do you have any idea how beautiful you are?"

Her face flushed as he approached. Swallowing became difficult. Each breath required active thought. She wanted to believe she'd finally seduced the unseducable, but the hard cock hiding beneath his waistcloth made her wonder which head he thought with. *Who's seducing who here?* "No, but feel free to tell me."

He stood so close his chest nearly brushed her nipples. "I can't eat. I can't sleep. You're the only thing I think about."

The room buckled. Sam swooned. *Jesus! I'm not a*

blushing virgin. She turned quickly and sauntered toward the rinse drain, reprimanding herself for wanting to give in so easily. Leaning against the cool stone, she opened her stance so he could see the outline of her wet lips. She pushed her ass backwards in a seductive tease. "Wash me."

Water splashed behind her as he filled the bucket from the pool. The anticipation of his touch made her moan before the warm water flowed over her shoulders. Hot drops ran over her nipples. They hardened, filled with blood until at the edge of bursting. The slow trickle down her thighs suggested the fluid there had more pussy juice than water. She only hoped the composition of the stream didn't elude his own imagination.

He squeezed the excess water from the washcloth behind her. She pursed her lips and blew out slowly. Hot, soothing strokes of rough cloth against her shoulders began again. Slow circles on her skin. Warm soapy water trickled between her ass cheeks. The drops skittered across her pussy lips and fell to the floor in a spout from her swollen clit. His free hand brushed her neck as the washrag rubbed her tight ass. *I'm losing control.* "Hands. You've only been given permission to wash. Not to touch."

"As you wish."

The painful loss of his stroking fingers dissipated as he worked the soap between her thighs. Gentle pressure slowly spread her outer lips and deepened. The slippery feel, mixed with rough texture sent shockwaves through her abdomen every time he bumped across her clit. After lingering minutes, she could feel an orgasm rising just beyond reach. "I believe my pussy is thoroughly clean. Perhaps I'll let you taste it later. You can give me your opinion. Until then, my legs need attention."

Gage knelt and stroked her legs with deft care. "I'd like that."

Sam pushed backwards until she could feel his breath cooling her skin and held it there. Just out of reach. *Control begins with temptation.* She smiled. The time he spent completing her legs revealed just how addicted he'd become.

This time you will kneel.

Sam closed her eyes in luxuriance as the warm water rinse poured over her body, bucket by bucket. She granted intermittent seductive shakes of her hips as a reward each time he refilled. Turning, she leaned her clean back against the wall, and placed her hands on top of her head. She opened her legs. "The front please."

He started high on her neck. Slow. His eyes

bored into her brain through her own, revealing his desires and transmitting them to her. Before he could take possession, she closed her eyes and moaned for his benefit. "Take your time. I'll just enjoy."

Lustful tickles radiated from her nipples every time the hot cloth bounced across them. A warm throb began deep within her vagina, spiking as her nipples sprung upright with the soapy fabric's movement. His hands roamed lower. She bit her lip as the to-and-fro strokes across her clit made her ass clench and raised the temperature at the apex of her thighs. Unbearable limits. "I believe that's sufficient." The words stuck in her throat and barely squeaked free. "Move on."

She looked down at his dark hair as he knelt, starting on her legs again. Placing her hands on the sides of his head, she moved his lips a whisper from her clit until he could scent her desire. "So that you behave. I wouldn't want you to take more than you're given."

The longer his breath grazed her pussy, the more she wanted him to lick her. To fuck her. After minutes passed, she couldn't take anymore. "Enough. Rinse me off."

As he poured, she stared into his eyes again. She pressed her breasts together and pinched her nipples hard. His attention never wavered from her chest. "You like these, don't you?"

His hand went to his crotch for a moment of adjustment. "Stupendous."

"My nipples are so damn hard. I almost come every time I pinch them." With another pinch for his benefit, she sidled into the pool.

She'd been hoping for refreshment, but dunking her head only made her hotter. As she cleared the hair from her eyes and squeezed the excess water from it, Gage gaped with deprived hunger. *You're mine now.* She rubbed her fingers over her clit as she exited the water. After pushing a single finger deep inside her pussy with a groan, she withdrew the wet digit and sucked it clean. "Damn. Every time I think of how hard I was fucked last night, I want it again. More men next time. At least eight, I think."

Gage didn't say anything. His mouth hung open in reverence.

Sam stood dripping on the wet cobblestones and opened her arms, trying to look exasperated. "Well?"

"Well what?" Gage tilted his head in confusion.

"Men." She groaned in mock apathy. "Dry me. You don't want me dripping all day do you?"

Gage jogged to the shelves and pulled down an absorbent cloth. He opened it and stepped to her side.

Wrapping it around her, he rubbed gently. The dry surface sucked the water from her skin. His obedience kept her wet. He moved slowly as he began working between her legs, accelerating his pace as she opened them wider. "Do a good job. My pussy is absolutely drenched."

He began licking his lips with greed as he stooped to dry her legs and stared at her hard clit.

She let him finish without further torment and then waited for him place the towel in an empty corner. Sam needed continuous concentration not to smile every time he adjusted his cock. She placed a hand on her naked hip and tapped a foot in faux consternation.

Gage stood admiring for another second before he recognized her conspicuous disappointment. He jumped toward the shelves and lifted her dress. Unfolding it, he held it out to her. "Here you are."

"You still don't get it, do you?" She held her arms above her head and considered how far his patience would actually stretch. "Dress me."

Submission means obedience in all things.

With awkward fumbles in unsure hands, the soft silk slid over her breasts before Gage tugged it into place at mid thigh. She giggled. "Wow. You don't put dresses on many women, do you?"

He looked hurt for a moment, but her chuckle infected him. He laughed out loud and walked toward the door. "I have a lot more experience taking them off. Shall we?"

His behavior struck her as beyond cute. She couldn't resist one last stab. She pushed out her bottom lip and tugged the hem of her dress down with both hands before looking down at the floor. "What about my kiss?"

His eyes scrunched together before he approached her with a lecherous smile. He leaned in toward her mouth, gripping her hips in his hands.

She tilted her head back and pushed his chest back with her palm. "No, silly." She rolled the hem of the dress above her hips and lifted one foot onto the bench. She pointed between her legs. "Here. I want to make sure she's clean enough to eat from."

He almost dove to his knees. Grabbing her hips with ferocity, he leaned in.

She touched his lips with a single finger and held the back of his head with her other hand. "One kiss. A simple taste and you're done. If you're a good boy, I'll give you more... later."

He pressed forward.

"Ah, ah ah. Tell me you understand."

The real test of obedience.

"I understand."

His words made her heart jump. Absolute satisfaction. She hadn't believed he could come so far. "Then kiss me, sweet boy."

Primed, his hot mouth almost brought her to her knees. She moaned as his long tongue pressed into her opening, delved deeply and slid upward for a soft kiss on her clit. He could have taken anything he wanted but he didn't.

Gage stood up straight and let his black eyes bore into hers with preternatural desire. His lips stayed only inches from her mouth for another heartbeat before he released her and moved away, holding out his hand.

With absolute surprise stealing her voice, Sam placed her palm in his and let him lead her into the sunlight.

The courtyard swimming pool reflected the sun's glare on its pristine, mirrored surface. A gentle breeze rustled the small trees without rippling the water's surface. The long night of pleasure had left her starving, but her focus failed to settle on the food-laden table set on the manicured grass. Instead, her gaze roved across the accoutrements standing behind it.

She'd seen pictures of the large X-shaped

scaffold. A Saint Anthony's cross. Beside it, a table piled high with devices of pain made her mouth water in anticipation. Paddles, canes, floggers, and contrivances of leather, the functions of which she could only guess. Close by, another table had been heaped in coils of silk rope, manacles, handcuffs, and other restraints more complicated than Gordian's knot.

She swallowed hard and stared at the padded benches between the two tables. She remembered them from night after night of porn fueled masturbation. Designed for positioning and immobilizing a subject before fucking them into semi-unconsciousness. "It seems you've a pleasure-filled day in store for me."

Gage licked his lips. One side of his mouth twisted upward in a leer. He swept his hand toward the nourishment-laden table. "Breakfast first. Then we'll see what the morning brings."

"Indeed." She sat in a soft chair he pulled out for her, trying to appear disinterested in his gallantry. "We appear to be alone this morning. No helpers today?"

Gage hefted a pitcher of coffee and began filling her cup. "I sent the seekers away. I wanted to be the one who cared for you today. If that's all right."

Sam's heart fluttered. Knowing her hands would shake, she didn't lift the coffee cup. "Ooh. Someone wants to be rewarded for good behavior."

His lips pinched together in an attempt to hide a smile. He handed her a basket of bread. "I guess that's entirely up to you, isn't it?"

"Of course. It always was." She pretended not to notice he'd used her own words against her. She selected a croissant and placed it on her plate. "I guess you can be taught after all."

"Maybe I just needed the right motivation."

She let him serve her, eating as if his ministrations meant nothing. His apparent change in attitude had flustered her. She couldn't deny it. If she let him know how excited his attentions made her, she would be giving away the control she'd worked so hard to obtain. *This is who I am now. I decide what I want.*

Finished, she blotted her face daintily with a napkin before rising from her seat. She ran her hand across the warm steel of the bondage cross and sauntered to the table filled with toys of punishment. His eyes never moved from her ass. "So. What are we to learn today?"

"Tools of the trade."

His hard cock lifted the fabric at his waist but she

didn't comment, enjoying the effect her presence seemed to have on him. She lifted a polished bone handle with foot-long strips of leather swaying back and forth below it.

"A flogger." Gage lifted an identical one and waved it in a compact figure-eight motion, which kept the fronds extended. "One or two at a time. It takes skill to entice without leaving a mark."

Sam wanted him to use it on her. Hot drops began to trickle down her thigh. She set the flogger down and pointed to object after object, staring at him with interest as he answered.

A long thin bamboo rod. "A cane. Many sizes soft to stiff."

A glove with steel fingertips sharpened to frightening points. "A vampire glove. In the right hands, no marks, only ecstasy."

She lifted a long feather. "This seems out of place. Don't you think?"

"Not at all." He laughed. "You alternate between pain and pleasure in a long session. The subject is blindfolded. Every sensation is new. Unexpected. Each touch increases desire until lust overcomes everything around them. Their mind can't even contemplate anything but more."

Her heart began to pound as the introduction to

the toys rolled on. She couldn't think anymore. He'd begun to seduce her and she wanted her control back. "So. Should I tie you to the cross and simply experiment? I think you're more likely to be injured rather than pleasured, but I'm willing to try." She tilted her head and batted her eyes, trying her best to look sweet.

"We are an enthusiastic pupil today." Gage set a long paddle down on the table. "I was going to demonstrate on you."

Sam raised her eyebrows with her best *you-must-be-kidding-me* expression and tried not to say yes. "Not this time, Gage. You'll have to think of something else or our lesson is done for the day." She didn't want the training to end, but she'd no intention of losing the ground she'd gained.

Gage's mouth turned down in disappointment for no more than a heartbeat. He looked over her shoulder and a lascivious expression lifted toward his ears. "I believe the answer to our problem approaches."

Sam squinted her eyes and scrunched her brow before following his gaze. Katherine leaned against a column on the other side of the courtyard. Her red hair blazed like fire despite being wet. The white transparent shift she wore couldn't hide the outline of her mons or the hardened nipples jutting outward. Her pale white skin shined like polished alabaster in the sun. A goddess of nearly perfect beauty.

Sam called to Katherine in sultry tones tinged with delight, "Good morning, sleepy head. You look stunning this morning. Will you join us?"

Katherine quick-stepped to her side in excitement, bouncing with glee as she stepped into Sam's arms and kissed her deeply. She moaned. "Morning, Sam. I missed you at my side when I woke." Her gaze shifted to Gage, grinning at his tented waistcloth.

Gage motioned to the table still laden with food. "Would you like something to eat? To drink?"

Katherine clutched Sam's hand in hers, swiveling her hips back and forth. "I've already eaten. I took a bath and grabbed a snack before I came searching for Samantha."

The slight embarrassment in Katherine's voice melted Sam's heart. Her innocent infatuation radiated the definition of 'cute as a kitten'. *My kitten*. "Would you be willing to help us with something today?"

Katherine's mouth fell open in awe. She looked up with veneration. "Anything for you, Samantha. Just ask. Anything."

Sam smiled, trying to assuage her own guilt.

Guilt that rapidly faded in the face of rising desire. She led Katherine toward the small bench between the two tables.

Ten inches wide, the padded top looked like a waist high massage bench. Much narrower, two padded rails paralleled the bench surface about two feet closer to the ground.

Katherine clamped her lower lip between her teeth, alternating her gaze between the bench and Sam's face. Squeezing Sam's hand tighter. "What is it?"

"A spanking bench." Sam ran her hand along the soft sheep skin covering. "Is that the correct term, Gage?"

Gage stepped to another table. He lifted a blindfold and two coils of rope. "Spanking bench. Pleasure bench. Paddle frame. No name more correct than any other."

Sam could see the hesitation rising in Katherine's eyes. *I need this, beautiful.* She turned the corners of her mouth downward and pushed out her lower lip. The pout had become her go-to seductive expression. "Don't you trust me, Katherine?"

Katherine clutched both of Sam's hands in her own. "I do." She turned to Gage. "Will it hurt?"

"Only as much as you want it too. You'll be

our...subject." He stepped closer. "The level of pain or pleasure is entirely up to you."

"Samantha will protect me." She reached out to the soft top and touched it with her fingers as if considering her words. "Won't you?"

The power Sam now wielded had become intoxicating. An aphrodisiac without equal. "Of course."

Sam moved closer to Katherine's soft body and rolled the hem of the woman's skirt above her hips. Katherine lifted her arms with a smile, letting Sam pull it free. Hard nipples. Shining skin. Succulent body. Sam focused on the tiny patch of red hair between her legs. The silky curls couldn't hide her outer labia or the thin pink inner lips peeking out between them. Sam ran the tip of her tongue across her teeth, remembering how delightful Katherine's cum had tasted. With a coaxing hand, Sam leaned Katherine forward until her stomach touched the bench and then bent her at the waist. The redhead exhaled as her chest pressed against the padded table top. Sam lifted Katherine's knees onto the lower rails, opening her wide. The position spread Katherine's legs and separated the outer lips of her pussy. Just enough to tease.

Gage's deep voice broke Sam's trance. "She'll

need a safe word."

Sam looked at Katherine's trembling lip, enjoying her trepidation more than she should have. She'd read about safe words but never had one of her own or asked someone else to choose one. "You need to pick a safe word, Katherine. If you say it, everything stops immediately. No regrets. No recrimination. Can you do that?"

Katherine looked deep in thought. "Can I use 'Samantha' for my safe word?

You are so delicious. I could just eat you. "Yes, Katherine. Of course you can." Internal guilt threatened again but Sam pushed it down. She wanted Katherine's submission more than ever.

Gage passed a blindfold over Katherine's back. "Cover her eyes. It amplifies the sensations."

Sam placed the blindfold gently before running her fingertips across Katherine's back and kissing her cheek. The beautiful girl trembled under her touch. A soft moan. *What have I become? Why do I want to fuck her even more as she submits?*

Gage held out a coil of black silk rope. "Bind her."

Sam uncoiled the rope in her hand. She pulled length after length though her hands so Katherine could hear the hiss of silk against skin. Without a word, Sam looped the rope around the woman's frail wrists, tying it with skill, which surprised even herself. Gripping Katherine's other hand, she positioned the pale white arms behind her back and lashed them together. Sam checked each turn, making sure they didn't pinch as she listened to the redhead's breathing rate soar.

Katherine licked her lips. She moved her head as if pleading for the visual cues completely denied to her.

Sam looped another coil around Katherine's elbows and tied the ends off to the eye bolts beneath the bench. Admiring her handy work, Sam let her hand slip beneath her dress and pressed a finger against her clit. Katherine couldn't roll. She couldn't move forward or back. Sam leaned in close to Katherine's ear. "Is that too tight, baby?"

Katherine's voice squeaked in eagerness and fear. "No, but...I can't move."

"That was my intention." Sam moved down to the smooth legs dotted with errant freckles. Sexy without distraction. She kept her face close to the rosy patch of hair and wet lips between Katherine's legs as she wrapped more coils of rope around her legs. Katherine wouldn't be able to close them if she tried. The redhead's sweet cleft already dripped and Sam couldn't resist a soft kiss. A taste. High pitched moans told her everything she needed to know. "My favorite flavor. She's ready."

Enraptured by her beauty, Gage reached out and caressed the white skin of Katherine's ass. "Soothe first. A soft touch. Everywhere you'll be working. This is the beginning. A necessity."

Sam swallowed, wishing his hands caressed her instead. She wanted to give herself to him but needed his submission more with every second. "Ask first."

Gage tensed his muscles as if struck. "What?"

"She's not your possession." Sam lifted his hot hand from Katherine's skin. "She's mine. You *will* ask first."

He stared hard. An icy glare threatened but passed as if blown away by a coming storm. "May I touch her?"

Sam leaned in again. Her lips inches from Katherine's own. Seduction. "Will you let him touch you, baby girl? For me."

The skin on Katherine's back prickled with visible goose bumps. "Yes, Mistress."

Yes. I am your mistress.

Sam began to rub her clit again, making sure Gage watched where her fingers strayed. "You may proceed, Gage."

His hard body twitched as he watched Sam work against her own sex. His hands moved back to Katherine's ass in smooth circles again. Touching each cheek. "Soothe first. Prepare her for what is coming."

Gage slapped softly. Each cheek. An upward motion. Focused strikes without pain before he began his slow circles again. Each tap caused Katherine's muscles to tense even though he hadn't hurt her. Sam slid a finger between her own sopping lips before circling her clit again. Fascinated.

"And then, harder." Gage slapped again. The same upward motion. A pink blush appeared on the pale skin. "Watch her body. Her reaction. Determine your next strike based on her breathing. Her moans."

He circled softly again before slapping again. Katherine stiffened with anticipation each time, but Gage waited until she relaxed before striking swiftly again. Katherine's fingers closed. White knuckles flexed and relaxed as she struggled uselessly against her bonds. Her moans had become a symphony of pleasure. The most beautiful sonata ever composed.

Gage stepped away from the bench. "Your turn."

Sam lifted her own finger and sucked it clean for Gage's benefit. Following his instructions, she rubbed her hand against Katherine's flesh. The blush radiated heat beneath her palm. Succulent. She slapped. Her strikes, though soft, forced every muscle in Katherine's skin to ripple. Wreathed in curly red hair, tiny drops of cum had begun collecting on the woman's hard clit. Harder. The drops fell to the tile as new ones formed again. Thicker. Sam watched her quiver. She listened to the redhead's breath, and when Katherine's muscles began to relax, she hit her harder. Her hand left red prints now. The flesh had become molten. Hot beyond imagining. She watched Katherine's pink outer lips contract and relax. Her cum had become a stream. Quick drops running off her clit to splash onto the floor below. Sam squeezed her ass. Lifted. Caressed. Harder. The slaps became pistol shots. Her fingers left imprints on the pristine skin. *Can a person cum by being spanked? Would she?* Sam already rode the edge of orgasm herself. Nothing had ever been more erotic. As Katherine's pink lips writhed again, Sam pulled back her hand to hit harder than she ever had before. *You are mine!*

Gage clutched her wrist with unbelievable strength, staying her strike as he gazed into her eyes with lechery oozing from his grin. Before she could speak he lifted a finger to his lips, halting her question. He held up a feather then stroked it over Katherine's back. The woman bucked against her bonds as if Sam hand landed the final blow.

Katherine's groans became scathing moans as she thrashed against the touch.

Gage held out the feather and Sam started where he'd left off. Overloading Katherine's senses. Their plaything had no idea what would come next. Pain or pleasure. Sam continued to run the plumage down Katherine's back. Goose flesh rose and fell on white marbled skin. The beauty's struggles became less. Accepting.

Gage lifted the multi tailed leather flogger, holding his finger's to his lips again. He let the fronds drag across Katherine's back, making her buck again. The whimpering from Katherine's lips had become Sam's aphrodisiac. The sensation deep between her own legs pulsed as if her womb had been ignited by a force beyond herself.

Gage moved behind Katherine and let the fronds touch her pussy. Katherine mewed like a lost kitten. He raised the flogger and brought it down with a soft flap from the top of her left cheek to the bottom of her right. The whimpers rose as he moved in a figure eight. Right cheek to left. Left to right. A rhythmic motion that fired every nerve in Katherine's body. As her voice rose into something just less than a scream, he stopped then dragged the fronds over her body again. He handed the bone handle to Sam with a nod.

Sam understood immediately. She took the handle in her hands and dragged it downward, watching the sides of Katherine's chest heave in near convulsion. She stepped behind her and repeated the rhythmic swings she'd seen Gage use. Right to left. Left to right. Top to bottom. Again and again. Harder. Welts began to appear but Sam didn't want to stop. The rising cries from Katherine's lips drove her like a slave before the lash. The contracting pussy lips and the puddle below them became her only focus.

Katherine sobbed as Gage stayed Sam's hand again. The sound nearly made her cum. Her own pussy alternated between pulsation and contraction as if she was being fucked. Hard. Aroused without touch. Without a cock buried deep inside of her. Her hands shook as she moved in close to Katherine, bathing her own ears in the sweet song of the redhead's tears. "Are you all right, my love? Use your safe word and this all ends."

Katherine sniffed. Cried and sniffed again. "No. Don't stop."

Sam ran her hands across Katherine's back. "You're crying. I don't want you in pain."

Katherine whimpered again. "It's not pain. It's... It's... Something else. Something, wonderful." Her body became wracked by tears. "Don't stop. Please don't stop. I'm so close."

Gage held a finger to his lips in answer to Sam's confusion. He wore the vampire glove on his raised hand. The sharp steel claws glistened in the sunlight. Sam didn't want him to hurt her, but the desire to see him use it on the soft skin became overpowering. She stared at Gage before reaching out to run her fingers through Katherine's hair. An attempt at comfort or, perhaps, an apology in advance. Sam no longer sought for answers to address her own needs. She simply let her heart pound and her mouth salivate with desire.

Gage lowered the claws with tenderness Sam didn't even know he had. He touched Katherine's shoulder. Only the weight of the metal pressed against the redhead's flesh and still Katherine thrashed against her bonds. *The bonds I tied.* He pulled the glove downward, crossing from Katherine's shoulder to her opposite hip before starting again on the other side.

He offered another glove and Sam took over. No marks. No scratches. Pure sensation. With her other hand, Sam pushed a finger inside herself as the ripples of Katherine's shocks began to subside and her breathing slowed. Each stroke of her finger made the wet walls of heat between her legs contract and squeeze, threatening release. Release she didn't intend to deny. She pretended not to notice Gage watching her as he squeezed his cock though the fabric at his waist. A warm flush between her legs foreshadowed the hot trickle of cum rolling down her fingers and into her palm as she stroked deeper, knowing what she had to do. "Push your fingers into her, Gage. I want to taste her essence on you."

Gage lifted his hand from the swelling between his legs and moved into position behind Katherine.

Sam traced Gage's lips with the fingers she'd used on herself. She grabbed his wrist and whispered as he sucked. "Ask. She's not your toy. She's mine."

Gage sucked hard until Sam pulled her finger free and pushed it into her own mouth drawing small circles on her tongue. Rocking her hips back and forth and pulling the hem of her dress downward like an innocent little girl.

Gage held his fingers close to the dripping pink cleft encircled in soft red hair. "May I push my fingers into you, Katherine? Your...Mistress wants a taste."

Katherine raised her head, turning toward their voices as if she could see them. She licked her lips and breathed her answer. "Yes. Please. Sir."

Gage gripped Katherine's hip in one hand and gently opened her with his fingers. He pushed softly, pulling in and out, milking the cum from between her legs until it dribbled down his fingers. As Katherine moaned louder, Gage forced his fingers in harder until the wet lapping of his strokes echoed in Sam's consciousness. Deep quick penetration. Slow withdrawal. Again and again until it was Sam who stood on the verge of breaking. "My turn."

Gage pulled his soaking fingertips free, glistening with clear promise. He held them beneath Sam's nose, letting her inhale with burning lungs before she had to take them in her mouth. The sweet flavor of Katherine became even more arousing when mixed with the salty tang of Gage's skin. She unpinned his waist wrap and let it fall to the ground. Any complaint he may have had disappeared as she gripped his hard cock in her hand and pumped slowly. So full, she could feel the swollen veins slide across her palm. Beads of sweet pre-cum fell from his cock's head and rolled across her knuckles, making her squeeze harder before she pumped again. Squeezing. Stroking. Sucking Katherine's nectar from his finger like a last meal. She didn't want to play anymore. She only wanted him inside her, but she could no longer resist the tease. The addiction. The power of seduction coursed through her blood and she would make it last.

As he reached for Sam's hip, she released his shaft, holding up a hand to stay his advance. "Not yet, Gage." She licked her lips. "I want to see you fuck her hard. The way you want me. If I'm impressed then, maybe, I'll reward you."

Sam ran her fingernails down Katherine's back as she walked toward her head, never letting her gaze waver from Gage's body or his massive erection. She put her knee on the bench and rolled up her dress. Her pussy almost touched Katherine's lips. "Katherine, I want you to have my scent in your mind as he takes you."

Gage gripped Katherine's hips in his hands. His biceps bulged and rolled. He smiled at Sam. "May I have you, Katherine? Your mistress's demands are my desires."

Katherine inhaled and stretched out her tongue, searching for Sam's flavor. "Yes. Yes! Please, sir."

Gage pressed into her with a grunt.

Katherine gasped. "Slow! Please slow!"

Sam didn't tell him to slow down. Instead, she fingered herself and fed Katherine her cum one lick at a time to calm her. She wanted Gage to fuck her hard. She wanted to hear Katherine scream as he made her cum. *The way you want me.* Sam reached with one hand and undid the knots securing Katherine's arms but not her hands. In one motion, she pulled up her dress and swiveled her hips beneath the redhead's plump lips and pulled her head down. "Lick my pussy, baby girl."

Katherine sucked her clit into her mouth and Sam moaned. The world ignited around her as Gage drove harder. Muffled grunts from Katherine's lips with every thrust made Sam's sensitive nub tingle. Electric shocks zinged deep into her vagina, radiating upward until the wet, throbbing walls began to pulse in wave after wave. Sam panted as sweat rolled down Gage's face and bounced across his muscled chest. His head had been thrown back in pleasure. His jaw clenched and unclenched as he groaned, hammering again and again. "Make her cum for me, Gage."

Katherine lifted her head from Sam's lap and screamed as Gage increased his power. A beast possessed. Katherine came, and the power of her orgasm twisted Gage's face as her contractions around his cock tried to pull him with her.

Sam supported Katherine's shoulders as her shuddering release rolled on in scream after scream. Sam decided to test the limits of her control. "Don't you dare cum, Gage! That pleasure is mine alone."

Gage's face shifted from ecstasy to horror. He pushed backwards and pulled his pulsing cock from

Katherine's writhing body. Gasping. His whole body became flushed. He placed his hands behind his head and bit his lip, trying to beat back an unstoppable force with concentration alone. He moaned and walked in a frustrated circle, stomping his feet, his cock bouncing in rhythm to his steps. "You're a cruel mistress. A little warning is all I ask...next time."

Sam could barely bite back her satisfaction as his torture continued and the visible throb of his cock began to slow. She pulled off Katherine's blindfold and brushed the hair from her eyes before kissing her forehead. Reaching behind her, she undid the knots binding Katherine's hands and held her. Rocking slowly. Comforting. "I'll think about it, Gage. Either way, you were a good boy. A very good boy."

Gage squeezed his throbbing member hard, milking the pre-cum from its tip. His eyes darkened with licentiousness, fixated on the women before him. "How good?" He paused and stroked again before finishing his thought. "Mistress."

He'd earned a reward of some sort. Sam just hadn't determined the form it would take. She let Katherine sit up before standing herself. *Control.* She kept her gaze on his and walked toward him. She tugged the hem of her dress upward with every step, stopping its ascent before her saturated pussy had been revealed and pushed it down again.

His hard body rippled beneath her hands. She kept her face close to his, tracing his nipples with her fingernails. Her heart thundered with need as her palms slipped downward. His erection seemed impossibly hard in her grasp. The veins coursing across its surface pulsed between her fingers.

Gage opened his mouth to say something and Sam silenced him with the press of her fingertip to his lips. "I didn't give you permission to speak."

She knelt before him and pumped his massive dick in slow motion, licking her lips as a clear stream of creamy fluid rolled from his cockhead and slid toward his tightening sack. He reached out to touch her hair and she stopped, glaring up at him with false anger. "I didn't give you permission to touch."

Gage looked perplexed at first but then closed his eyes, moaning as her tongue lapped the clear stream from the sensitive skin below the purple head and sucked the residua from the open hole. Delicious nectar teased her palate but she wanted more. She needed him to force her against the ground and fuck her the way she'd wanted since seeing him the first day. It seemed so long ago. She took his cock between her lips and sucked, letting her tongue swirl against the velvet skin. Moving her head, she polished his cock in half circles, taking him deeper. She released and began again, letting him farther into her throat each time until his size threatened to gag her. Her hand pumped in counterpoise to her bobbing head. The other encircled his tight sack just above his balls, tugging with gentle passion until he began to shake and moan with ferocious need on the edge of release. The drink she craved approached with unstoppable force.

Gage laced his fingers behind his head and closed his eyes. Thrusting against Sam's mouth as she took him to the precipice. "Yes, Mistress. Don't stop! I'm almost there! Don't stop!"

A vanilla breeze laced with lavender tickled her senses and woke her again. Her skin became hot, inflamed by the memory of delectable passions from the past and dreams of the future. She lifted her head from the hard spigot and found Nova staring down from above. Her face flushed as she wiped her lips with the back of her hand. She stood with something between confusion and embarrassment.

Before Sam attempted to explain, Nova lifted her chin with a single fingertip and ran her tongue across Sam's lips and chin, cleaning Gage's pre-cum from her face. Nova's arms wrapped behind Sam's neck and she surrendered to the soft pull. Their lips pressed together so their tongues could dance and play. Sam gripped Nova's ass in her hands and pulled their hips together.

"Mmmm." Nova pressed her forehead to Sam's. Their lips separated by a breath. "The taste of my lover upon your lips is the sweet wine I desire more than any other, my delicious girl."

Sam could only stare at the ground as they parted. She remembered Gage's pulsing need and the drink he'd almost poured down her parched throat. "You're even more cruel than I am." Sam turned from Nova's soft lips to stare at Gage's dripping cock. His face had twisted in a mixture of frustration and disappointment. His gorgeous chest still heaved with the pain of denied release. "He was about to empty his sweet cum down my throat and now you've left us both in limbo."

Nova slipped her hand beneath Sam's dress and pushed two fingers deep inside her pussy. She grinned wickedly at Gage. "I'm sorry, lover. She's so wet right now. I bet she was going to let you fuck her before you came in her mouth. Did I guess right, Samantha?"

Nova's fingers slid in and out with rapid strokes. Her thumb pressed against Sam's clit. "Yes." Sam could barely breathe let alone answer, but Nova had continued to press Gage's desire intentionally. She hadn't appeared by accident. "He was going to be allowed to have..." Sam groaned as the orgasm washed over her. She placed her head on Nova's shoulder, holding her hips as the blonde angel's fingers continued their skillful penetration. "Anything he wanted."

"Shame." Nova removed her slick fingers from between Sam's legs and sucked them clean. "I would have liked to see that."

Gage growled before picking up his waistcloth and wrapping it angrily around his hips. "You continue to deny me then? My torture is to continue indefinitely?"

Nova tried to look appalled as she pressed her chest against his and lifted her wet fingers to his mouth. "Not at all, my lover. I believe you're ready to return to my bed."

Gage gripped her waist and pulled the tiny nymph against his hips. He inhaled Sam's scent on her fingers before sucking them softly. "More than anything. I've missed you, Nova. My body aches to have you again. Even an hour is too long."

"I agree." Nova kissed his chest before slipping her hand beneath his wrap and making him whimper. "You have just one more thing to do and my body is yours to pleasure as you will."

"Anything. Simply ask." He took her face between his hands and kissed her with passion only lost love could elicit. "Ask, my love."

A twinge of jealousy skittered across Sam's heart as the supernatural lovers rekindled their thousand year old romance. Sam had broken him. Hardened him. Seduced him. Even knowing he belonged to Nova, Sam wanted him inside her. She needed him to use her body as an example to all those who had sought to deny his want. She'd earned the right to quench his thirst after he'd been refused release for so long. It'd been her who'd stoked his smoldering match of contempt into a blazing inferno of unrequited lust. Nova could enjoy him after he'd torn Sam's body apart and shot his molten seed deep inside her throbbing pussy.

Nova continued to stroke Gage but turned to face Sam with a smile. "Are you ready to take the last step, my sweet Samantha?"

"Me?" Sam forgot her anger. She had no idea what Nova meant.

Gage stiffened. He lifted his black eyes to gaze at Sam in confusion.

"Oooh..." Nova removed her hand from his cock and kissed his chest again. "So tense, my love. I thought I had but ask? Did I hear incorrectly?"

"Of course not. But... I thought..." Gage didn't seem to know which of the women he should be looking at.

"But what?" Nova's voice hinted at rising anger and yet somehow remained sweet. Irresistible. "The choice has always been yours, Gage. Do you accept or has she yet to bind your heart?"

Sam had no idea what they talked about. She watched the two beings strip the clothes from her body with their eyes. Their silence threatened to buckle her knees beneath the weight of their inspection.

Gage licked his lips like a hungry wolf that hadn't eaten in days. "She has. I accept, without reservation."

"Excellent." Nova walked to Sam's side and gripped her hand with palpable zeal, bouncing like an excited child. "Come, Samantha. You must prepare. Katherine? You can help us."

Sam let herself be pulled along by the bubbling blonde package of exuberance. She turned to see Katherine dressing quickly with a confusion that matched her own before jogging to catch up. Looking over her shoulder, Sam watched the tattoos on Gage's body begin to pulse and writhe. He squinted in the sun, fixated on the women retreating from his side. He raised his upper lip like a feral animal in heat. A dominant who took what he wanted from his mate and left nothing behind.

Nova jerked Sam's arm again, pulling her toward the arched building and jolting her back to reality. "What is it I am preparing for, Nova?"

The gorgeous blonde twittered as if she'd heard the funniest thing in the world. "My lover's test. It's time for you to show us what you've become."

Sam's mind went blank. The sound of her own bare feet slapped on the cold marble beneath them, echoing in the silent hallways. "I don't understand."

"It is time for Gage to submit and you, my sweet Samantha, are the mistress to whom he'll bend."

Chapter Thirteen
Becoming

Sam turned before the full length mirror as Katherine and Nova looked on. "I look ridiculous."

Dark as night, the leather top hid nothing. It pushed every inch of her ample cleavage together until her nipples threatened to pop free with the slightest movement. Beneath her bulging tits, a silver zipper strained to hold the two sides of the tiny blouse together and left her midriff bear. Her tight leather skirt didn't even reach mid thigh, as if it would ride up at any moment and uncover the freshly shaved, pristine smoothness of her outer lips. Sam groaned in disbelief as she tottered on eight-inch heels. Black latex boots rose just above her knees.

"On the contrary." Nova licked her strawberry-red lips. "You look positively scrumptious."

From behind, Katherine wrapped her arms around Sam's waist and rested her chin on her shoulder. Their eyes locked in the mirror's reflection. "I could eat you."

"You already have. Multiple times." Sam caressed Katherine's hands with her own and chuckled with obvious discomfort.

Katherine released her grip and kissed Sam on the neck. "What's the matter? You don't look happy."

"Ugh..." Sam groaned. "I just don't know if I can do this in front of an audience. Why can't it just be a small number of people? Just you two. Maybe Khan. I've already had each of you and I wouldn't be so...self conscious."

Nova stepped in front of her reflection. She held Sam's face between her palms. "The rules, Samantha. The council demands proof his submission isn't false. Witnesses. His peers. His submission means nothing in private. He must yield and all must know he did. You can do this, Samantha. For him. For me."

"I'll do my best. That's all I can promise." Sam's nervousness seeped into her bones and crawled through her skin. Every minute they stood only made the tremor in her hands worsen. "I'm tired of waiting. Let's get this done."

"That's my girl." Nova kissed her lightly and led the way out of the room.

Sam tried to picture Gage's face as she walked

through the halls. The click of her heels only reminded her of the task ahead. *What am I doing?* Her mouth seemed filled with cotton. She wanted a drink. A lot of drinks. *What am I going to do?*

The sun had dropped below the horizon hours before. The dark sky was filled with stars. An orange moon hung low in the sky, lighting their path with a burning glow. An ethereal torchlight placed by gods to mark the significance of this night forever.

They passed beneath a massive stone archway. The air rarefied around her. A stone walkway yielded to a massive raised dais carved from a single piece of marble. On her right, enormous walls rose up like a medieval hedge, bristling in ropes, restraints, paddles, whips and every piece of hardware Gage had ever shown her. A Saint Anthony's cross held center stage, bordered on two sides by a spanking bench and a padded table with eyebolts designed for ties she'd been trained to secure.

Sam looked off to her left. Stone benches faced the stage in a half circle. They climbed toward the sky beyond her sight. She gasped with sudden fear as she realized every seat was occupied. An uncountable number of souls muttering among themselves. Staring at her. Only her.

Before Sam could run and hide, the stadium

erupted in cheers and whistles. A deafening crescendo of a million voices screaming in unison. Nova and Katherine gripped her arms as her legs weakened beneath her. "I can't... I..."

Nova wrapped her in soft arms with impossible strength. She pierced her soul with blinding hazel eyes. Blue. Green. Blue. Green.

Samantha began to hyperventilate.

"Breathe, Samantha. Breathe."

She tried to decipher the sounds assaulting her ears. "I... can't..."

"They scream your name." Nova's voice seemed to come from within her head. "They announce your rebirth."

"What?" Sam canted her head. It didn't make sense.

The sound began to crystallize, pounding in her head like a swarm of insects released within her ears."Domina! Domina! Domina!"

"Who?" Sam righted herself, finding strength in her limbs again as the noise increased in volume beyond understanding. "Who's Domina?"

Nova opened her hands and fussed with Sam's outfit. Straightening and smoothing imperfections only she could see. "You are, my sweet child. If you choose to be." Nova held up a golden loop. A thousand strands of braided gold glistened in the starlight. The crowd became as silent as the darkness. "Bind him to me."

Sam took the priceless treasure from Nova's hand. Her eyes focused on the thing of beauty she didn't understand. A silver padlock fastened the two ends together. A jeweled key glistened in the keyhole. "Bind who?"

Nova touched her cheek. "The key is yours, Samantha. The collar is mine. The reward is ours."

Sam hefted the weighty artifact, understanding its significance at last. Before she could protest, Nova took Katherine's hand in her own and led her from the stage. Sam longed to follow, but her feet had become welded to the stone floor. She wanted to call to them, but her vocal cords no longer vibrated with intelligible sounds. Her mind became empty of tangible thoughts.

The crowd erupted again. Sam jerked her head away from the glittering bauble as if a noose had tightened around her neck. Gage stood in front of her. His skin shined as if oiled. His black eyes had come to life. Dark embers burning in a face cleaved from heaven. The multicolored tattoos on his arms moved, writhed and stopped again. Wicked muscles tightened and relaxed as he flexed his arms and stared at her with profound intensity. The cloth around his waist had already begun to lift but his erection seemed to have grown in size. Massive beyond belief. Impossible.

As she stared, a hush fell across the crowd. Profound presence without sound. The blood rushing though her ears roared. Her own heartbeat slammed into her skull with deafening pulsations. Her breath raged like an overflowing cauldron of boiling oil.

She lifted the chain on her finger and swallowed as she reached for the words she had to utter. "Will you submit?"

Gage tensed his jaw. Every muscle in his face seemed to ripple. His hands clenched and unclenched without rhythm. Without reason.

Sam gulped. His silence began to kill her inside. The pain became heat. The heat became fury. Unrequited lust she'd waited too long to taste. Worked too hard to nurture. She clenched her hand on the hammered links and raised her voice, enunciating every word with a syllabic hiss. "Will? You? Submit?"

His eyes widened. He glanced at the crowd and back at her. His posture began to relax. "I will."

Sam held her breath. She wanted to scream. To dance. To laugh. Every emotional variation of happiness she'd ever experienced flooded into her body at once. The crowd disappeared from her mind. Only Gage remained. With shaking hands she unlocked the collar and walked toward him, holding an end in each hand. "Kneel."

Gage took a single knee and raised his chin. Proudly. With defiance. He whispered so only she could hear. "Do you hope to bind me with my lover's collar?"

The answer came to her from an unknown place. An unknown time. With her entire being she finally understood with absolute clarity. A soft smile rose on her lips. "No, Gage. This collar sets you free."

Gage lowered his eyes and pushed his knuckles against the stone. Sam clasped the collar around his neck and locked it. She pulled the jeweled key free and squeezed it in her hand before hooking it to the zipper at her chest. *At last.* "The collar may be hers, but tonight, you are mine. To do with as I please. Rise. I want to play."

The perfect male stood before her. She looked at the stage, tapping her lip as she considered. *Where do we start?* She no longer cared who watched. The world outside the two of them ceased to exist. *My turn.* "The cross." Turning her hand palm upward, she waved in the direction of the St. Anthony's scaffold.

"If you'd be so kind."

Her pussy already throbbed. The leather corset pressed against her swollen nipples. She'd been born again.

The wall of toys seemed too imposing. Too many selections. She'd never be able to choose. Exasperated, her mind found what her eyes had become too scattered to see. The perfect choice. She rushed forward and lifted the two-foot riding crop. Thin and black with a one-inch leather tip. She flexed the thin rod in her hands and turned to her charge. Satisfied. Elated. "Remove your cover. I want access to everything."

Gage stared at her. Expressionless and unreadable. His hands moved slowly. He undid the clasp at his waist and let the fabric fall. His massive cock already pulsed. Shining with the thin stream of cum emerging from the head.

"Delicious." Hot cum slid down her inner thigh. She swirled the crop in her hands. "Turn. I wish to see my dessert."

Gage raised his hands and turned in a circle. The muscles in his ass had been chipped from stoned. His back, a veritable anatomy textbook, had every muscle defined as drawn in place. A sculpture. A masterpiece.

She tapped her lip with the tip of the crop. "Grip the scaffold." She sensed resistance. Tightening in his muscles. She whispered for him alone. "Please."

He turned his back toward her and placed his hands at the upper corners of the cross. He shuffled forward until his toes touched the lower corners.

Satisfied by the click of her heels and the rippling of his muscles the sound seemed to invoke, Sam sauntered toward him. She touched the tip of the crop to his neck, gratified by the stiffening of his body. With a light touch she dragged it across his back. Lower. She traced every muscle group until she reached his perfect ass and tapped each cheek, stiffening him again.

She strapped his right hand in the restraint and pulled it tight for effect. Sam looked at him once more then slipped a blindfold over his eyes. He faced forward and breathed through flaring nostrils. She moved her lips to his ear and licked with the tip of her tongue. "Are you going to fuck me like you own me? Will you take me apart, thrust by thrust?"

She inhaled his musky scent and dragged her tongue across his neck. Her body had become a burning flame. White hot and needing. Salty. Sweet. Man. *My treasure.* She tied his other hand and bent to secure his ankles. Tugging at the straps as she moved her tongue across his lower back. *My toy.*

Standing, she moved the crop between his legs and brushed his balls until he strained at the wrist straps. She pressed her leather encased tits to his back and gripped his massive erection in her hand. Pumping. She purred in his ear. "Will you ravish me? Will you savage my pussy until cum drains down my thighs? Or will you fuck my ass until I scream for mercy and then deny me respite?"

She stepped away before she came. His breathing had become ragged. She smacked his ass hard with the crop. The red welt only drove her lust. "Answer me!"

He shook, tightening his hands on the straps. "Yes."

"Good boy. I knew you could obey. You only needed the right incentive." She slapped his other cheek. Harder. A moan rose on his lips. Her clit pounded. She'd never wanted to be fucked worse in her life. "Don't you dare scream! I want a man who can take me over the edge. Not a mewling boy." She bit his shoulder, sinking her teeth until his body tilted in an attempt to relieve the pain. "Are you that man?"

He righted himself again. "Yes!"

She walked to the wall and drew her hand across the choices before her. No longer complicated, only fun. "Yes what?" She lifted the bone handled flogger they had used a few hours before and flashed it through the air. Satisfied.

He moaned. "Yes...Mistress."

She let the fronds hang over his shoulder and pulled them until they dropped across his back. "Good boy." She struck lightly at first. Shoulder to ass. He bucked. She struck again across the other side. Harder. His cries began to rise. Her arm moved in a figure eight. Shoulder to ass. Faster. Shoulder to ass. Harder. The rhythm became easy. Powerful. Red marks appeared and still she continued. Needing him more with every stroke. Wanting him with everything she'd ever been.

His head tipped backwards. He howled.

She stopped her onslaught and pressed against him again. "What's the matter, baby boy? Aren't you mine to do with as I please?"

He hung limp from his wrist restraints. Shaking. Sobbing. His words came in broken breaths. "Yes...Mistress."

She used her nails. Dragging them across his back. Deep angry furrows cut into his skin. Marking him with drops of fresh blood. She needed him inside her. Breathless, her kisses fell upon his flesh. Biting. Licking. Tasting. "Are you man enough to take me to the limit?"

He lifted himself onto his legs again. His head fell forward. Warbling moans leaked from his throat.

She kissed the steaming welts on his back and gripped his cock hard. "Are you ready to break me or do you need more instruction?"

His muscles tensed. He jumped at the strength of her voice. "Yes, Mistress. Whatever you want. No more instruction is necessary."

"Exactly. Whatever *I* want." Breathing hard, she pressed her cheek to his back. "Good boy."

Sam bent and undid his leg restraints. He turned his head toward her, as if able to see. As if able to understand. She undid his wrist straps.

He held the frame for balance and turned to face her. He cocked his head, searching for her by sound. "Mistress?"

She pulled his blindfold free and dropped it on the ground then stared into his infinite eyes. "I am here."

"What is your wish?"

"One more task and you will have your reward." She stepped to the table and lifted a loop of black silk. Unwinding it, she let one end fall to the stage and pulled it through her fingers with a hiss. "You taught me to bind, did you not?"

He breathed, wondering what fate awaited him. "I did."

"And I was an adept student, was I not?" She moved toward him. The sway of her hips so easy now. Programmed from birth.

He watched with fascination. "You were."

"Cross your wrists." She pulled the silk through her hands again. Another hiss. Erotic beyond measure.

Gage obeyed without a word. His eyes never wavered from hers.

"I will tie you with the most complicated knot I know. If you can free your hands, I am yours. Do you understand?" She breathed and tried to calm herself. Trying not to shake.

He clenched his jaw. "I do...Mistress."

"Good boy." She stepped forward and turned the rope around his wrists, leaving the loop loose. She tied a simple bow and pulled the ends until the loops hung like large dangling ears. "I expect you'll do your best, but I've learned well. I know what I want and exactly how to get it."

Gage looked at the binding with an open mouthed stare. His eyebrows rose as he searched her for understanding. A truck could have driven through the gap between his wrists. A pretty wrap binding no one.

Sam walked to the spanking bench and pulled the jeweled key downward, unzipping her top and freeing her swollen breasts. She pulled the leather corset off and let it dangle from her finger before dropping it to the floor. Her hips wiggled back and forth as she pushed her skirt to the ground and kicked it free with her toe. Boots in place, she sat on the padded bench and lifted her feet onto the lower railings. Legs open, she ran a finger over her cum slicked clit. "Try to escape. I dare you. You're not man enough to take me where I need to go."

Gage moved his hands. The rope fell to the floor. He walked to Sam with purpose, never taking his gaze from hers. "May I have you, Mistress?"

His hot hands found her thighs. He stepped between her legs. She wrapped her legs around his waist and pulled until the head of his cock pressed against her wet opening. Locking her fingers behind his neck, she tried not to drown in his obsidian gaze. "I was always yours. All you had to do is ask. Now you must fulfill the promises you made me."

The crowd erupted as his huge cock slipped inside her. His thrusts weren't kind. He wasn't gentle. The burning stretch opened her wide. She clawed her nails into his back and dug her heels deep as he found depths she didn't know existed. Pounding.

She screamed his name until her throat seemed blistered and the sound of her voice drove him harder. Unimaginable length. Indescribable width. Tearing her apart while he hammered again and again. The pain became pure pleasure. She sunk her teeth into his shoulder, mewling as she climaxed. Clawing. Pleading as her body contracted, released and contracted again. Orgasm flowed into orgasm. Pinnacles of pleasure climbed higher uncovering impossible zeniths. Her muscles burned as reality tipped, skittered away and solidified again. The air became waves of surreal dreams. False. Reality. Release again. On and on.

As Sam whimpered for more, Gage pulled from her thrumming pussy. He lifted her from the bench forcibly and turned her on her stomach. He pinned her head hard against the cold fabric and pried her legs apart with his knee. Like a demon possessed, he drove his cock into her brutally. She clawed at the bench and screamed as he pounded into her with unimaginable savagery. No safe words. No end.

Hot liquid ran down her thighs in a continuous stream as she came in unending storms of climax. He tangled his fingers in her hair and pulled backwards with barbaric violence, driving her onto her forearms as he battered her pussy with merciless ferocity. Her vagina erupted like a broken dam. Gushing fluid sprayed from her pussy and poured onto the ground. Stars swirled in her eyes. Punishing flashes of light beat against her broken mind.

He slowed his stokes and relaxed his hold on her hair. She gasped for air in strained breaths that merged with the roar of the crowd. Her fingers dug into the cushioned top of the bench and tore the fabric as she tried to pull herself forward for relief.

His fingers slid up her thighs, capturing the running stream and transferring it to her ass. He pressed his long digits into her tightest hole, lubricating her as she moaned and pleaded.

Burning. Searing flesh stretched to its limits.

He pulled his cock free and milked the cum from her dripping pussy with his hand. He pushed two cum slicked fingers into her ass and filled her with her own essence. Sliding in and out hard. Deep. A guttural growl left his lips as he continued to prepare her. "One more promise, Samantha."

Before she could question his intentions, he pushed her head against the bench's padding hard and held it there. Her knees fought for purchase on the lower rails as the head of his cock pressed into her ass. He gripped her hip and entered without patience.

Grunting, he pushed in farther, reversed and slammed deeper over and over.

The world flickered. Sam no longer possessed the strength to scream. Her knees slipped. She dug into the rails with the toes of her boots but his assault continued. Her throbbing pussy gushed again. Release after release. Harder. He tore into her as he'd promised. The way she'd wanted.

Her consciousness flickered. Disappeared and returned again.

He roared from somewhere far away. His cock plowed into her. His limit. Balls deep. Pulsing waves of heat filled her as he came inside her. Molten seed seared the inside of her body as it filled her. The sensation rose. Her stomach. Her chest. Complete awareness. Satori.

Her mind bent, slipped away, returned, and left again, but his unremitting hammer strokes raged on.

Sound no longer came to her ears.

She searched for air.

Unable to think, she could only exist. She drifted among the stars. Planets came and went. Reality faded.

Black, infinite universes of beauty beyond comprehension.

Chapter Fourteen

A New Reality

W*here am I?*

Flash. Flash. Flash.

Muffled sound.

Gone.

Indistinct voices.

The world teetered. A mirage. A dream.

Walls.

Sunlight.

Wasted.

Sam's fingers dug into the bed. She pulled her eyes open and they closed again. So heavy.

Am I blind?

She clawed her way upward through consciousness determined to elude her. The world pulsed. Formed. Flickered away and reformed.

Where am I?

No part of Sam's body remained unscathed.

Everything hurt. She moaned, gasping for life once again.

Memories flooded back to her.

It couldn't have been real.

"You slipped away from us."

Nova's voice pulled Sam back. Called her. Told her to return.

Sam woke in the place in between worlds. The soft bed she'd shared with Nova and Katherine. Open walls letting in sunlight to sear her retinas. The cool breeze against her skin helped invigorate her and prodded her muscles back to life.

The world began to make sense one image at a time. Nova sat on the bed by her side and rubbed her back with light fingers. Gage came into focus. He stood with arms crossed over his chest. Tapping his foot. Nervous.

Sam didn't get to ask him what had gotten him so ruffled. Gage rushed to her side and kissed her cheek before she could open her mouth. "You came back. I thought I'd lost you." He kissed her again and pulled her into his arms. Rocking her as he pressed his cheek against her own.

Even with her pained limbs and muscles protesting movement, his embrace lifted her spirits and began to make her whole again. His scent lingered in her mind and now filled her nostrils again. The golden collar remained on his neck, sparkling in the sun, amplifying the beauty of his tanned skin. Sam wrapped her arms around him and returned his affection to the extent her weakened state would allow. A newborn kitten in the paws of a lion.

Gage's worry seemed excessive but having him in her arms lifted her heart. She smiled. "I wouldn't have thought a long sleep after last night would have surprised anyone. A girl's gotta recharge every now and then."

Gage furrowed his brow and lowered her back to the pillow again. He looked at Nova with a pained expression before he spoke again in soft reassuring tones. "You've been out for two days, Samantha."

Sam bolted upright. "Two days! What do you mean two days?" The aches in her body made even more sense.

Nova pressed her fingers against Sam's chest. "Shhh. Yes, my love. Two days. Sometimes a mortal reaches too far in this place. They never find their way back. After a thousand years, Gage never fails to satisfy me. Humans may be too frail for his particular...talents." She flashed a soft smile at Gage. "My husband never left your side. He bathed you. Worked your muscles and kept your joints limber."

Sam tried to imagine having slept for more than twenty four hours. She could recall the night of Gage's submission but no other dreams came to her. The thought of Gage as the minister of tender affections while she slept made her blush. "I bet he did."

Nova's laughter lit the room, a complex wind chime tinkling in the afternoon breeze. "I assure you it was worry, not lust. However, now that you mention it, I didn't monitor his care twenty four hours a day. Maybe I shouldn't have left him alone with you."

Gage couldn't meet their eyes. He stared at the ground in silence.

Sam caressed his back with her fingertips, glad it'd been him. Elated she'd had such a profound effect on another soul. "I'm sure his affections were conducted with absolute purity of heart. Thank you, Gage. For everything. Thank you both."

Sam swiveled her legs off the bed with a groan. The world spun for a moment and came to a stop. Thirst. Hunger. Nothing else mattered but food.

Gage offered his hands. "Take it slow. You're profoundly weak. Would you like something to drink?"

Sam nodded as she pulled herself upright with his assistance. Her legs wobbled and threatened to falter. Gage moved in close. He supported her with his arm before she tumbled. She stood in place until the world stilled before taking tentative steps forward. As the kinks and cramps began to work themselves out, she could stand straight again. Her balance improved with every step and she could almost walk unsupported by the time they reached the courtyard. She clutched Gage's hand in her own, needing assurance more than a shoulder to lean on.

A mob of people surrounded an opulent table heaped with food. Khan. Katherine. Jace. Joshua. Faces of men and women she had a vague recollection of and those she didn't remember. All welcomed her with open arms, kissed her cheek and told her how glad they were she'd returned. She sat down at the table and realized her face hurt from smiling but the succulent aromas made her stomach twist and growl. As the people around her heaped her with affection she began to eat. Slowly at first and then with hunger driven by days of starvation. Everything looked scrumptious. It tasted even better. In the company of friends and lovers, she began to heal, one bite at a time.

Sam ate her fill before taking a long, luxurious bath that flushed the majority of her pains away. Gage tended to her with a soft touch and careful hands. Helping when she needed it. Just being there when she didn't.

Nova helped her dress. A blood-red sundress with pleats swirling just above her knees. It fit perfectly, outlining her figure and enhancing her curves. The décolletage didn't dive deep, it only hinted instead of teased. The woman who stared back at Sam from the depths of her mirror's silvered surface had changed from the girl she'd known for a lifetime. She no longer needed to show skin in order to feel sexy. Confidence dripped from her pores. Her attire no longer defined her. Clothes had become tools of seduction, nothing more. She glanced around the room, searching for the outfits they'd purchased a few days before. "What happened to all the packages?"

"I've already sent them to your home." Nova wrapped her arms around Sam's waist and peeked over her shoulder. "Are you ready?"

Sam placed her hands on Nova's soft skin. Sadness filled her heart even though she'd never been happier in her life. "I have to be ready."

From the other side of the room, Gage cleared his throat. "One more kiss then?"

Nova's hands opened and Sam ran into Gage's arms. She kissed his lips with every ounce of passion she'd ever known. He squeezed her tight and lifted her from the ground. Hot tears ran down her cheeks. She recalled the things he'd taught her. The things they'd taught each other.

Sam wiped the salty drops from her cheeks as Gage lowered her to the earth again. She held his hands tightly and stepped backward, searching the obsidian depths of his eyes for emotions reflecting her own. She found understanding there. A twinge of regret perhaps. "Thank you, Gage."

He squeezed her hands tightly. "You saved me, Samantha. I can never repay you for that."

Her heart ached. She didn't want to lose him. *Why do I feel like this? I'm supposed to be free now. No more pain. No more loss.* She couldn't hold back the tears anymore. As the sobs began, she released his hand and scurried back into Nova's arms. Wanting her to know how she felt.

"Shhh now, baby girl." Nova held her close and stroked her hair before addressing Gage. "I'll take her home. We have things to discuss."

"As you wish, Nova. Goodbye Samantha. My heart is yours. It always was."

Sam couldn't turn to face him. Her heart wouldn't survive it. She pulled Nova tight and let her tears come without restraint.

The world shifted. Ripples cast upon the air to

shimmer in multicolored beauty. Her stomach lurched.

***

The oppressive heat of the Phoenix sun beat down upon them mercilessly. Sam unfolded herself from Nova's embrace and dried the wetness from her cheeks as best she could. They stood in her apartment complex parking lot next to Sam's beat up car. Morning had come and gone. Only a few cars remained, those without jobs or school to drive their day.

"Are you going to tell me where your tears come from, Samantha, or should I tell you?"

Sam sniffed again and wiped her face with her palms. "It's not fair. I'm not supposed to feel like this. Gage was never mine. You shared him with me, but he was always yours. I knew that from the beginning. So why do I feel this way? Why do I feel so hurt? As if something has been ripped out of my soul. I don't want to be sad. I have no right to be."

Nova pushed Sam's hair back from her face and tucked it behind her ears before laughing.

Sam jerked her head back from the woman's touch, shocked by Nova's cruelty. She'd poured out her heart and received mirth in turn. "Why would you laugh at me? How could you?"

Nova held her hand in front of her mouth but couldn't suppress the continued twitter. "I thought you were done with love, Samantha. Isn't that what you told me? Isn't that what you wanted?"

"Love?" Samantha realized where she'd found these feelings before. How much they hurt. "It can't be—"

"Love?" Nova cut her off sharply. "Call the feeling you're experiencing whatever you want. Love. Longing. Loss. It's irrelevant. It feels the same. Do you remember what I told you?"

The words had been seared into Sam's mind forever. *The quest for love drives everything we do. We may spurn love, hate it, and even turn our backs on it, but love always returns. Pain and pleasure. Inseparable. Lust and desire. Indivisible.* She looked at the ground and twisted the ends of her hair as the painful storm of anxiety she'd almost forgotten approached with relentless fury. She mumbled, realizing she'd been warned before she'd ever met him. "Yes but... But it was only sex. Only lust."

Nova touched Sam's chin and lifted it until their eyes locked on each other. "Was it, Samantha?"

Samantha turned away, not wanting Nova to see her cry again. "I don't want to feel this way anymore,

Nova. I don't want to love anyone. It hurts too much."

"I taught you control, Samantha. I taught you seduction. You will never escape deep emotional connection no matter how hard you try. Remember that. You have to decide who you want to be. Are you Samantha? Are you Domina? Or, are you something else entirely? Only you can determine who you'll become."

Sam understood the words even if she didn't want to hear them. She raised her head and gazed across the heat rising from the pavement. She could barely utter a whisper. "Will I ever see you again?"

"Perhaps."

Sam didn't want her to leave. She didn't want to forget. She turned, prepared to tell Nova how much she needed her. How much she needed both of them but the goddess had already gone. Without a sound, her teacher...her heart...had simply vanished.

Chapter Fifteen

Born Again

Sam sat with her newest acquisitions. The club had already reached its peak for the evening. Sweaty bodies ground against each other in every corner. Music blared from speakers above her head. Riotous laughter mixed with a hundred voices buzzed in the background.

Sam closed her eyes. She moaned with delight as Andrew rubbed her feet. Paradise. His tanned skin glistened with sweat still fresh from their trip to the playroom. She demanded his muscled body be uncovered and on display when he craved her dominance. Tight biker shorts were all she allowed tonight and none doubted he belonged to her.

She held her empty wine glass out to Philippe. A chiseled specimen from Spain, his gifts above and below the sheets had made him her current favorite toy. He didn't speak English, but Sam didn't keep him

as a pet for the words he spoke. Eye candy.
Submission. A fuck toy she could sink her teeth into.

Philippe jumped to his feet and pulled the chilled
wine from the ice bucket. He poured a single finger
depth into her glass like a good little boy. He knew
he'd be punished if her drink warmed before she
finished it.

As a professional bodybuilder, Philippe enjoyed
wearing a Speedo and nothing else. Sooner or later
she'd have to remind him who his owner was by
exerting control over his wardrobe but, the fact of the
matter was, he looked delicious. Besides, he'd licked
her pussy for hours earlier in the day and only the
movement of her hips were needed to keep him on
task. Men able to satiate her appetites for even a few
hours were a rare breed.

Sam placed her six-inch heel next to Philippe's
balls. The pose opened her legs for his viewing
pleasure. She'd stripped to her panties and leather
corset hours ago. She didn't wear more than two
pieces of clothing anymore. Seduction in all things.

Her fingers danced across the jeweled key
hanging from the black lace choker at her neck. She
never took it off. Nothing else from the Place Between
remained except her memories.

When the pain of her preternatural lovers began

to subside, Sam opened a studio for the exploration of pain and pleasure. It was the only way to keep her newly acquired skills sharp and still satisfy an unending line of those who craved her talents. For a price concomitant with their desires, she taught her clients control and perfected her own abilities. She granted them the pleasures they deserved and fucked those she wanted, when she wanted, the way she wanted. As a result, the collection of men and women begging for her touch had grown beyond counting.

"Samantha?"

Sam turned toward the familiar voice. Kelly stood next to her table with a gorgeous blonde hanging on his arm. He looked younger than she'd remembered. Immature perhaps. Smaller. Unimposing. "Speaking of men who can't be taught."

Kelly possessed the playboy look Sam used to crave. He wore an expensive dark blue suit jacket unbuttoned over a stark white shirt with its collar undone. His face still carried the perpetual five o'clock shadow he worked so hard to maintain. Beneath his dark eyebrows, brown eyes made him appear rough and untamed. A catch for sure, but something less than spectacular. He ran his eyes over Sam's relaxed pose and let his eyes linger on the tight silk between her legs. He licked his lips. A wild animal determining how to separate the weak from the heard. "I've thought about you a lot, Sam. You're the last person I would've expected to run into here."

Sam smiled with faux disappointment. She let her knees open further, drawing his eyes between her legs. *Control in all things.* Her finger traced the swollen lips beneath her panties in slow circles."That's funny. I haven't thought about you at all."

His eyes lingered on the wetness her caress had begun to evoke. He squinted in confusion. "I just mean..."

"I know what you mean, Kelly," Sam cut him off mid-sentence. "But I'm the one who should be surprised. I offered you the opportunity to explore the pleasure of another's flesh once. A long time ago. You refused." The memories flooded back to her. Not with anxiety but rising anger instead. A desire to cause him pain.

Kelly's blonde companion looked at him with concern. "Did you two used to go out or something? I didn't realize you were close."

Sam couldn't take her eyes off the young woman's breasts. They threatened to pour from her low-cut blouse at any minute. The short plaid schoolgirl skirt invoked a sensual flower in need of picking. "Oh? He didn't tell you about us? About the things we did?"

The blonde stepped away from Kelly with a glare. "No. He didn't." Her voice sharpened."He said he knew you. That's it."

"I see." Sam sipped from her glass. She held it out in her hand and Philippe jumped to fill it again. "I guess I wasn't that memorable."

The woman stared at her in awe. "I can't believe you two were a...thing." Her eyes widened as she realized what she'd said. "I mean, you're so gorgeous..."

"No need to explain." Sam licked the cum off her fingertip. "I understand exactly what you mean."

Kelly shifted with discomfort, alternating his gaze between the two women with reddening cheeks. "Tina." He reached out a hand but she batted it away."We were together for a while. She didn't look like..." he motioned to Sam with his hand, "...*this* when we were together. I didn't tell you because I wasn't even sure it was her."

The fury in Sam's chest began its upward climb. "Two years is *a while*. That's for sure. Tina, did he ask you to come here or was it your idea?"

"It was his idea, but I wanted to come." Tina's mouth dropped open. "Two years?"

Kelly tried to take Tina's hand, but she jerked

away. His voice warbled. "We just wanted to check it out. You know? To see what all the fuss was about."

Before Sam answered, two arms wrapped around her. Wearing nothing at all, Melissa placed a soft kiss on her neck. "Samantha, when are you going to let me play with your new toys?"

Sam turned toward the dark-haired beauty and kissed her deeply. She pushed her tongue into the woman's mouth with a moan, making sure she had Kelly's attention. "When is your husband going to fuck me again?"

Melissa giggled. "Anytime you want. He adores you and your...talents."

"Thank you, baby." Sam rubbed Melissa's shaved pussy, bumping against her clit. "How about I eat this pretty pussy while he takes me from behind? I miss the way you taste."

Melissa kissed her again. "That sounds perfect. I'll find you later and we can play. Bring your new toys. I want a ride."

Sam watched Melissa walk back to the dance floor before she spoke to Tina again. "Come sit by me, Tina."

Tina glared at Kelly again before stepping to Sam's side. Andrew and Philippe bounced to their feet. Andrew pulled out her chair. Philippe took her fingertips in his and helped her sit. Together, they pushed her chair in.

Crimson roses bloomed in Tina's cheeks. "I could get used to this."

"You have no idea." Sam leaned forward and inhaled the skin of Tina's neck. "Have you ever been taken so hard and so many times that the world around you ceases to exist?"

Tina giggled like a little girl. "No. I mean... I've never done anything like...that before."

Kelly looked at the floor and growled out, "Let's go, Tina. Nice seeing you again, Samantha."

Sam kept her eyes fixed on the gorgeous blonde's green eyes. "I think Tina may want to stay a while."

"Whatever." Kelly raised his voice. He held out his hand. "Now, Tina! Let's go."

Philippe and Andrew stood with gritted teeth and angry stares. They moved between the table and Kelly before crossing their arms. A muscled barricade.

Tina couldn't meet Sam's eyes.

Sam reached up, swept a lock of soft blond hair from Tina's face and tucked it behind her ear. "You have an important decision to make tonight, Tina."

"You really are a piece of work, Samantha." Kelly stepped to the side so he could see the women around the human mass of flesh blocking his view. "Now,

Tina!"

Melissa's husband, David, sidled up next to Sam. He placed a hand on her shoulder. His hulking form cast a shadow over the table. He seethed, burning Kelly with an acid scowl. "Do we have a fucking problem here?"

Sam kissed Dave's massive hand. "No, my prince. My *ex*-boyfriend was just leaving."

"Fuck you!" Kelly roared. "Good luck finding a ride, Tina. Fucking cock tease." He stomped off toward the exit, cussing the whole way.

Dave raised an eyebrow. "Nice guy." He looked down at Tina cowering below him. "You okay?" His voice softened. "Don't ever let anyone treat you like shit. After a while you'll start to believe their words. Life's too short for misery. You have a problem with anyone in here, you call me. Men who disrespect women are the lowest form of scum." He kissed Sam on the cheek. "I believe we have a date tonight."

"We do." Sam kissed him back before squeezing Tina's knee. "May I bring a friend?"

Dave laughed. "Anything you want, Samantha. You know that." He merged with the crowd and disappeared from view.

Andrew and Philippe returned to their seats.

Sam could see the excitement rising on Tina's

face. She ran her fingers up and down the woman's leg. "We are friend's, aren't we, Tina?"

"Yes."

"How wonderful." Sam let her fingertip rise across Tina's stomach and higher. She drew soft circles between her pale breasts.

Exhilaration pumped through Sam's veins. *Control. Seduction.* "Friends trust each other, don't they, Tina? I would be so sad if we didn't trust each other." She pushed out her lower lip and cupped Tina's face in her palms.

Tina swallowed hard and forced a smile. Her knee bumped against Sam's. "I do. I mean hell... I just let my ride walk out the door."

"You don't need him, baby girl. You're coming home with me." She drew her hands downward, lingering at Tina's breasts again before moving on to her knee and calming its nervous bounce. "I'm a purveyor of fantasy. Multiple men. Multiple women. Pain. Pleasure. All you have to do is ask and I will make your dreams come true."

Tina opened her legs, accepting the upward climb of Sam's hands. She whispered. "I've never been with a woman."

"No?" Sam let her fingers trace across the wet cotton between Tina's thighs. "Such a shame. We'll have to correct that deficiency immediately. Will you do me a favor? Between friends?"

Tina began to pant. "Of course. Anything."

"Oooh," Sam purred. "Anything? Such a good girl." She leaned forward and whispered in Tina's ear. "Will you take these panties off for me?"

Staring at Andrew and Philippe, Tina blushed. "Here? Now?"

"Don't worry about them." Sam looked at her two pets and pointed to the table. They pressed their foreheads against the hard surface. "It'll be our little secret."

Tina's mouth fell open at the control Sam possessed. She looked around surreptitiously. Lifting her butt from the chair, she pulled the pink lace free and handed the panties to Sam under the table.

Sam lifted the damp fabric to her nose and inhaled deeply. "Yum. My favorite flavor."

"Oh yeah?" Tina pressed her fingertips to her mouth and stifled an escaping giggle. The blush in her cheeks spread across her chest. "And what might that be?"

Sam let the panties dangle from her fingertip then leaned forward and kissed Tina's lips softly. "Innocence."

Chapter Sixteen

Who You Want To Be

Eyes heavy with sleep, Sam pulled her new Lexus into the apartment complex. She never brought conquests home with her. Her bedroom allowed her to rest in peace, recharging before another night of pleasure began.

She was relieved she didn't have to go to her studio today. She didn't have the energy for a long training session and, quite frankly, felt fucked out for the first time in months.

Tina had been insatiable. The woman had overcome her initial nervousness with alacrity and eaten Sam for hours. Even Dave's massive size couldn't restrain her. In fact, his relentless pounding seemed to increase her hunger rather than satiate it. Ten orgasms in, covered in cum and sweat, the newbie lust whore had matched Sam man for man until dawn. An impressive task to say the least.

She fingered the key at her neck and sighed. Her despondency was more than just a lack of sleep. She'd known it for weeks and could no longer deny the facts. Lust had begun to disappoint her. The conquests she claimed now were little more than a means to an end. Toys to provide her with orgasms. Brief moments of release in which the trials of this world were lifted and memories of The Place Between were forgotten.

The quest for love drives everything we do.

"No!" Sam struck the steering wheel with her hand. Her chest tightened. She could have any man or woman she wanted. They crawled because they needed her. Love had nothing to do with it.

We may spurn it, hate it, and even turn our backs on it, but love always returns.

Damp tears formed in her eyes. *Nova, why did you do this to me?* She choked back the sadness of losing Gage.

Pain and pleasure. Inseparable.

"No!" Sobs raked her lungs. "No!" She jumped from the car and locked the door.

Lust and desire. Indivisible.

Realization struck. She couldn't breathe. It wasn't the fact her conquests didn't have the fortitude to keep her; each of them *needed* something from her.

They only desired her because she promised to fulfill their tiny, insignificant fantasies. Her own hopes and dreams meant nothing to them.

You have to decide who you want to be.

She gripped the roof of her car and pressed her head against the hot metal while tears of pain flowed. *No love.* She shook her head back and forth. *Never again.*

"Ma'am?"

The deep male voice startled her. She stood up straight, sniffed and wiped her tears with the back of her hand then turned slowly to see he was tall. His dark blue three-piece suit and red tie seemed out of place in the middle of a rundown apartment parking lot. Short brown hair and brown eyes. His strong face was shaved clean except for the tiny triangular goatee that graced his chin. The single stud diamond in his left ear caught the light and twinkled. Handsome. Rugged. Sam could think of a million words to describe him but she couldn't think of a single thing to say.

"Are you all right?" He kept his distance but his expression radiated concern.

Sam wiped her cheeks again. "I'm fine."

"Okay. I didn't mean to intrude, but I saw you crying so I had to ask. Sorry I bothered you." As he turned and walked toward an old red Mercedes, he pulled a ring of keys from his pocket.

Who does he think he is...a white knight to the rescue? She watched his back as he unlocked his car door. He'd been the only person to offer her assistance without a catch for longer than she could remember.

As he pulled open his door, she shouted, "Thanks! Thanks for asking about me."

He smiled at her. "You take care, now, ya hear?" He turned away.

As he climbed into his car, she squinted against the bright morning sun. *I don't need a white knight.* "Do you live around here? I don't remember seeing you before."

The man got out again. "Yeah. 205. Right over there. I haven't been here long. I'm sorta...between jobs right now. I have an interview today so I'm hopeful."

Love is transient. Sam bent sharply at the waist to unlock her door, reached in and grabbed her sunglasses from the center console while rocking her hips back and forth. It was second nature now.

She closed the door and locked it again. "I'm in 412. Over there. Right across the way from you. Good luck on your interview."

Control is forever. She started a slow walk toward

her apartment, working her pose as she moved, knowing he watched.

"Hey! Uhm..."

Sam pushed the sunglasses up into her hair and turned with a seductive half smile. "Me?"

The man paced across the parking lot to catch up with her. "Would you like to...you know...get something to eat later or something."

She liked the fact he'd already become uncomfortable. She sucked her lower lip between her teeth. "Well, that depends."

He shifted from foot to foot, looking down at the ground and back up at her with a hopeful gaze. "On what?" His interest had been piqued.

"On what you like to eat." She touched her upper lip with the tip of her tongue.

He looked down again. "Oh...anything...anything you want."

She cocked a hip and pulled each word out with emphasis. "Anything? I? Want? I don't know if you're ready for that."

"Well... I mean, you can decide."

"Of course. I always do." She watched him squirm for a minute. "Shall we say five?"

"I can't make five. Is six okay?"

She pushed out her lower lip and pouted. "That's

too bad. I really wanted to eat at five. I don't know if I can hold out until six. I should be enjoying dessert by then. Perhaps another time."

She pulled her sunglasses down, turned on her heel, and swayed toward her apartment.

"Wait!" Desperation thickened his voice. "Five would be great. I'll meet you here at five...er...I didn't get your name."

Sam pulled her sunglasses down her nose and glanced over her shoulder. "Domina." She fingered the jeweled key around her neck and licked her lips. "I *am* Domina."

About the Author

Patrick Khayler is the pen name for a closet erotic romance writer who burst onto the publishing stage in 2016. He writes with passion in every word, thus immersing readers in characters they understand and relate to, people they may already be like or may want to become. Within the pages of his stories, readers are transported to a world of fantasy and fulfillment, a time they don't want to end and a place they never want to leave. He understands that human dreams and desires dictate how far his characters want to go, how close to the edge they dare risk, and the consequences of going over the brink. Patrick lives in Texas with his wife of many years and two sons. When he's not writing, he enjoys travel, scuba diving, and the outdoors.

Other Novels by Patrick Khayler at
www.patrickkhalyer.com

The Present

Valentine Dreams

Bound by Cotton

Amelia

Enjoy More Erotic Romance from Amore Moon Publishing, an imprint of TWB Press

No Limits
An erotic short story by Ashley Adams
amoremoonpublishing.com/nolimits

Army Buddy
An erotic short story by Ashley Adams
amoremoonpublishing.com/armybuddy

My Valentine Cowboy
An erotic short story by Ashley Adams
amoremoonpublishing.com/myvalentinecowboy

White Stallion
An erotic short story by Theda Hudson.
amoremoonpublishing.com/whitestallion

My Sweet Entity – Book 1
An erotic short story by Soliel De Bella
amoremoonpublishing.com/mysweetentity

Entity Mine – Book 2
An erotic short story by Soliel De Bella
amoremoonpublishing.com/entitymine

Entity's Rival – Book 3
An erotic romance short story by Soliel De Bella
amoremoonpublishing.com/entitysrival

The seduction of Lexie Dane
An erotic romance novel by Soliel De Bella
amoremoonpublishing.com/lexiedane

Claiming Holly
An erotic romance short story by Soliel De Bella
amoremoonpublishing.com/claimingholly

Fire X Ice
An erotic romance short story by Soliel De Bella
amoremoonpublishing.com/firexice

Slump Buster
An erotic romance short story by Brian Smith
amoremoonpublishing.com/slumpbuster

The Vacationing Wife
An erotic thriller novel by T. A. Malone
amoremoonpublishing.com/thevacationingwife

www.twbpress.com

www.amoremoonpublishing.com

www.ingramcontent.com/pod-product-compliance
Lightning Source LLC
Chambersburg PA
CBHW051447260626
47162CB00001B/296